Lili

A Novel

Always believe
in yourself!
Michelle Lane

by

Michelle Lane

AMAXIM
Alpharetta

Lili is dedicated to all the girls who struggle with who they are and who they will become. You are not alone.
MLV

Amaxim
3000 Old Alabama Road, Suite 119-221
Alpharetta, GA 30022
visit our website at ***www.michellewrites.com***

First Electronic Edition: June 2012
First Paperback Edition: June 2012

This book is a work of fiction and its characters and events are fictitious. Any similarities to real persons, living or dead, is coincidental and is not intended by the author.

ISBN-10: 0963110527
ISBN-13: 9780963110527

10 9 8 7 6 5 4 3 2 1

Printed in the United States of America

Hi Friends,

I'm Michelle Lane, and I'm so happy to share Lili's story with you. When I was growing up, my best friend Suzanne stood by me when times were tough and I went through much of what Lili did at school. We laughed together, we cried together, and we celebrated big moments side by side. She's the first one I told that I would write novels one day, and she shared her artistic dreams with me. I wouldn't trade those best friend moments for anything in the world.

Friendships are so important, and in my next book you'll meet ***Mitch and Andie***, a couple of really good kids whose lives have them stuck in a rut of responsibility. A tragedy throws them together and tests their strength at every turn. But when the final straws break and they can't take it anymore, a bit of soul-searching rebellion is in store for the pair. They ditch their cozy Maryland digs for the bright lights and night life of New York City, and all havoc breaks loose. You'll just have to read ***Mitch and Andie*** to find out what happens to them next!

And next winter, you'll meet ***Grace***, a smart, witty runaway with a troubled past and too many stories to tell. When she arrives on her estranged grandmother's doorstep on a Michigan winter day, there is no turning back. Life must change, and that means digging in and learning to deal. And it also means figuring out a way to leave her road memories behind her while she tries her hardest to fit in at high school.

I'd love to share your stories. Please write to me at **www.michellewrites.com**.

Happy reading,

Michelle

"Beauty is truth, truth beauty."
John Keats

1.

"And . . . *arabesque penchée*, ladies. Concentrate on the most *beautiful* body lines," Margaux said while she scrutinized the class. "Elongate every muscle."

She was so very French, and so very much the ruthless drill sergeant in *pointe* shoes. The line of dancers tried to exhibit perfect form while she tapped our bodies into submission with her baton. We held our legs high, toes pointed toward the ceiling and bodies tight.

The maneuver was excruciating.

"Grace, ladies! I must see graceful poses! Hold it. Keep holding. Do not move a single muscle until I say release," Margaux warned. "You must *enjoy* discipline to dance. Beauty takes great pain. Performance is an art you must embrace with your whole being."

My whole being felt nasty. This dance class had ceased to be fun long ago. My hair was falling out of my ponytail in heavy chunks. Beads of sweat dripped down my face and between my breasts to make my sports bras a soggy mess. The studio was on furnace blast to compensate for the September chill in the air, and my Aunt Margaux was a perfectionist with a sadistic streak. She loved to torture us with these end-of-class rituals.

I know ballet was good exercise, but good God this was agony.

A girl in front of me grunted, wavered, and collapsed to the floor.

Margaux uttered a 'tsk-tsk' and shook her head. "You cannot be weak, ladies. You must endure if you are to become true dancers. Ballet is not an afternoon fancy for silly girls. It is a passion. A *life* you must breathe."

Another girl gave a big sigh. My muscles shook as my aunt approached and pushed my extended leg until blazing pain shot through my calf.

I groaned and stared at the floor, concentrated on the scuffed hard wood that had held up far better dancers than me. I breathed in the studio's smell, part talc, part sweat, part dusty memories of other girls' performances.

"Keep those muscles tight, ladies. Might I remind you that *Cinderella* is less than one month away? Not all of you will be cast to appear on stage. That right must be earned. And you will look like cows if you do not strive for absolute perfection."

I felt the raw, hot pain of a blister bubbling on my right heel. Why was I enduring this torture exactly? Oh, yeah. My mother. She wanted me dancer thin.

Behind me, a thud and a groan. Two more fallen ballerinas.

I stretched harder, determined to prove my worth though my breasts were sliding toward my chin in an amazing show of gravity as I leaned over. I sucked in my gut. Daring to glance up at Aunt Margaux, I caught her eye. She studied my lines. The raised eyebrow and the subtle frown on her lips told me she was not pleased.

I'd seen her wear that look before, and it was never good.

She cracked her baton against the practice *barre* three times. "*And* relax."

Groans and sighs filled the space as we all collapsed to the floor to massage achy muscles.

"Work harder, ladies. *À demain.*"

Just 23 hours until I get to do this all over again.

Sophie slid across the floor to sit next to me as I undid my ponytail and shook out my sweat-damp hair. She dug into her dance bag.

"That was intense. My ass hurts in places I didn't think it could," she said. She slipped her glasses onto her nose and blinked a few times.

"You got that right," I told her, laughing. I mopped my chest sweat with a smelly towel from the bottom of my bag. "She's pushing hard, isn't she?"

"Lili, *ma chérie*," my aunt said to me in her lilting oh-so-French voice. "I am afraid we must talk. *Alone*."

"What'd you do to piss her off? You looked good." Sophie asked me under her breath as she unlaced her *pointe* shoes and pulled them off. She plucked off the wad of lamb's wool on each foot, rubbed her bloody toes and winced. In practically the same motion, she unwrapped a granola bar and took a huge bite.

Sophie was the company's shining star. She always stretched, always extended herself with perfect poise, always made every landing look effortless and graceful. My friend was born to be a prima ballerina. If it weren't for the bug-eye glasses she wore after school to give her eyes a rest from her contacts, she'd be pretty much perfect.

Me? Not even close to perfect. I was a certified clod in comparison, let into these coveted classes at the most prestigious dance school in Connecticut out of a warped sense of family obligation.

But I suspected the joyride was coming to an end. Quickly.

I swiped the sweat from my brow as I pulled off my own pink satin shoes. "Who knows what I did? I breathe wrong and she disapproves. She's too much like my mother. It's in their genes."

"In my office, Lili. *Maintenant*. Gather your belongings."

I rolled my eyes at Sophie so my aunt couldn't see. "I don't know what's worse. Sucking at my arabesque or the fact that I'll be cramming all night just to pass my geometry test tomorrow."

Sophie laughed and pushed back her glasses. "Definite toss-up. Geometry sucks."

I got to my feet. "See ya, Princess."

"Call me later," Sophie said, smiling. She tucked a strand of her platinum hair behind her ear. "Good luck."

As I followed my aunt's lithe steps into her office, I felt the weight of my own body as I moved. I wasn't sleek as a swan, like she was. I didn't have the height and grace and angular beauty of the French heritage she shared with my Mom and their other triplet, Nina. And I had not one speck of the elegant presence of my statuesque *Grand-mère* Camille. Four times the female gorgeousness in my family, and I had to face their images every day of my life.

No. No such luck for Liliana Carracino. I'd inherited the genetic predisposition of the other half of my family, my Dad's Italian *abbondanza,* with all the curves and the gobs of dark hair and the fleshy abundance that just didn't play well with other ballerinas.

But my mother had been a dancer, she *wanted* her only daughter to be a dancer, and *mon Dieu*, a dancer she would have. Or so she tried to convince herself.

When I saw my aunt perch delicately on the edge of her desk and drape those lovely slim arms over her toned legs, I had a sinking suspicion.

My curvaceous body wasn't part of her grand plan for perfect stage presence.

I sat down hard on a chair and ran a hand through my damp hair. She stared, and I folded my arms across my chest to cover the sweat streaks on my pink leotard.

"My dear, Lili," she began. "You are my most precious *joie de vivre*, but I am afraid we have a bit of a problem."

I cleared my throat and tried not to sound defensive to the drama queen who was my aunt. "What's that?"

She tsk-tsk-tsked. "Your lines, my dear." She shook her head and pursed her lips into a pout. "You are not . . . not so much like the other girls in the company. I am afraid this level of class might be . . . how you say . . . beyond your range."

I bit my lip. This hurt. No matter how you sliced it, this was still a personal attack, and nobody wants to be told they look bad. Especially by family that's supposed to support you.

My aunt pressed a button on her computer and brought up a video of the class dancing. "Come here, my dear."

She extended that graceful hand with the manicured nails toward me and I wanted to smack it away.

"No. I'm fine here, thanks." Hiding behind the veil of my heavy hair and layers of fat.

She gave me a pained expression. "Let us watch together, then."

I swallowed hard. "You actually taped us?"

She raised her brows. "But of course. I tape every class to evaluate the dancers before company roles are assigned."

I don't know why this surprised me, but it did. And when I stared at the screen, I did not like what I saw. In fact, my appearance was horrifying. My chest bounced, and I hit the ground like an elephant on my *grand jeté*. I looked like a jiggly, corpulent mess compared to the other dancers.

My aunt waved a hand toward the screen and frowned. "You are so . . . how you say . . . *full*? When we look at you alongside the other girls, Lili . . . well, it just will not do. Those breasts. . . too *grande* for a ballerina."

I shrank against the chair. "What are you saying, Aunt Margaux? That you don't want me?" I bit my cheeks to keep from crying, as those very breasts heaved with frustration. My own aunt, my *family*, was throwing me under the bus. "Just come right out and say it. Get it over with."

"This is very difficult, my sweet. Perhaps you should —"

Emotional agony. That's what this session was. Slow torture.

Suddenly, I couldn't take one minute more. I just did not want to hear it. Not now when my calf muscle was cramping and my back ached and my new blister popped when I moved my foot.

"I'll save you the trouble, Aunt Margaux. I quit. I'm done. No more classes four days a week, no more bloody feet, no more blackened toenails. You don't have to worry about me ruining your ballet line again." I paused to point at her. "And *you* can tell my mother. I can't deal with her reaction."

Margaux looked distressed. "But, Lili. Let me—"

"Save it."

I was already headed for the door.

2.

With the streetlights just beginning to come on downtown, I slung my dance bag over my shoulder and turned onto Main Street, head down against the rain. It was a short walk home, and downpour or not it was better than waiting for my mother to show up . . . or not. My dad's schedule made him completely unreliable. They'd both stranded me more times than I could count, and I didn't feel like hanging around the scene of the crime.

As I walked, I noticed a new art quilt display in the Kerry's Cottage window, but I didn't want to study stitching techniques. Not tonight. I was too preoccupied with my own misery.

Still stinging from my Aunt Margaux's words, I fought tears on the ten-minute walk back to our house. I'd forgotten a coat and umbrella, my leotard and sweat pants were drenched and clinging, and my thoughts circled back to the same conclusion.

I. Hate. My. Stupid. Body.

Cars drove past as I swiped the rain and tears from my eyes. Why couldn't I have been born long and lean and beautiful – *and flat*– like my French ancestors? Why did I have to be the only ninth grader pushing her way toward porn star sized boobs? My days had been bad enough in fourth grade to be the only one forced to wear an actual bra.

Life just wasn't fair.

A pickup truck with roll bars and fog lights pulled out of Artie's parking lot, came toward me and slowed to a crawl. Two guys stuck their heads out the truck's windows and wolf-whistled. At the same time I saw a few quick flashes of light.

A shiver ran up my spine. I knew that truck. It was Jimmy Barnett's.

Oh, no. This was not good.

I hurried and tried to look busy by staring into the jewelry store window as I passed.

Tricky maneuvers wouldn't make a difference. Tyler Jackson and Joe Sanderson had spotted me.

I started to run away and quickly realized my mistake.

"Nice rack, Carracino!" Tyler yelled. "Keep running, baby! Bounce those titties for me!"

"Love those high beams!" Joe added making disgusting squeezing gestures with his hands. "Woo-hoo! Let me get my hands on them!"

"In your dreams," I snapped. As the truck passed, I glanced down to my chest and realized the chill in the air and everything else was showing clearly through my wet leotard and sports bras. Mortified, I flipped them a bird, crossed my arms tightly and ran-walked as fast as I could.

Another obnoxious whistle later and they mercifully left me alone.

My legs felt leaden as I trudged up the hill to my house. This was becoming an unwelcome daily ritual, me dodging comments and gestures from boys who only saw me for one thing – and it wasn't my brain.

My breasts had taken over my life.

I just wanted to get home and forget this day ever happened. And no way could I even think about concentrating on geometry.

Tomorrow, I'd deal with another F, but tonight, I'd have to face my mother.

And no doubt she'd talked to Margaux.

3.

Slipping my key in the lock, I opened the front door a fraction of an inch. I listened.

The house was blissfully quiet as I stepped inside.

A second later a foam football whacked me in the head, and my 10-year-old wannabe jock star brother burst into hysterical laughter as he aimed his video camera.

"Gotcha!" he said, doing a little victory dance.

"Tony, I'll kill you one of these days if you don't cut it out! And quit taking my picture!"

I picked up the ball and winged it back. The rat was too quick. He ducked expertly, and I watched in horror as the ball sailed into my mother's crystal vase.

I gasped as he followed its trajectory with the camera.

Before we could even move toward it, the vase wobbled, tipped, hung in the air for a breath-stealing moment, and then shattered on the tile floor to spill water, daylilies and broken bits of sparkling glass everywhere.

Tony sucked in a sharp breath and started to laugh in that annoying little brother way. "Oh, this is going online. And I'm going to tell Mom! You're in trouble now, big time!"

Before I could react, he'd bolted from the room with his camera and screamed for my mother.

My only sibling was such an unbelievable brat.

I stood there dripping, staring at the mess, and the tears I held back started to leak from my eyes.

I just couldn't deal with this, too. Not on top of everything else.

So I stepped over the debris, climbed the stairs to the bathroom and locked myself inside.

"Lili! Get down here this instant!" my mother shouted up the stairs. "Clean up this mess! I do not have time for this! I have an important meeting in just a few moments!"

A stream of unrecognizable French curses followed.

"Liliana!"

It took all my strength, but I double checked the door lock and ignored her. I turned the tub on hot and dumped a load of bath bubbles into the water. Soothing steam began to fill the air, to warm my bones while my mother made noise downstairs.

When I looked into the mirror, my reflection began to cloud. So much better to look at myself now that a large part of me was obscured. Soon enough, all that remained in the glass was the image of my tired eyes, and when those had vanished in the mist, I finally turned away.

I peeled off my sweats and leotard and stuffed them with great ceremony into the trash. Next came the tights, and out of my duffel, the *pointe* shoes, the talc and the lamb's wool. The tiny can overflowed with remnants of my miserable failure.

I stared at the pile for a minute, feeling rotten, then opened the window, picked up the trash can and threw it onto the lawn.

When the entire mess thunked onto the grass below, I could finally breathe a little easier.

Purging was such amazing therapy.

Turning off the bath water, I dipped a finger into the tub.

Perfect.

My brother stuck his mouth to the door's keyhole and chanted. "You're i-n trouble. You're i-n trouble. Na-na-na-na-na-na!"

"Get out of here, Tony," I snapped.

My nightly wrestling match with the wet sports bras began. Tugging at the elastic band of the first one, I stretched it wide and yanked hard, pulling up toward my face. The first one caught me on the chin and made me bite my lip.

"*Merde!*"

I pulled off the offensive garment and threw it to the ground in a soggy heap. Only one more to go. The process was agonizing, but when it was over, I was free in all my floppy naked glory.

As I massaged the deep grooves the elastic had cut into my skin, my mother pounded on the door and scared the life out of me.

"Lili, you must get out here and take care of the mess. You cannot just walk from your responsibilities!"

I quickly dove into the bath, panties and all, sloshing water over the rim. "I'm sorry, Mother. I'm already in the tub. I'll clean later."

She cursed furiously in French, pounded the door once more for effect. "We are not finished, Lili."

I tuned her out and submerged.

Finally, she gave up on getting me to respond and headed down the stairs screaming something I couldn't understand with my ears full of water.

That was the exact moment at which I realized the bath water was scalding my skin so much it actually hurt.

And I didn't even care.

4.

Sophie called me on my cell at 7:00. I was bundled in one of my dad's oldest silk robes and pajamas, inspecting waterlogged pruny skin. The rain and wind rustled leaves from the trees outside my window, blowing them with wet slaps against the panes.

I was supposed to be studying. Instead, I contemplated my misery.

"So what gives?" she asked. "I couldn't wait after class anymore. My brother and his girlfriend picked me up and they were pretty steamed, as usual. He already had a giant hickey." She paused a second. "So tell me already. I'm dying here!"

I groaned. "It's totally too embarrassing."

Sophie laughed. "Just spill it. BFF, remember?"

She was right. We promised to tell each other everything. "I got the boot. She kicked me out of the company 'cuz I'm too fat."

Sophie gasped. "Seriously? She's your aunt!" A pause, then, "You're kidding . . . right?"

I flopped on the bed and pulled my comforter over my head. "I wish. She told me I don't fit in."

Silence. "Lil, that's so brutal."

"Tell me about it."

For some weird reason, I didn't feel like crying. Now I was just . . . numb.

Sophie asked the standard good friend question. "Are you sewing?"

I stared at the headless mannequins lining my wall, pinned with half-finished projects and draped with fabric. Sophie knew I sewed when I needed to work out a problem, or stall, or fill the dawn hours when I couldn't sleep because of too much diet soda and French coffee. She knew I worked with a needle and thread to divert attention away from whatever was bugging me. The more upset I was, the more detailed my work.

I studied the multi-layered embroidery I'd embellished on a pair of jeans and wondered why I hadn't reached for them as soon as I came into my room. If anything qualified as a major upset, today would be it.

"So, are you? Sewing?" Sophie asked again.

But today I couldn't even concentrate on my needlework. "Sulking."

"I know you're not cuddling with geometry proofs. Embroidering?"

"Doing absolutely nada 'cept feeling sorry for myself."

"Whoa. This is really serious. You're scaring me. Should I come over? I can be there in, like, five minutes. Wait. *Crap.* I've got to pick up another pair of contacts." She sighed."Never mind. I'll cancel and come over."

I rolled over and hugged my pillow. "Naw. Get your lenses so you can still read at school, but thanks. I just feel miserable. Fat. Ugly. Unwanted. Social reject. All of the above."

She laughed. "Stop it. You're none of those and you know it." Sophie lowered her voice to a whisper. "So have you talked to her yet?"

Her.

"My mother? No. I'm avoiding." The thought actually made me sick.

A rapid series of knocks sounded at my door.

"My dad's coming in. Gotta go. Meet me in the morning at the stop sign."

"You need major therapy, sister. I'll bring bagels with *shmear,*" Sophie promised like the good friend I could always count on. "And I want details. Send me an email. *Ciao* baby."

"*Au revoir.*"

From the hall, Dad asked, "Are you proper?"

Ever since I grew boobs, he made a rule to completely respect my privacy, in spite of his liberal European upbringing. This habit was old-fashioned and sweet, and I appreciated him all the more for it.

"Sure."

Pulling the comforter to my chin, I watched my father come toward me. Handsome, suave, and impeccably styled, I still thought he looked like Italian royalty with his thick black hair and sparkling brown eyes. When I was little, my friends joked that he was a king come to rescue me in his custom-made suit and shoes. And this is how I thought of him now, the perfectly dressed executive popping in to put in an appearance for his kids. It was sad, actually, how little time we spent together.

When he saw my expression, his face registered concern. "*Bella*, what's wrong?" He was by my side in an instant, sitting on the bed, laying a hand on my forehead. "Your skin is so flushed."

I shook my head. "Just tired."

He pushed a damp lock of hair from my forehead.

"You need more rest, ah?" he said, making that clucking noise that all my Italian relatives seemed to enjoy. "Dinner is almost ready."

"I'm not hungry, Daddy."

"Ah, but *Bella*, you must eat. To keep up your strength for dance and for school. You are a growing girl."

I pulled the covers over my head. "I can't eat. Not tonight."

He pulled back the covers and laughed. "And why not, may I ask?"

"Because Mother is mad at me."

"She will get over it," he said with a grin and a wink. "The mess is already gone. She makes a temper, but she always comes around." He shrugged and made that noise again. "It was just an accident, hmm?"

"No. It was Tony's fault for being such a pipsqueak."

He kissed the top of my head. "Get dressed for dinner and join us. We have much news to talk about."

He stood to leave and loosened his silk tie.

He gave me a wink and a smile. "*Andiamo*, Lili. Do not keep your mother waiting."

5.

I steeled myself before I entered the kitchen. My parents were chatting in their odd mix of French-Italian-English. Just 15 years off the immigrant boat and they'd made up their own language that I could understand a little more every day. Sometimes it was helpful they didn't know how much I could actually decipher, like around birthdays and Christmas when my brother and I could win Academy awards with how convincingly dumb we pretended to be.

Even dressed casually, my parents were both stunning. Glamorous. Successful. Independent. My mother, long and blonde and lean, wore tight black leggings and super high leather boots with a slouchy belted cashmere sweater that would have made me look a well-fed pig. On her it accentuated her absolute Frenchness. Dad, in his dark wash jeans and un-tucked but crisp button-down shirt, looked worthy of a fashion magazine spread as he poured two glasses of red wine.

Sometimes these two made me feel positively gnome-like by comparison.

While they shared nibbles of the *bœuf bourguignon* from the kettle on the stove, I slipped in and took a seat at the table.

A few minutes later, my brother bounded into the room like the bull-in-a-china-shop he was, knocking a baguette from my mother's hands as she turned toward the table. She sucked in a breath, studied his impish "sorry, Mom" expression, then ruffled his hair and smiled.

She would have killed me if I'd done that, but that soft spot of hers for him seemed to grow right along with him. It annoyed me that he got away with bloody murder, and I was scrutinized for every hangnail.

"Dust off the crumbs, *mon chére*," she said. "And where is your sister?"

"Duh, Mom," he said, hitching his thumb toward the table.

This time five whole minutes passed before they noticed me. Nowhere near the record of 17 minutes and 37 seconds, but still, impressive. It was a fact. When my parents cooked or talked business, I ceased to exist.

My mother turned to me and her expression grew pained. "Oh my dear, what are you wearing, Lili? It is truly dreadful!"

She hated when I dressed like a slob, and the 5X bright yellow sweatshirt I bought at a yard sale didn't help. "I'm comfortable, Mother. Just leave it be, please."

"You look like a fat lemon," my brother said snarkily.

I smirked at him. "Exactly the look I was going for. Thanks."

My mother studied me. "Push your hair back, Lili, and sit up straight. You do not have a dancer's posture."

I'm not a dancer, Mom. I'll never be a dancer.

I'm just your great disappointment.

She tsked and dished the stew into colorful pottery bowls.

My dad turned and finally noticed me.

"Ah, Lili! We're all here! *Molto bene!"* he said. "Come, *mi famille*. Tonight we have much to celebrate."

Celebrate? No, thank you. My day sucked.

My mother, the one and only Adrienne Carracino, leather goods designer to the uber-wealthy and fabulously famous, was beaming at my father, the true love of her life.

My father raised his glass. "Tonight we toast. To your mother's and our family's success. *Salute!"*

My mother got tears in her eyes and clinked glasses with my father. "*Salute, mio Antonio. Ti amo."*

They only had eyes for each other.

My brother and I stared as they kissed both cheeks and hugged. It was so embarrassing they were still so in love. And that they showed it. All the time.

Finally, I lifted a glass and elbowed my brother. We clinked a few times, loudly, to get their attention and interrupt the parental smooch-fest. "Congratulations for what?"

They turned, tapped their glasses to ours, and sat.

"This is a very big day for our company," my dad said.

Uh-oh.

My dad went on. "Adrienne Carracino Inc. is expanding!"

Double uh-oh.

My brother smacked a fist into his palm. "Did you crush some little guy and take him for all he's worth?"

My brother was too blunt for his own good.

She laughed. "No, no, no, my sweet boy. But we *are* signing the deal to purchase Chianzi Leather."

Dad took over. "This is a momentous day. Our new supply chain and manufacturing will allow us to launch entire product lines as well as the handbags and leather goods."

My mother rubbed her hands together with glee. "Shoes! I will finally design the shoes of my dreams! Is it not glorious?"

I slouched in my seat, realizing in no uncertain terms what this meant. Planning sessions. Art meetings. Shorter tempers. Louder yelling. Hours and hours at the design boards. More tension until they worked through the start-up problems. Even more when they finally went retail. *And –*

"We'll leave tomorrow," my mother explained giddily. "But only for two months."

--much more travel.

"Oh, man!" my brother whined. "Who's gonna take me to my football playoffs?"

"I'll be there," I said, feeling momentarily sorry for him.

He glared at me and pouted. "You don't count. You're just my sister."

I had to try even though I knew my efforts would be useless. "Can't you stay home, Dad? Just this once?"

He clucked. “I am afraid not, *Bella*. Building a business requires sacrifice. I am needed in Rome to negotiate contracts. They require a certain . . . subtlety.”

This was terrible. Abandoned again.

“This is like the fifth time this year already! Why don’t you just ship us off to boarding school with the other orphans and be done with it?”

They laughed, but I was dead serious. At least then they wouldn’t have to pretend they enjoyed the job of being parents.

“So who’s our warden this time?" I crossed my arms. They wouldn’t ask Margaux.

Uh-oh. “Not a babysitting service again.”

“Nonna Lena is in Italy until Christmas,” my father explained.

“Didn’t tell me that,” I snapped.

My mother had the grace to pretend she’d be concerned during their extended absence, even though she wouldn’t take her mind off her designs. My mother was unstoppable, much like her sister Nina. Once she made a plan, she went for it all the way.

“You will be so pleased, *ma chérie*." She took my hand. “It is someone very special.”

Triple uh-oh.

I gulped. “Who?”

My mother smiled too brightly.

“Grande-mère Camille.”

6.

My brother and I stared at each other in shock.

"You can't be serious," I said.

"*Absolutement*," my mother assured. "She arrives first thing tomorrow from Paris. Even Margaux and Nina do not know. Her arrival will be a surprise for them, too."

I began to envision my bleak future. "Mother, no offense, but we hardly know her."

My mother scooped an extra dollop of stew into my bowl. "She is your grandmother and she loves you very much. And she *wants* to know you."

"Then why hasn't she even tried?" I asked. "It's not like she's made an effort, staying in France and traveling with Christophe all the time. Letters and presents don't count for much."

My mother looked taken aback by the all-too-true accusation. "Lili, that is simply not nice. She consults with Christophe on his new designs and she is very busy with her work."

I speared a mushroom with my fork. "Aren't we all?"

"She has taken a leave of absence to be with you as long as is necessary."

Tony whined, "But the last time Grand-mère stayed she was a dictator."

"That was five years past," my mother said. "How can you even recall?"

He had a fit. "But she made me take a bath EVERY single day! And I HATE eating carrots!"

My dad laughed. "And this is a problem? Why?"

Tony rolled his eyes and covered his head with his dinner napkin while he grumbled.

I stabbed at a hunk of meat and pushed it into the gravy. Nausea rolled through me. I could feel my mother staring at me, waiting for me to respond. But what could I say? That it freaked me out to be in the presence of the woman who single-handedly inspired an entire era of French fashion? That I felt like a bridge troll when I stood next to her with her perfectly coiffed chignon, her dewy skin and her fabulously famous long limbs? That she was more beautiful as a senior citizen than I could ever hope to be? *Ever?*

No, I couldn't tell my mother any of that. She was the byproduct of the woman with enough super genes to produce three identical beauties at once, and then resume her fashion career and slip right back into her designer size zero dresses.

"Well, Lili?" She arched a perfect brow. "Will there be a problem?"

I shook my head and forced a good-daughter smile. "No, Mother, of course not. We'll greet her with open arms. What time does Grand-mère arrive?"

She ignored my sarcasm and chatted about logistics for a few minutes. Then my mother casually dropped the question bomb I'd been dreading.

"So how was dance today, Lili?"

Her cell phone rang and she punched the dismiss button. "It is Margaux calling again. Oh, Antonio, I cannot talk to my sister tonight! She will know about our surprise!"

I nearly choked on a spoonful of potatoes. I forced myself to swallow, and fought the urge to heave right on the checkered tablecloth.

My mother pursed her lips. "She has called four times already, but if I talk to her she will soon realize I am not telling her something."

"Maybe it is important?" he mused while he read his Blackberry. "Why she calls?"

My mother sighed. "No, I am certain she just wants to talk." She tore off a piece of bread and nibbled the crust delicately.

Relief washed over me when she forgot she had asked me about dance class.

One glance at the notepad beside her, and her focus turned to my father. "Oh, Antonio, I nearly forgot to tell you about the call with Marco. There are so many things we must do before we leave tomorrow, and we have another conference call with the lawyers –" she glanced at her wristwatch and swore in French "—in five minutes! We must hurry. *Vite, vite!*"

And in one breath she was on her feet and ranting in that hybrid language they'd invented about business that didn't involve me and that I cared nothing about. I folded my napkin and excused myself from the table.

When I cleared my dish to the sink, I glanced into the backyard and spotted my ballet gear glowing pink and scattered forlornly across the lawn.

"You can eat later," she scolded my father as she took his bowl and he clucked. "It is just food. We must attend our call, Antonio!"

She clearly hadn't seen my stuff outside on the lawn or she'd have said something.

Thinking quickly, I grabbed the trash bag and headed for the door. "I'll take out the trash."

My father smiled at me as he tore off a hunk of bread. "*Grazie mille*, Liliana. You and your brother clean up while your mother and I work, hmm? We will talk later?"

"Sure." I scooted out the door and scrambled across the grass to gather my clothes before anyone noticed. The rain had stopped, but the ground was soggy. I stuffed the muddy clothes into the trash bag alongside the beef wrappers and carrot peels and breathed a sigh of relief.

From the shadows of the backyard, I called my Aunt Margaux on my cell.

"*Âllo*," she said.

"Aunt Margaux, it's me. Lili."

Upstairs, my parents' home office light flicked on.

My aunt's sigh was audible. "And how are you doing, my darling? Are you all right? I was so worried about you when you left. You did not let me explain."

"You still don't have to." I waited until my parents sat at the conference table. "I'm fine. Just fine. But you've got to do something for me."

"And what is that?"

I went for it. "You can't tell Mom that you fired me."

She sucked in a breath. "Lili, I did not *fire*—"

"Whatever. Call it what you will, but don't tell her yet. Please. She's got too much going on at work and she doesn't need the distraction."

Margaux seemed to weigh the request. "And why should I not tell my sister? We do not keep secrets from each other."

I paced the lawn, thinking about tomorrow's surprise visit from my grandmother. "I know, I know. Family honor and all that." It was such bullshit. "But you owe me this at least."

She let out a measured breath. "And if I agree, when will *you* tell her?"

I sighed. "When she and my dad get back from their business trip to Italy. They leave tomorrow, and I know they wouldn't want to be preoccupied by my failure."

"You are not a failure, Lili." She let her words linger. "But all right, *ma chérie*. I will make you that promise."

"Thanks."

I hung up. When I got back inside the house, my twerp brother had disappeared from sight.

And as long as I didn't have to talk to my mother about my fat butt and my massive mammaries, I didn't care if I had to wash every single dish in the entire house.

7.

While I shoveled two bowls of frosted sugar cereal into my mouth, I'd patiently listened to the lectures from both parents on doing my schoolwork, keeping up my grades, behaving to make them proud, doing what Grand-mère says, always being polite and not talking back, minding my brother, being helpful around the house . . . all the basic good daughter stuff.

But even while they went through the motions to prep me for their departure, my parents were fully preoccupied with their impending corporate acquisition. My mother kept making notes, and my father barely looked up from his stack of contracts. I knew they were preoccupied because neither one of them scolded me on my blatantly inappropriate food choice. In fact, I don't think they even noticed I was stress eating enough for twelve people. And they definitely didn't notice I was wearing a hole-ridden faded flannel shirt and ripped jeans to school.

An hour later, while they counted suitcases in the front hall and double checked their passports and e-tickets, we'd said our goodbyes. Hugged. Kissed on both cheeks. Hugged again.

After they confirmed their limo's arrival time, handed us a wad of money for emergencies and made absolutely certain we knew what to do when Grand-mère arrived, my brother and I had finally been released to walk to school like we did every morning. Out on the front path, we gave each other a resigned look and a half-hearted we're-in-this-together wave. He went one way while I went the other.

Thankfully, the subject of dance had never once been mentioned during my parents' 'be-good' speech. My secret was still safe.

It was damp outside and blustery, with fat raindrops falling from the night-wet trees onto my head as I walked beneath them. My retro green slicker fluttered against me with every step, making that scrunchy-crackly noise plastic makes when it's cold.

When I met Sophie at the corner, I was deep in thought and attempting to dry off my cheeks by rolling my shoulders onto them. The move only succeeded in making my face wetter, and my frustration must have showed.

"Relax." She handed me a cream cheesy bagel wrapped in a flowered paper towel. I handed her an espresso in one of the paper to-go cups I kept stashed at home.

She looked svelte in a black wrap coat and stylish rain hat that accented just how glossy her platinum hair was. I looked like an overgrown watermelon. I sighed. "Can't relax."

She clearly read my mind.

"You don't look so bad," she said, swiping at her bagel's overflowing *shmear* with her tongue. She licked the blob of cream cheese with precision.

"Did you get your new contacts?"

"Yeah. I'm blind as a bat without them, but they're still not right and I'm wearing them anyway. At least I don't have to wear my glasses," she complained, blinking.

"I know you're stuck on not wearing specs to high school, but seriously. If the contacts aren't working, at some point you might have to bite the bullet and give in."

"No way. For years, I've been called every name in the book, and I'm sick of the abuse." She turned toward me. "But I must say, you *are* looking mighty fuzzy."

"And now we know why I don't look so bad," I concluded.

Sophie shoved me. "Cut it out. So did you handle her?"

I shook my head as I chewed. "Too busy. She didn't even notice me."

We stepped over a fast food bag and debris floating in a puddle on the sidewalk. Cars whizzed past as we drank the hot coffees and ate in a most unbecoming, unladylike manner. My mother would be horrified.

"That kinda sucks," Sophie said with her mouth full.

I stared at her. "How can you eat so much and never gain an ounce? You're such a bitch!"

She grinned with her teeth full of cream cheese.

"That's gross!" I said, giving her a shove in her all-too-sculpted abs. "It's so unfair."

Making a great show of it, she polished off the bagel and wiped her mouth, then stuffed the paper towel into my raincoat pocket. "So what's unfair? Your aunt?"

Margaux was only the smallest part of my worries.

I shrugged it off. "That, and . . . . I don't know. It's just. . . ." What I'd been feeling for weeks now was so hard to put into words. I was seriously out of sorts and I could barely stand to look in the mirror anymore. How do you tell someone you're starting to hate yourself more every day? "It's not important, Sophie. It doesn't really matter."

She pinched me so hard on the arm I nearly dropped my coffee.

"Hey!"

Sophie gave me the Jewish mother guilt look she'd mastered. "So, tell me already. You expect I'm a mind reader? What exactly is your problem?"

I stalled for time by sipping the last of my espresso. Sophie noticed, but didn't nudge.

"Well, besides the fact that my grades are tanking . . . it's just . . . well, it's other stuff, too."

"I'll quiz you on social studies and English this weekend, but you're on your own for science and math," she offered. "As much as I like alternate universes, you know I'm no good at bio. And I totally suck at proofs."

I shrugged. "Well, that will help . . . *some*. Thanks."

"You gonna pass your geometry test today?"

I sighed. "I won't be getting one of the first three letters of the alphabet on my paper, that's for sure. But I've got bigger problems."

"Dance?" she asked.

"No." I shook my head.

Up ahead the road dead-ended at Middleton High. I scanned the rows of cars in the student parking lot. And there it was, in all its redneck glory, parked halfway into the handicapped spot by the flagpole -- Jimmy 's truck with the huge tires and roll bars and fog lights. And there *they* were, Tyler Jackson, Joe Sanderson and Jimmy Barnett, standing beside that horrible truck smoking cigarettes like they didn't have a care in the world.

My body tensed and I shivered against the damp breeze.

Sophie followed my gaze. "Oh. I get it. The terrible threesome giving you trouble again?"

I nodded, embarrassed by how much I'd let them get to me. It had been a downhill slide since they saw me in a bathing suit this summer. "Last night. Walking back."

Sophie swore under her breath. "Damn, I shoulda made my brother take you home." She leaned close as we walked. "I'm sorry, Lil."

I gave her a half-smile. "It's not your fault. It's mine."

She pulled away. "How do you figure? They're the cretins who keep hassling you."

"Yeah," I said softly. "But at the end of the day, they still have all the power around here. And I'm still *me*."

8.

Ninth grade was the bottom of the barrel at Middleton High. In a 9-12 school like mine, where 1,638 official students roamed the halls and climbed the walls on a daily basis, being the new kids on the block had no advantages. Seriously, none. Lockers on the hall near the reeking dumpsters, trailers for classrooms, lunch at 10:15 in the morning and absolutely zero respect from upper-classmen. I repeat, ZERO.

This sad state of affairs was never more apparent to me than during class change before first lunch, when I got caught with my hand on my vibrating cell phone, not by one of my teachers, but by Joe Sanderson.

Joe Sanderson. Jock. Junior. Resident asshole.

He snatched the phone from my hand and held it over my head as it buzzed.

“What ya got there, Carracino?” he mocked. “Call from your loverboy?”

“Not likely." I reached for the phone but couldn’t stretch far enough. He was basketball tall and I wasn’t. And when I stretched, he accidentally-on-purpose rubbed up against my chest with his free hand.

The touch made me really mad. “Give it back, Joe. I’m serious.”

I scanned the hall for teachers and saw none, but two older boys snickered as they walked past us. And if my miserable failure in math hadn’t done enough to wreck my mood, this atomized it.

Joe played keep-away, tossing the phone back and forth between his hands. “Why don’t you jump for it? Come on, let me see you jump.”

He glared at my chest tugging the buttons on my flannel shirt, and I felt my face flush. I refused to give him the satisfaction of humiliating me. Instead, I tried to relax, held out my hand and hoped he'd cooperate. Prayed, actually.

He spun away from me and pushed a few buttons on my phone, calling up the incoming text. He read it out loud.

"Just want to say I love you one more time."

He raised his eyebrows. "What is *this*?"

I yanked on his tee shirt as he held the phone over my head. My frustration was mounting. "Give me my phone back. Please."

Joe looked down at me, grinning. "Got yourself a lover, huh hot stuff?"

I wanted to punch him where it counts but he got away from me.

He ran a few feet with my phone, slipping between a group of science club kids blocking the hallway and the open doors to the cafeteria. He was doing something with my phone that I couldn't clearly see. By the time I caught up with him, I realized he'd been texting.

Mrs. Alban, the gray-haired lunchroom supervisor everyone suspected of being a lesbian, blew her shrill whistle and pointed at him with a crooked finger. She practically barked at him with her man voice. "Is that your cell phone, young man? Give that to me right this instant."

She advanced on him, but Joe put on his best All American imitation before tossing the phone back to me. "No ma'am. It's Carracino's phone."

The scary teacher with the pinched face turned her glare toward me, and seconds later Joe slipped into the crowd and disappeared.

I cowered.

"Young lady, must I take that telephone away from you for the remainder of the year?" she asked through gritted teeth. "You know school rules."

I shook my head and slipped the phone into my backpack. I tried to think fast. "I'm sorry, Missus Alban. My phone . . . fell out of my bag and he picked it up for me. That's all." I swallowed hard. "It won't happen again. I promise."

I backed up a few feet and tried to give her a smile, but the expression died before it reached my face. Turning quickly, I fled, pushing past students rushing for the pizza line. Ducking into the music wing, I made my way around the hall monitors to the girls' room in the corner to wait out my lunch period alone. I couldn't handle being surrounded right now, and the smell of greasy pepperoni pizza was turning my stomach.

Inside, I could still hear the violins trying to play in sync but not quite making it. To the muted sounds of a classical strings disaster, I slipped into the farthest stall and locked the door. Perching on the toilet seat, I leaned back, closed my eyes and tried not to breathe in the scent of the stinky school bathroom with bad plumbing.

After a minute, I took out my phone and dared to look at my sent texts.

My stomach seized when I saw what Joe had written.

You make me so hot, baby. Let's do the nasty right no--

"Oh. My. God," I muttered.

I blew out a long breath when I noticed the flashing envelope at the top of my screen. Clicking a few buttons, I checked the incoming text.

Lili?

Breathing a sigh, I tapped out my reply.

Sorry, Daddy. Boy stole my phone. Wasn't me saying that.

I imagined his relief and waited for his response. When the note came, it didn't exactly offer the sympathy I'd hoped for.

Ah. What can you do, Cara? He was just having fun. Boys will be boys, right?

Right.

I shut off my phone and leaned back against the tiles to stare at the graffiti covering the stall door. The usual distracted me.

Susan loves Jason.

Fuckwads rule.

John was here.

Beavers ate my shoelaces.

Then my sights landed on bold red letters that proclaimed the one thing I did not need to see right now.

Lili Carracino is a raging slut.

9.

"No way can I do this alone," I said to Sophie as she lay on my bed and alternately flexed and pointed her toes in the air. Her gray NYPD tee shirt puddled around her like a blanket, but her leggings fit like a glove to her dancer's legs.

I picked up a basket of loose buttons and trim, and pawed through the odds and ends until I found the amethyst-colored brooch I bought at an old man's yard sale last month. "You'll stay for dinner, won't you? I need reinforcements and my brother is no help. Lasagna's already in the oven."

She plopped her legs on the bed. "Yeah, whatever. I could eat. But I must say I'm curious about the almighty Camille Le Jeune."

"My grandmother is a force to be reckoned with," I groaned.

"What about your grandfather?"

I shook my head. "We don't talk about him much. He died when my mom was little. I never knew him. She raised the triplets on her own and she never remarried."

Digging into the bag of extra hot taco chips on the desk, I grabbed a handful and stuffed them into my mouth. Chasing the fire with a cold diet soda, I stifled a fizz burp.

"Give me some of those," Sophie said, motioning with her fingers. "I need crunch."

I gave her the bag and moved toward one of my mannequins. She chomped the chips noisily.

The denim jacket I was working on still didn't look right, even after I'd embroidered violets and given them petals crafted out of the palest of lavender tissue faille. The colors needed more oomph, a little sparkle maybe. Wiping the taco dust from my fingers, I held the pin up to a cluster of blooms and nodded toward Sophie. "What do you think?"

She shrugged. "I can't see it without my glasses. Besides, you're the expert. And don't be such a drama queen. Camille can't be that bad." She snorted. "You've never had to contend with the likes of my Bubbe Ruth when she's kvetching with my mom. They'll needle you to death if you're not careful."

"At least they talk. My grandmother doesn't *say* much," I said. "It's impossible to know what she's really thinking."

"That's tough." Sophie rolled over onto her side and began to do leg lifts.

I stared at her. "Do you ever stop moving? I'm exhausted just watching you, and you just got out of two hours of dance."

"Can't help it," she said without stopping. "Want the lead. I *will* be Cinderella if it kills me."

"You're not even breaking a sweat. You're a freak of nature." Stuffing three more chips into my mouth, I buried my guilt in calories I didn't need. Then I pinned the brooch to the jacket shoulder and stepped back a few feet to study while I chewed. Better, but not the best. "Did I ever show you the album? I didn't, did I?"

We'd been friends since sixth grade, when Sophie moved to Middleton from Long Island. One day on the playground at recess we collided headfirst in a game of tag and almost knocked each other out. Her thick glasses broke and we'd compared goose eggs all day and had been best friends ever since.

Sophie breathed hard, twice. "What album?"

In one swift motion, she flipped positions on the bed and began to lift the other leg.

"*The* album. My childhood obsession." I walked over my stack of untouched school books to my closet. On the shelf I moved my hand to the gilt-edged binder. I slid the book out and opened it. "When I was little, I started a scrapbook on my mother's family. This one was for Grand-mère."

I hadn't opened these pages in years. They were too hard to look at for long, too much of a reminder of the person I could never be. Her genetics had not trickled down the family tree to me. Not one little bit.

"Camille has her own book, hmm?"

"Several, actually," I said, sighing. "Did I ever tell you how she got started?"

"Besides being born beautiful with amazing bones?" Sophie finished her leg lifts and pulled herself to a sitting position. She spread her legs into a perfect V and leaned onto her elbows. "Put it here so I can see," she said, patting the bed a few feet in front of her. "I still need to stretch."

Without moving her legs, she flung her body sideways over the bed to reach her dance bag on the floor. When she righted herself again, her eyes were magnified in huge hot pink frames.

I stared at her face. "Interesting."

"You like?" she said, pushing them back on her nose. "Picked them up when I got my contacts. Thought they were kind of funky. Neat, huh?"

I smiled. "Definitely . . . *progressive.*"

Sophie laughed. "They are too cool for school, that's for sure. I'd never hear the end of it. But they're fun. So show me the book already."

I sat and opened to the first page. "When my grandmother was only fourteen, she was walking along the banks of the Seine in Paris by herself carrying a bouquet of pink peonies. Notre Dame was all shimmery in the background, it was June, it was breezy and her white dress was billowing out around her like a sail," I explained, repeating the story I'd heard a hundred times. I showed Sophie a picture of her in the early years. "She was the same age we are now."

Sophie mocked. "Absolutely *disgusting.*"

"Christophe St. Pierre saw her in the sunlight looking all golden and gorgeous and knew she was his muse." I nodded. "She inspired his genius. Because of her, he completely redefined casual elegance with his designs. The rest is fashion history, and now she's a legend."

"Wish I could inspire someone like that," Sophie groaned. "I knew she was famous, but *sheesh.* I can't even get Adam to notice me."

"You have to stop exercising long enough for him to. And what do you see in him anyway?"

Sophie sighed and gave me a big smile. “I don’t know. He’s sweet. He loves corn dogs with mayonnaise. I saw him eating them at the pool on Fourth of July,” she said dreamily. “And he’s into classic sci-fi, just like me. I heard him talking to his sister about *The Martian Chronicles*. And you know that’s my all-time favorite book! We like the same stuff!”

I shook my head. “My friend, your interests are an ongoing juxtaposition. But you are a dichotomy.”

She held up her hand and showed four fingers. “Bonus score for using the English vocab in sentences. Only twenty-eight more concepts to go." A picture in my grandmother’s album distracted her. “This is sick. She’s got naturally great lines.”

“Tell me about it.”I flipped a few more pages, moving past the sketches of my grandmother that inspired St. Pierre’s first collection. I’d found them on the Internet when I was seven, and had been tortured by them ever since. “She became *the* face of Paris before she even turned sixteen.”

“No pressure there,” Sophie said, finally sitting up and relaxing her posture. She rolled her neck to work out the kinks until the bones cracked loudly.

Together we stared at the images on the pages. Camille in *Vogue*. Camille in St. Pierre couture on the red carpet at the Cannes Film Festival. Camille wearing Balcroix diamonds . . . and her flawless skin. Camille . . . *being Camille*.

“The limo is here!” Tony screamed up the steps. “Battle stations ready!”

I closed the album with a snap and jolted to my feet.

“Jeez, will you relax already?” Sophie chided. “She’s just your grandmother.”

“You don’t understand." I pushed back the hunks of hair hanging in my face. Tugged on my flannel shirt and fastened the button that had popped open. Wiped off chip crumbs. Ran a finger over my teeth. “She’s way too scary.”

“But she’s *old*, Lil. How scary can she be?”

I shook my head and wiped my sweating palms on my jeans. “You have no idea. She hasn’t seen me in years and I’m sure she's every bit as gorgeous as I remember. And I've gained, like, twenty pounds."

"Of curves, maybe. I should be so lucky."

"But *she's* perfect. *Worse* than my mother."

Sophie ran to the window and pulled back the curtain. "This I have to see."

Peering over her shoulder, I watched the limo driver hold open the back door for my grandmother.

When she stepped out, he helped her to her feet. She was at least three inches taller than him.

Sophie gasped when my grandmother turned her face toward us, saw us in the window and smiled. "*Wow*. I didn't think real people could look that good." She pushed back her glasses and grabbed her nose. "Think I could get my nose bobbed like that? Would it look okay on me?"

"Sophie, you have to stop obsessing over your nose. It fits your face." I stood behind my friend. "Guess I better go greet her."

"I'd kill for legs that long," Sophie moaned, following me. She tossed her glasses onto the bed. "Can you imagine the leaps she could do?"

I sighed. "Did I mention that she was a dancer, too? Balanchine himself saw her dance and offered her a supporting spot in the New York Opera Ballet, but she turned him down. Retired her dance career to be a full-time muse and mom."

Sophie gasped while we took the stairs to the foyer two at a time. "She gave that up? Is she a whack job? That's like my total dream!"

I shrugged. "Passed the torch to her daughters. Margaux's the only one who stuck with it. Mom blew out her knee and Nina liked playing with make-up and hanging with boys way better."

"Now *I'm* even intimidated," Sophie said quietly, smoothing her long hair.

Downstairs, Tony pulled open the front door so hard it banged into the wall and rattled the family pictures hanging there. I scolded him as I walked out onto the porch. "Behave yourself."

He stuck out his tongue and blew me a raspberry. “You’re not the boss of me.”

I swatted him in the back of the head as we stepped onto the walk then sucked in my stomach and tried not to look terrified. Sophie hung in the doorway to watch, but my grandmother hurried toward us with long strides.

“Grand-mère,” I said, opening my arms to greet her in a hug.

“My darlings!" She pulled my brother and me into a hug and kissed us on both cheeks. “We have been apart far too long!”

Her accent was still as strong as I remembered, her words slow.

She inspected my brother first, smoothing a lock of his dark hair and cupping his cheek with her hand. “Just like your father. Such a handsome fine boy.”

I studied her. At 62, her skin was still dewy and the tiny lines around her eyes only added to a look of refined elegance. Her bones were sculpted with perfect symmetry. Her golden hair was swept up into an understated twist. Her crisp clothes . . . impeccable.

The woman had just traveled across an ocean, and she looked camera-ready.

My flannel shirt and jeans were a huge mistake. I should have changed. I hugged my arms to my chest and stood up straighter but it didn’t make a difference. She still knew her granddaughter was a total slob.

Grand-mère turned to look me over and her chin jutted out ever so slightly. Sophie may not have noticed, but I did.

“Ah, my Liliana,” she said sweetly, dropping her gaze to glance quickly at my thickened middle. Her eyebrow arched just a bit. “You have grown so.”

She didn’t need to say any more. She might as well have told me I swallowed a horse.

10.

After we made the introductions and I attempted to do some social studies homework with Sophie, she'd settled into the guest room and freshened up. My aunts were descending on us tomorrow, but for tonight, we were alone.

When my grandmother walked into the kitchen to join us, she'd traded her navy travelling suit for celery colored cashmere and wool slacks that somehow brightened her complexion.

She wore pearls. My grandmother wore pearls to dinner in my kitchen.

We sat around the table and listened to each other breathe, Sophie and my brother at the ends, my grandmother across from me. I cut the previously frozen lasagna into squares and slid one onto my brother's plate.

"This is so kind to have . . . dinner .ready," my Grand-mère said. She stared at the bubbling pasta in the foil pan and her smile kind of froze on her face.

"You've had a long day," I told her as I scooped a heaping portion onto her plate and handed it to her.

She looked at the five-layer feast of cheese, pasta and meat and tried to smile. But her gratitude seemed to be replaced by horror. Beside her, my brother stuffed his face greedily.

"Nice manners," I scolded. "Why don't you wait for the rest of us?"

He shrugged. "I'm starving! Give me a break."

My grandmother did smile then, at him. "*Adorable.* I know why you have become so tall. You eat already like a man!"

Sophie handed me her plate. "So, Lil tells me you were a ballerina."

I swallowed hard and dished out the food. I didn't want her to think I was gossiping behind her back. But she didn't flinch.

"Ah, those dancing days were such a long, long time ago. It is hardly worth mention, my dear."

"But Balanchine?" Sophie said excitedly. "He was the greatest of all time!"

Grand-mère stood and moved to the wine rack to select a bottle. She trailed her fingers across the bottles until she found one that piqued her interest and removed it to study the label.

"Sophie is a dancer, too," I said.

Just as Grand-mère turned to look at me, the enormous piece of lasagna I'd balanced on the spatula slipped off and landed face down on my plate. Sauce splattered all over me and my shirt.

My brother snorted. "Nice one, klutz!"

I glared at him and tossed the spatula into the pan. My shirt was a lost cause, so I left the stains.

"You dance *pour* Margaux *avec* Liliana?" my grandmother asked Sophie while she uncorked the wine.

Sophie shot me a worried look. "Um. . . yes. Ma'am. Two years now."

"She's the best in the company," I said, stuffing a forkful of melted cheese into my mouth. "Doing *Cinderella* and she's a shoo-in for the lead."

My grandmother looked perplexed as she poured a glass of wine for herself. "Shoe in? What is this? *Comme des chaussures?"*

I wiped sauce from my mouth with the back of my hand. I'd forgotten to give everybody napkins and I'd forgotten not to use slang with my French grandmother. "No, not like shoes."

"More," my brother demanded, shoving his plate toward me.

"Get your own," I snapped back. To my grandmother, I explained. "No one else can compete with Sophie. She's the best there is."

"Ah," she nodded. "The lead. *C'est dans la poche."*

I smiled. "Yeah. It's in the pocket."

I watched as she took her seat, somehow descending to the chair with a fluidity that defied description.

Sophie clinked her fork against her plate. "Lil's being too kind. I have a ton to learn. My *plié grand jeté* falls way short. I need distance in my leaps."

My grandmother set down the glass she'd been delicately sipping from and put a hand over Sophie's. "Do not give up, my dear, and you will find your feet."

They exchanged knowing glances and nods, some secret ballerina code I couldn't grasp.

Grand-mère Camille turned to me. "And you? How do you do?"

I knew she wanted to know about dance, but I didn't want to make my failures dinner table conversation just yet. So I told her exactly what Margaux had said to me.

"I'm actually too full," I said as I took another forkful of food.

Sophie choked on her milk and sprayed her plate. "Oops! My bad!"

Tony started laughing as she wiped her food.

My grandmother looked between us, lost, then back at me.

"You have had enough?" she asked, confused. "Then why do you eat?"

A sigh escaped me. "I'm not *full* full. Just . . . *full*." With a vague gesture toward myself, I shrugged. "Never mind." I gave her a smile that was a little too big. "More food?"

Grand-mère sipped her wine and studied me. "We must work more hard to help me understand, Liliana."

While I added another heaping portion to my plate and dug in, my grandmother took a tiny nibble of her food, grimaced, and pushed her plate away.

"C'est tout," she declared with a smile and a gentle pat to her stomach.

She was finished eating. After only one bite.

And she didn't even finish her wine.

Sophie and I traded looks as we continued to shovel in the lasagna.

This would be a long two months.

11.

"Take your places on the court," Mr. Walden said, blowing the whistle hanging around his beefy neck. He clapped his hands together three times. "All right, let's see some hustle today. I want you all to break a sweat, and no holding back. I don't see sweat shining on those faces of yours, you fail."

I ducked my head and crossed my arms over my chest. There was nowhere to hide in this blazingly bright gym with the volleyball nets strung across it. We'd been divided into boy-girl teams, and I'd forgotten to pack a clean sports bra for my gym locker. The one I wore barely fit me anymore.

And it was co-ed volleyball day.

"Look alive, people! Remember, three touches then over the net. Bump, set, ATTACK." He blew the whistle again. "And . . . serve."

Balls went flying over the nets on the four courts as Mr. Walden barked orders and rubbed his buzz cut.

I didn't have time to think. One solid hit from the other side and the white ball sailed toward me in the back corner. I put my hands in front of my face to block it and shrieked. The ball smashed straight into the ground and the other team cheered.

"Nice one, Carracino," Billy Martin groaned. "Way to waste my serve. Why don't you try actually playing instead of just standing there?"

"Sorry." I shrugged. He was a baseball player I didn't know very well. He was cute, but that didn't make up for the fact he was apparently competitive, and maybe a little bit mean.

I watched another volley that thankfully didn't include me, and our team got the ball back.

We switched positions on the court and our server announced the score. I moved up to the front row and found myself across the net from Tyler Jackson.

The sweat in my armpits grew slick as he sucked in a breath and taunted me quietly through the net. I tried not to look at him.

"I'm gonna make you jump, Carracino. Gonna make you jump high for me," he said in a low voice, flicking his tongue like a pervert. "I'm gonna watch those babies bounce."

I didn't respond. Instead, I tugged on my too-tight gym shirt, turned toward my team and tried to ignore him.

But Tyler kept going, biting away at my confidence like a pit bull on crack.

"You're looking so *sweet* today," he said. "Nice and juicy."

Nobody else paid attention to him in the noisy gym, but his words were getting under my skin. I willed myself to tune him out and cheer for my team. I gave a few lame claps. "Let's get a point! Come on."

I'd volunteer for two years of geometry classes instead of this abuse. Tyler wasn't distracted from his mission to torture me, but Billy Martin nodded at me in approval from the back row on my court.

"Go for it, baby," Tyler hissed. "*Jump!*"

The ball went flying over the net and was spiked back to our side. Billy bumped it into the air, a girl named Sally set it up . . . to me. Too high.

Mr. Walden was watching me. He shouted through the bullhorn, "Carracino, attack that ball!"

My team went crazy and I leaped to spike the ball over the net. I smacked it onto the net instead, it teetered, and tipped back to our own side.

And then I landed. *Hard.*

My breasts bounced with a triple reverberation.

"Yo, baby!" Tyler called out, clapping and whistling through his teeth. He leaned toward me and pulled on the net in front of his face. "Now that's what I'm talking about, Carracino. Bustin' out all over, all in the name of the game."

By the time I stopped the fleshy aftershocks on my body, I looked down at my chest . . . and instantly knew why Tyler had said what he did.

They all noticed, and laughter came my way.

My face burned. My boobs – my hideous ginormous boobs - were oozing over the tops of both sides of my useless bra. One nipple was even poking out.

I was quadroboob.

Exposed.

Humiliated.

“Going to the nurse!” I yelled to the coach, not even bothering to look in his direction or wait for permission.

And then I bolted through the gym doors clutching my chest, leaving the cackles and sneers behind.

12.

The battle-axe nurse, who wasn't really a nurse but just some cranky woman with a badge, denied me. I'd changed back into my regular clothes, and she didn't believe I had a pulled hamstring, which, of course I didn't. My acting skills clearly lacking, she allowed me exactly two minutes to collect myself in the sick room before sending me back to gym class with a stern look, a pointed finger toward the hall and a "good and healthy" pass.

I refused to go near the gym, and no way could I even think about studying. Instead, I slunk into the back door of the sewing room and tried not to interfere with the students working on projects at their stations. Mrs. Russell spotted me and gave me a curious "what's going on?" look. I pleaded with my eyes. She hesitated for a moment, seemed to come to terms with my presence, then turned back to her class.

For the rest of the hour, I grabbed a bag of scraps and busied myself at a spare sewing machine, clipping the pieces and shaping the fabric into a crazy pattern I'd embroider later.

My breathing slowed and my calm returned as I listened to the quiet hum of the machine and watched the needle slip in and out of the fabric to make something interesting where nothing before existed. I was in my zone, concentrating only on the emerging shapes and the colors and textures rippling beneath my fingertips.

Someone tapped my shoulder. "Time to get to your next class, Lili."

I looked up at Mrs. Russell. "Huh?"

"It's time to go or you'll be late," she said. She ran a hand over my hair to smooth the loose strands then gave me a warm smile. "Hard day?"

I shrugged at the teacher who'd moved up from middle school to high school at the same time I did. She'd always allowed me the freedom to create.

"Just the usual stuff," I said. Looking down, I added, "Thanks."

When I shut off the machine and stood up I handed my work over to her, but she shook her head as she admired the intricate design.

"You keep working that. I think you may be onto something with that technique."

Walking through the door into the busy hall, I listened to lockers slam and stared at the fabric in my hands. The piece was the beginnings of something. I didn't know what yet, but the combination of silk scraps, cotton ticking stripe, damask and crisp linen was intriguing.

A hand grabbed my arm and I shrieked.

"Got ya!" Sophie said with a laugh.

I slugged her in the shoulder. "You scared the crap out of me! Quit doing that!"

She laughed. "You're a walking space cadet."

She threw an arm around my shoulder and leaned against me as we walked.

"I couldn't resist. You hear from your parents?"

I grimaced at the memory of my father's texts. "Yeah. Safe and sound on Italian soil. Already up to their ears in meetings. My mother actually scheduled a conference call with me."

"Time management *is* important to success," she said, quoting my mother. "How'd the math test go?"

I shook my head. "Dismally."

Sophie nodded. "Okay. Next subject. How'd last night go with French grandma after I left?"

I sighed and scooted around an oblivious couple devouring each other's tongues against the lockers. "Strained. We survived. I did the dishes and retreated."

The hallways were crowded and noisy, but thankfully Tyler and Joe were nowhere to be found. And I hadn't seen Jimmy Barnett all day.

"So what's doing after school?" Sophie asked.

No dance. That's what.

"Not sure. I'll figure out how to fill my time somehow. Wander the streets aimlessly. Eat plenty of saturated fat and clog my arteries. Avoid going home as long as possible and figure out a way to get out of studying." I sighed. "She'll have talked to Margaux by now, no doubt. So she'll know I got kicked out."

I looked up at her. "Hey, your eyes are really red. You're not . . . *high* . . . are you?"

"Yeah. Like that would happen. It's just the contacts," she told me, blinking.

"Go back to your glasses, Sophie," I said. "This is stupid."

"No. I refuse to give in. Changing the subject now. What about your Aunt Nina? Where's she?" Sophie asked.

My shoulders stiffened. "They are together right now."

Sophie let out a low whistle. "Ooh la la! That's trouble in French pants."

I sighed. "Don't I know it."

13.

Two hours and one triple fudge ripple double scoop ice cream cone later, I walked into the kitchen and tossed my backpack of un-cracked textbooks into the corner. My Aunt Nina and Grand-mère Camille were sitting at the table sipping espresso from delicate china cups and nibbling dainty cookies, chatting in rapid-fire French.

At first glance, they could have been twins. Perfect highlighted blonde hair, smooth French twists, elegant features and flawless skin. The fact that my grandmother was 26 years older didn't make much of a difference. Their similarities were eerie.

And all I could do was stand there and think which girl in the room is not like the others? Dark haired, olive-skinned, chubby, curvy me. The one wearing somebody's old Yale sweatshirt and baggy jeans.

Aunt Nina turned. "Lili! *Bonjour*!"

She got up and bent to kiss me on both cheeks. I smiled. "Hey."

As the founder and artisan behind her own makeup line, Splendor, my Aunt Nina's physical presence was breath-stealing every time I saw her. She was the great beauty of the triplets who had modeled for years like her mother before her, making a name for herself by showcasing designer cosmetics on her luminous skin and dating hordes of scandalous men. She positively radiated glamour from her invisible pores, and her face was known to millions. The natural extension of her fabulous career was to launch her own makeup line.

But, of course, ma chérie. Let us be more famous than we already are!

The kitchen felt too small to breathe with so much French elegance in the room.

"You have dark circles under your eyes, Lili," Aunt Nina said tilting my chin up for a closer inspection. "Are you using the concealer I gave you?" She turned my face to the side. "And *mon Dieu*! When was the last time you moisturized?"

I shook my head. "I keep forgetting."

Aunt Nina released me and threw up her hands.

"Leave the girl alone," my grandmother said in my defense. "She has had school today."

Folding my arms across my chest, I smiled weakly.

Aunt Nina gave my clothes aonce over and sighed.

"We all could use some improvement, *Maman,"* Nina said. "Is that not what you always say?"

Grand-mère smiled. "Liliana is beautiful just the way she is."

When my grandmother and I exchanged glances, I wondered.

Did she actually believe what she said or was she just trying to make me feel less ugly?

"Why are you not at dance?" she asked suddenly, killing my interest in what she'd said. "Do you not have class every day?"

Clearly, she hadn't talked to her third daughter yet. I grabbed a package of cream-filled cookies sitting on the countertop and started for my room. "I don't dance anymore."

"But why not?" Aunt Nina asked as she refilled her espresso cup.

I paused to stare into her beautiful face. "Because Margaux said I'm too fat."

Stuffing one delicious cookie into my mouth, I turned on my clumsy heels and left the room while I listened to them gasp.

14.

Sneaking out my bedroom window wasn't hard. With a room on the back of the house overlooking the woods, I could slide a few feet onto the garage roof, then slip onto the wide limbs of the tulip tree. A few dicey footholds and a minor jump onto the lawn later and I'd be free.

I'd only attempted an escape twice before, but my room felt like a prison this afternoon, with so much speculation going on in the kitchen. And I was far too distracted to do my assignment on the foundation of the American democracy. Worse yet, Margaux was coming for dinner.

I couldn't bear it. There was only so much Frenchness I could take when I was feeling so low.

With half a dozen cookies in my pocket and another four and a full sugar soda in my belly, I walked along the edge of the driveway toward the Fergusons' house and took the shortcut through their backyard toward Main Street. Mrs. Ferguson was standing at the kitchen sink, looking out the window as she washed dishes. We went through our daily routine. She gave me a nod and I gave her a smile. I could count on one hand the number of times I hadn't seen Mrs. Ferguson at the sink doing dishes. With eight kids and no dishwasher, if she wasn't at church, she was perpetually changing diapers or recovering from dishpan hands.

Within minutes, I was walking through the front doors of Kerry's Cottage. The smell of cotton and wool greeted me as the door's bells began to silence. I drew a deep breath and smiled as calm came over me.

"Hey, stranger," Kerry London said as she set a basket of trim onto the work table. "Haven't seen you in a week. Where you been?"

"The usual. School, dance, parents," I said. My eye was immediately drawn to the display of bold new silks cascading a softly lit wall. I rushed past the barrel full of linings to touch them. The fabrics slid beneath my fingertips in a way that nothing but silk could. “Wow. These are absolutely amazing.”

“They’re ikat weaves,” Kerry said. She unrolled a few yards of beaded organza from a bolt and began to measure. “It’s a resist-dyeing process, kind of like tie dye. But the difference is they dye the threads before they’re woven. The technique’s been around for centuries in southern Asia. I fell in love with them when I was a kid.”

“These patterns are incredible,” I said, holding one to the light. Shades of cerulean blue blended seamlessly into deep aquamarine and then again to the palest of shimmery turquoise before the pattern reversed then repeated. The design was intricate, yet subtle. I glanced at Kerry. “Dare I look?”

She shrugged. “They’re not too bad, for hand work.”

I flipped the price card over in my hand. Sixty-five dollars a yard.

I sighed and let the fabric fall with a whisper toward the wall.

“Hey. I’ve got something for you,” Kerry said.

“What?" Pulling up a stool, I sat at the work table and helped her re-roll yards of pale gold crystal beaded fringe.

She handed me a paper bag. “Thought you could use these."

I opened the sack and glimpsed a jumble of satin ribbon, cording, brush fringe trim and fabric scraps. “Thanks, Kerry. These’ll come in handy.”

“What do you make with them anyway?” she asked. “You’ve never shown me anything you’ve done.”

Kerry’s newest art quilt hung at an angle in the window so it could be admired from the street or the store. I studied her technique. The quilt was a showpiece of her endless creativity, depicting a New England winter scene on a moonlit night. No matter how hard I tried, I could never match that kind of talent. And I never shared my work with anyone other than Sophie. Not even my mother. It was too . . . private.

"Oh, my sewing isn't very good. Besides, I just mess around with clothes."

She picked up a pair of shears and pointed toward me. "Well, you're always in these huge sweatshirts and jeans. Why don't you ever wear any of the clothes you make if you spend so much time working on them?"

Wear them? No way.

I glanced again at her quilt. "I just like to look at them."

Kerry shook her head and sighed. "I'll stop giving you my scraps if you don't show me something pretty soon."

This kind of pressure I didn't need.

Hopping off the stool, I grabbed the bag and held it up. "Thanks again, Kerry. I really appreciate it."

"I want to see your work!" she called after me.

When I gave her a wave from the sidewalk, she was still shaking her head as she unrolled a bolt of plum-colored taffeta.

Three shops down, the thrift store offered a full view of the broad windows into Margaux's dance studio. I ducked inside to wait for Sophie and avoid my aunt.

"Got a new load from some Stamford widow's attic," Brian said to me. "Saved the best for you."

I smiled at my friend in flannel as I walked toward the cash register. Mr. Brian Worthington owned my second favorite shop in town, Worthington's Wonders. He was a Yalie in his sixties, with a head full of Einstein hair and specs resting on his forehead. I'd never actually seen him use his horn-rimmed glasses. They were always just propped there, ready to fall onto his nose, but they never seemed to move from their perch above his eyes.

"What do you have for me? Anything good?"

"Haven't even priced the lot yet." He pulled a hat box from behind the counter and handed it to me. "Scarves, a bit of cashmere and a few old nightgowns."

Nodding, I glanced toward the studio. The dancers at the barre were going through their last set before the class wrapped up and Sophie would be free. "Cool. I'll take these over to the window to look at them in the light."

"Make me an offer," he said, returning to his cup of tea and copy of Kafka's *Metamorphosis*. The cover showed a cockroach crawling toward a man in a shaft of light.

"Nice book," I said with a laugh.

He lifted the novel toward me. "It's about a salesman who turns into a giant bug and worries how he'll get to his job. Heavy reading."

"Shouldn't it be the other way around?" I asked, settling in on the windowsill with the hat box on my lap. "The bug turns into something better?"

He shrugged and slurped from his tea. "Yeah, but I'm just getting to the good part. His family ignores him, he gets sick, he dies and they get along just fine without him. The end."

"Charming." I laughed as I pulled a bundle of scarves from the box. "Not exactly a Cinderella story, is it?"

Brian laughed. "I guess Kafka was making a grand point about change."

The faded scarves in my hands smelled like dust and lavender, but they'd make a beautiful ruffled collar. "What's that?"

He sighed and scratched his forehead. "If I figure it out, you'll be the first to know."

Across the street, the dancers began to filter onto the sidewalk.

I stuffed everything back into the box and got up quickly. "How 'bout eight bucks for the lot?"

"Twelve," he bartered.

"Ten and I pay cash." I reached into my pocket and pulled out a bill.

He nodded. "Deal."

I handed him the money and gave him a wave on my way out.

"Don't go changing." Brian punched a button on the vintage cash register and an old-fashioned bell rang as I left.

Outside, my eyes scanned the crowd of sweaty dancers. I whistled between my fingers, and Sophie turned to look at me in her big sunglasses.

I motioned for her and she darted between cars to cross the street.

“Hey, you,” she said, leaping onto the sidewalk. “Missed you in there. It’s not the same.”

I rolled my eyes. “Whatever. No fresh blisters, so I’m cool." Then I pleaded. “But you’ve got to save me, Soph. Can’t go home for dinner." I sighed. “Triple threat on the menu." I paused. “They’ll *all* be there.”

She groaned in sympathy. “Let’s walk and talk. Leo’s got a hot date and won’t pick me up. He took my dad’s car.”

I laughed. “We know what that means.”

“Yeah. Jaguar sex." Sophie rolled her neck. “So you’ll come to my house and we’ll kvetch about *your* relatives for a change.”

15.

Bubbe Ruth was about four-foot-nothing in her tiny heels. As I walked into Sophie's foyer, I towered over the old lady with the sleek frosted blonde bob and hunched shoulders coming toward us.

"Sophie!" she shrieked, throwing up her hands when she noticed that her granddaughter was wearing dance clothes and not much else. "You need a little sweater! You'll catch your death!"

Sophie wrapped her grandmother in a fierce hug and readjusted the cardigan draped over the older woman's aging shoulders. "It's like sixty degrees out there, Bubbe. I'm fine."

"I'm just saying," the older woman pulled away with a pained look. "Don't come to me when you get pneumonia from running around half-naked. I should know. I had double pneumonia last year, in case you should forget."

"Hi, Missus Goldberg," I said with a smile. "How are you today?"

She gave me a shrug. "Who can know? Dinner's on the stove."

Sophie nodded as she watched her grandmother walk away. "We'll be right in."

I darted onto the Persian rug in the living room and sat on the high-backed cream sofa opposite a polished ebony grand piano.

"Don't futz with the pillows or Ma will freak," Sophie said in a whisper, glancing over her shoulder. She pulled off her sunglasses and blinked. "They're like her children."

I laughed. "Why do you even have this room if no one is ever allowed to come into it? Who even plays the piano in your family, anyway?"

"No one. It's just for the neighbors." Sophie straightened the needlepoint pillows behind me. "Just get off the sofa, will ya? You're making me nervous."

I purposely stretched out along the prim sofa's length, dangling my street shoes over the damask while I called my house on my cell.

She tried to scoot me off my comfy spot, but I wouldn't budge. Instead I held the phone to my ear and listened to the rings while I stared at the lit four-foot portrait of a seven-year-old Sophie. She was Princess Odette in *Swan Lake* that year, looking every bit the ballerina angel with her pale blonde hair swirled into a feathered crown, and her long limbs draped around a classical tutu and beaded bodice.

But right now, in her ordinary practice leotard and her tight and worried expression, my friend looked one short hiccup away from major apoplexy.

My brother answered the phone and I shot to my feet so Sophie could finally relax. "Tony? What are you doing home?"

Sophie fiddled with the pillows until she arranged them just right, exactly three inches apart with the center one turned on the diamond.

My brother crunched loudly in my ear. "We got out of practice early."

"Are you eating my Doritos?"

He laughed and crunched again. "Found your secret stash in the front closet. *Ha!*"

"Those were mine!" I groaned. "You owe me. Just for that, you tell Grand-mère I'm staying at Sophie's for dinner. I'll be back before nine. Don't forget to tell her!"

I hung up before he could object.

"Sophie! Dinner's *on the table*!" a woman shouted from the kitchen. "It'll be *ruined*!"

"So what do I look like, a clock? Godforbid we should be three seconds late or she'll have a conniption," she said, yanking me into the fray.

"Where have you been?" Mrs. Fishkin, a.k.a. Sophie's Ma, was frantic. She shooed us toward the table in the gleaming kitchen. The former Lois Goldberg looked exactly like her mother, only a few inches taller, a little more blonde and a lot better preserved by the ladies at the La Prairie counter at Saks. She gestured again with manicured hands. "Eat, eat already, girls. The roast will get cold and your brother's not even here to eat it!"

"We wouldn't want cold meat," Sophie said, sliding into an upholstered chair that my brother would have destroyed with a single meal. In her kitchen, it worked.

The Fishkins' gourmet kitchen was a designer's dream with bisque Italian plaster walls, aubergine and gold draperies and plenty of custom-made ironwork and pottery dotting glossy granite countertops. And of course the design scheme included the requisite professional portrait of Sophie, the only girl in the household, this time wearing a crisp white blouse and jeans and holding a casual bunch of wildflowers in the middle of a luxurious summer garden. Her golden hair caught the sunlight.

I stood there staring at her image and wondering why they'd never photographed her in her glasses, but her mother was indeed having a fit.

"Lili, *the food, already! Meh!* It's getting cold!"

All of a sudden I sneezed violently against my sleeve. I said "excuse me," and sat in Sophie's dad's chair next to Bubbe Ruth.

She glared at me.

"What?" I said to the little woman with the tightly puckered mouth. "Am I not supposed to sit here? I thought Murray was in San Francisco all week?" I turned to Sophie. "Isn't your dad out of town?"

She shrugged. "'Til Saturday."

I sniffled and fought another sneeze.

"She has *a cold*," Bubbe Ruth said to her daughter. "Now we're all going to get sick." She let out a sigh. "I shoulda known."

Mrs. Fishkin looked worried. "It's not a chest cold, is it, Lili?" She shook her head while she talked to her mother. "You know, she could have gotten it from the paper boy. I saw him blowing his nose last week and we all know what *that* means. He spread his germs, probably all over the papers. And we've been touching them every day! Now we're all going to get sick."

Sophie gave me a thick slice of roast and a mountain of mashed potatoes. "She's not sick, Ma."

"I feel fine, really," I protested as I poured gravy on my meat.

Mrs. Fishkin got to her feet and headed for the stainless refrigerator.

"Bring her a nice glass of juice, already," Bubbe Ruth demanded with a crooked finger. "She needs some vitamins."

I shook my head and cut a bite of the meat. "Really, I'm –"

Mrs. Fishkin plunked a huge glass of orange juice on the table before I could object.

"So you'll drink it," Bubbe Ruth said with a smile and a hand gesture, "and be healthy."

I knew enough to not argue with these women. They were on a mothering roll and it was unlikely this train could be stopped.

The phone rang and Sophie flew to her feet. She answered with her mouth full. "Hello?"

Sipping my juice I watched my friend.

"Is that Bertie? If it is, tell her I'll call her back," Mrs. Fishkin said. She turned to her mother. "Bertie always manages to interrupt our dinner. That woman, I tell you, she always knows when I'm trying to eat."

Sophie put a finger in her ear. "Who is this?"

"Tell Bertie I'll play tennis with her on Thursday morning, after my nail appointment," Mrs. Fishkin told Sophie. "No, wait. That's not going to work. I have the cardiologist at eleven. I can play after lunch instead, but only if I get home in time to watch Oprah. She's having that Jennifer Grey on, and we all know she hasn't looked like Baby since she did her nose. The surgery was just too much, I tell you."

"So what's wrong with you now?" Bubbe Ruth asked with a hand over her heart. "Is it Doctor Finegold you're seeing?"

"Sure, sure." Mrs. Fishkin shot to her feet and went to the sink for a dishrag and the spray bottle of bleach. "You know I've had those pains lately. With all this stress lately it could be angina. And I wouldn't want to have a coronary with Murray gone all the time."

"She never sits, this girl!" Bubbe Ruth said to me. "Sit already, will you, Lois? It's not good for your heart!"

I shoveled in the pot roast and smiled.

Spritzing bleach on an invisible spot on the table, Mrs. Fishkin wiped the smudge away until the surface shone. "I'm just saying. It could be serious."

"Is he a specialist?" Bubbe asked skeptically. "I could make a call to someone better."

"Will all of you be quiet?" Sophie yelled, covering the phone and rolling her eyes. "I can't hear!"

"I shouldn't play." Her mother turned toward her. "Just tell Bertie I'd better not--"

"It's not Bertie!" Sophie yelled, exasperated. "It's for me!"

Her grandmother kept talking, undeterred. "My neighbor's nephew is top in his field. He runs cardiology at Mercy General in Greenwich." She looked at Mrs. Fishkin and nodded. "I'll make the call and he'll squeeze you in. He went to camp with your cousin Benjamin, and *mein gott* he was a chubby one when he was young."

Mrs. Fishkin sat and put a hand dramatically on her chest. "I should see the best. After all it is my heart we're talking about here."

"So, it's decided. I'll make the call," Bubbe Ruth said with a shrug."You'll go tomorrow."

Sophie ducked into the other room, stretching the phone cord to its limit.

"From your lips to God's ears, I should be okay," Mrs. Fishkin said.

I smothered a laugh. The dialogue was the same every time I came to her house. Twelve conversations going at once and everyone picking at everyone else.

I loved every minute of it.

Sophie rushed back into the room and motioned for me to hurry up. “Ma, we’ve got homework. We’ll be upstairs.”

In one motion, Sophie’s mother and grandmother threw up their hands. “They never eat, these girls! Just all skin and bones, I tell you!”

16.

Sophie pulled me up the stairs.

"Jeez, what's your hurry?" I tried desperately to keep up before I face planted on the broadloom.

She yanked me into her room and slammed the door. Then she flopped down on her four poster bed and smiled. *"He called."*

"Who he?"

She lifted her head and beamed at me. "Adam. That was him on the phone."

I rushed to sit next to her. "This is big. He's never called you before." I smiled. "He finally noticed."

She nodded and bit her lip as she sat up. "I know. He said he just wanted to say hey. See how things were going."

"He likes you, Soph."I gave her a huge hug. "Are you . . . *crying?"*

She swiped the tears from her eyes. "It's just these stupid contacts. I'm ready to rip them out of my eyes." She smiled broadly as she got up and grabbed a bottle of solution from her nightstand. "Isn't it cool? Adam is *so* cute."

"So what'd you talk about?" I wanted to know.

As I watched her pull on her eyelids and remove each lens, I realized something horribly sad. No boy had ever called me before at home. The only person besides my brother I really talked to on the phone was Sophie, and our conversations were so familiar we didn't even finish our own sentences. What would I ever talk to a boy about? And how strange would that be?

Sophie put drops into her eyes then flopped back down on the bed, blinking furiously. She hugged a silk pillow to her chest as she slipped into her standby glasses. "We just talked about stuff. He told me all about the new steampunk book he's reading. Said he'd loan it to me. Then he asked me about dance. When *Cinderella* was opening."

"He knew about that? That's good," I said. I had only a vague idea what steampunk was, but I assumed it was related to her obsession with science fiction and all things weird. And I didn't want to get her started on a big discussion, so I avoided the topic. "He's keeping tabs on you, Soph."

Her grin was infectious. "And I thought he hadn't been paying attention. He *likes* me, Lil. I can tell. Adam likes me!"

"And he's a--"

"Nice Jewish Boy," she said, beaming. "Ma might even approve. His dad owns a law firm in Greenwich. We'll just keep the sci-fi stuff a secret or they might freak a little. They still don't get it."

"Even better," I said. The awareness that my best friend might soon have a boyfriend and I wouldn't left me feeling a bit unsettled. I got to my feet and ran my hands through my hair. I had to do something. Keep busy to avoid thinking about the changes coming our way. "Can I check my email?"

She waved me toward the desk as she fell back against the mound of fancy pillows on her bed. "Whatever. Adam Brock called me. *Me!* Is that not the best ever?"

"Don't tell your brother or you'll never hear the end of it." While Sophie purred, I sat at her desk, an opulent French affair with curved legs and polished surfaces, like it was never meant to be used, but admired instead. As I opened the web browser and called up my email account on her laptop, I suspected Sophie's mother made hourly runs to her daughter's room with the lemon furniture polish. I could smell it as strong as perfume.

"Maybe he'll ask me to the after party on opening night next month," Sophie fantasized. "Do you think he might? Wouldn't that be awesome? It'd be my first dance! With a boy!"

I snickered. "Not exactly your first dance, twinkle toes."

"Okay *shiksa*, you know what I mean." She sucked in a breath. "Maybe we'll slow dance!"

I tried not to feel jealous, but that feeling was there, filtering in to be noticed. The green-eyed monster kind of gnawed at me. "You'll need a dress if he asks you."

"My God, you're right." Sophie flew to her feet and opened her walk-in closet.

One glance toward her clothes palace and I was reminded of how different our apparel habits were. Sophie's closet was neat, organized, evenly spaced and color-coded. A small crystal chandelier hung overhead to light her daily selections and a baroque mirror and dressing table housed her assortment of perfumes, scented oils and jewelry.

As odd as she was in some ways, my best friend was not fashion deprived.

"I have absolutely nothing to wear." She stared at the immaculate space and looked deflated. "I feel like I'm staring into my mother's closet. I mean seriously, look at these old lady clothes! They're awful! She doesn't get me at all!"

I laughed. At least two hundred items hung in that closet room, many with the Neiman's and Saks' tags still dangling from them, yet she wore a different dance leotard and sweats practically every day. Go figure.

"I'm sure your Ma will pick up a few dozen outfits for you to try," I suggested. "Just look at what she did for your bat mitzvah."

Sophie groaned. "Don't remind me. I might as well have been turning forty."

The rite of passage celebration had been bigger than any wedding I'd ever hope to attend, except Sophie's own of course, and Mrs. Fishkin was not going to be outdone by her friends. She'd taken Sophie to New York for the weekend and they'd visited designer after designer until they'd found the perfect dress that made her look exactly like a young Lois Fishkin. Sophie hated the outfit, but her mother wouldn't listen and insisted she wear it.

She rustled the hangers while I clicked on send/receive and my emails started to download.

"Ma keeps trying to dress me like I'm a housewife ready to play mahjongg. Lil, this is a disaster," she said dramatically. She waved at the computer. "I need something hot. And fun. Hurry up with that so we can look at some dresses online before you go home."

"I'm hurrying already," I said. "Besides, he hasn't even asked you to the after party yet."

"Details, details." She rolled her eyes. "I'll guilt him into it."

I clicked on an email from my mother and sighed.

Lili,
Our meetings go very well, and we will share great progress these months in Italy. Are you a wonderful girl for Grand-mère? Always remember to be sweet and to help her with the housework. And kiss your brother for me. He will need his big sister, my darling. Remember our videoconference on Sunday at six in the evening.
Je t'aime.
Maman

"Yada, yada," I said, deleting the message without responding. I'd answer my mother later when I was in a better mood. Sophie's ramblings behind me were getting under my skin.

I thought my dad's email would cheer me, but I was dead wrong.

Cara Mia,
The pasta is perfetto, the streets are noisy, the paesanos are friendly and we miss you every day.
So you have a boyfriend, eh? He flirts with you at school? You are Liliana Carracino after all! Be proud!
Ciao Bella,
Papa

Flirt? I'd hardly call what Joe Sanderson did flirting. Torment was more like it.

"You almost done?" Sophie asked, hovering over my shoulder.

"Just one more." I clicked on the next post. The subject line said "just a reminder" but the message itself was blank. "That's weird."

She poked her head next to mine and the computer screen reflected on her glasses. "Who's it from?"

I shrugged. "Don't recognize the address. There's an attachment though."

I pressed the button just as Sophie shrieked "*Don't-click-on-that-it-could-be-a-virus!*"

Too late.

The full-color image uploaded to the screen and we gasped.

It was a little out of focus, but it was definitely me. Soaking wet. Nipples showing through my pink leotard. Shocked look as the flash went off on my face.

Across the picture someone had written a note.

Thanks for the peep show Carracino.

"Oh. My. God," Sophie said softly, pulling up a chair. "Who did this?"

I took a deep breath and closed Sophie's computer.

"Joe and Tyler," I said. "The other night when I walked home after dance. I saw the flash but didn't know what it was."

She was serious. "You can't let them do this to you. What'll you do?"

I thought about what my mother said. *Be sweet.*

I thought about what my father said. *Be proud and be good.*

I couldn't do either. Instead, I moved toward Sophie's door and opened it. "I'm gonna go home and cry."

Before she could stop me, I was down the stairs and out into the night.

17.

The house was quiet when I slipped inside, the kitchen dark except the stove light casting a warm glow over the burners. The room smelled like something delicious and French they'd had for dinner without me.

"Grand-mère?" I asked quietly as I set my hatbox and bag of fabric on the bench by the back door. "Tony?"

Her voice drifted toward me from the living room. "I am reading in the *salon, chérie*. Your brother has gone to bed."

I sucked in a fortifying breath and rounded the corner. My grandmother was curled into a wing chair by the window, her satin-slippered feet tucked beneath her long legs. A paisley shawl draped her shoulders and pooled around her waist in soft folds. She looked so pretty sitting there it almost looked like a painting.

"Hey."

She set aside her book and reading glasses. Her voice was a touch somber. "Your aunts stayed as long as they could to see you tonight, but you were not here."

Guilt hit me hard, right in the gut. I folded my arms across my chest and hugged my sweatshirt to me. "Sorry. I had a . . . project to do with Sophie. For school. It was kind of important."

The lie came too easily, and I'm sure she knew I wasn't telling her the truth. I could read the disappointment in those beautiful eyes.

She gave me a tiny smile and folded her hands across her lap. "I did not even know you had gone away until I went to your room to invite you for dinner."

I stared at my shoes. "I'm sorry, Grand-mère. I'll let you know next time."

"Please," she said, letting the word drift away.

She was so cool, so reserved. An uncomfortable silence fell between us. I could tell she wanted me to talk, but I wasn't in the mood to have another guarded conversation with her.

We stared at each other for a minute more, not knowing what to say or how to break the silence.

Finally, I looked toward the stairs. "Well, I'd guess I better go to bed. Got to get up early for school in the morning."

She let out the tiniest of sighs and smiled. "Certainly. Good night, Liliana. *Faix de beaux rêves.*"

Sweet dreams. From my grandmother's to my mother's lips, my childhood goodnight.

I gave her a nod as she picked up her book again and ran up to my room.

When I threw myself on the bed, my face hit something hard that didn't belong there.

An envelope.

I held it in my hands. The cream stationery was crisp and expensive looking, like the kind they used for fancy wedding invitations. Across the envelope, my name was written in my grandmother's beautiful script.

Sliding my finger under the flap, I opened the envelope and withdrew a note card, embossed in black with the name Camille.

My dearest Liliana,
A lady carries herself with dignity and pride.
Je t'aime,
Grand-mère Camille

I read the note at least five times, searching for more, looking for hidden meanings, trying to understand. But there was nothing. She'd written me a letter with just the one statement. Not even an explanation.

I could not have been more different from my grandmother if we'd been born on different planets.

Tossing her note onto my cluttered desk, I covered my eyes with my arms. It didn't help. In the darkness behind my eyes, my thoughts flashed to the ugly image of myself glaring at me from Sophie's computer screen, hanging out for the world to see.

And there was not one quality in that image to be proud of, that's for sure.

Nothing at all.

Finally, the tears I'd been holding back came and I just let them flow.

18.

We had an all-school "Character Counts" assembly fifth period. As I moved head-down through the halls with the buzzing swarm of kids going toward the auditorium, I ran into Billy Martin, the baseball jock from my gym class. Literally.

He spun around to stare, looking pissed. But when he saw it was me, his expression softened.

I shrugged. "Sorry."

He gave me a smile. Sort of. His lip kind of lifted halfway, like he thought about it, then decided against it. "You should watch where you're going, Carracino."

Then Billy Martin did the strangest thing.

He reached out and ruffled my already messy hair.

I blinked and he disappeared into the crowd.

Sophie's arm slipped through mine. "So get this. Adam ran into me accidentally on purpose outside my homeroom. He gave me his copy of *Ender's Game*," she said in a whisper. "I didn't have the heart to tell him I've read it like ten times. But he is way cool! We just stood there against the lockers talking like we did it all the time until Missus Bouvier made me come inside and she shut Adam out."

I was still looking for Billy Martin, but I'd lost sight of him as we entered the auditorium and found the closest seats together. We climbed over knees and backpacks until we hit the middle of the row.

"Are you listening to me?" Sophie whined as she *shlumped* into her seat. "You're a million miles away and I'm talking about my love life here!"

"Sorry," I said, trying to get comfortable in the crowded space. Mrs. Alban was up at the microphone, tapping out a sound check. "So you saw Adam."

"He *likes* me," she said with a smile. She plopped her backpack on the floor, put her feet up and pulled a cream cake from her pocket. "Want a bite?"

The cake was smashed in its wrapper and cream oozed all over the cellophane. "Definitely, no."

Sophie put half of the cake in her mouth and slipped on a new pair of invisible frame glasses.

"Those are new. But you're wearing them in public?"

"Can't see today and it's dark in here. Contacts have been giving me major headaches," she said between bites. "Doesn't mean I'll wear these in the halls."

"They're nice." I glared at her. "But you'll pretend to focus in class even though you can't?"

She licked her fingertips. "Not an issue. I can still listen. And I don't have to see to take notes."

I shook my head as I looked around at the teeming throng in the dimly lit cavern. The girl to my left was deep in conversation with her BFF and the other girl next to them. Sophie was sitting next to some other kids I didn't know. In front of us a couple of kids argued over whether .999 repeating actually does, in fact, equal one.

Sitting back in my chair, I sighed. "I hate these sessions."

With a mouth full of cream, Sophie smiled and adjusted her glasses. "Getting lectured *again* on how to be a better person?"

"Yeah." I thought of my grandmother's note then. It still struck me as weird, and I wondered what she was trying to tell me with her cryptic handwritten message. I thought about asking her, but I didn't know what to say.

A second later, hot breath on my neck sent a shiver up my spine.

"We're all alone in the dark, Carracino," the guy's voice said.

Jimmy Barnett.

I stiffened and tried not to react to the voice I'd recognize anywhere.

"Oh, the things I could do to you in the dark. You'd never forget it."

He made sucking sounds in my ear and I leaned forward.

Sophie noticed what was happening and smacked him on the head with her notebook. “Get away from her, you perv! You’re totally disgusting!”

“Bite me, Fishkin,” he said a little too loudly. “I wasn’t talking to you, dweeb!”

“*Barnett!* Come with me,” Mr. Walden barked. From the aisle he motioned with a beefy paw.

Though I didn’t turn around to watch, I could hear Jimmy’s pitiful attempt at self-defense.

He wailed like a sixth grader. “But she started it, coach! I--”

Mr. Walden hiked his thumb toward the door. “Outside. Now! You’re skating on thin ice with me as it is.”

Jimmy got to his feet, grumbling, and dumped a wadded ball of paper in my lap.

As he pushed past a row of kids toward my newly beloved gym teacher, I made the mistake of uncrumpling the paper.

My picture again.

Only this time, Jimmy had added a personal postscript.

You’re all mine.

19.

The days were getting dark earlier now, as summer faded away and the leaves were starting to change. September was sweater weather, and I loved it. This was the season to wear clothes to hide in, and today I had on two of my favorite sweaters. One was soft and baggy and cuddly against my skin, while the other was a huge knit cardigan with brown leather buttons.

With Sophie immersed in dance and me with nothing specific to do except homework, I had no choice but to walk home alone after school and spend some time with my grandmother. Long overdue, I knew. I'd been beyond rude. I just didn't know how to have a normal conversation with her, so I dawdled on the way home to put it off as long as possible.

I walked on the sidewalk beneath the shady hardwood trees, noticing streaks of deep red coursing through the canopy of green. Soon, the walk would be littered with brittle leaves, crunching beneath my feet with every step, and I'd be bundled in even more scarves and heavy coats and my favorite buff leather gloves.

A car rumbled past and blew a whirlwind of dried bits my way.

Hugging my cardigan to my chest as I walked past a thick hedge, I breathed deeply, inhaling the fall-comfort scent of burning leaves from a nearby yard. When a motorcycle roared up the road toward my house, I followed it with my gaze but the engine noise drowned out the sound of footsteps behind me.

I didn't realize they were gaining on me until I felt a boy's arm around my shoulders and another hand giving my butt a squeeze.

"Looking hot today, Carracino," Joe Sanderson said. "Nice sweater meat."

"I wasn't finished talking to you this afternoon," Jimmy Barnett said. "And you got me detention from Coach Walden. That made me really mad."

He squeezed me harder, inching his fingers toward my breasts.

"Please stop touching me," I said, trying to writhe out of Jimmy's grip and turn away from Joe.

I nearly dropped my books when Joe pulled me toward him. "I'm thinking you should be my girl from now on. No need to fight it. We're destined to make it."

These boys were older, and stronger, and they had me wedged between them in a truly horrible way that made me feel dirty. And I could smell the booze on their breath. They'd been drinking.

I swatted at them with my free hand while I tried to catch my breath. "Just leave me alone, please," I pleaded, trying to make a run for it.

Jimmy's hand was on my waist under my sweater now, snaking up my skin, and I knew he'd try for a full grab at the front of my bra if I gave him even the slightest opening.

"Come on, guys. Why me?" I asked, squirming. "Why do you always pick on me?"

"Because you're smokin' hot," Joe said. "And we know you want us."

Joe reached his hand up under the back of my sweater and grabbed my bra, yanking the band until it snapped against my skin.

They were coming at me from both directions and I didn't know who to fight off first. Panic rose in my chest.

"*STOP* touching me!" I dropped my books, lunging with my fists. "I will scream if you don't get your *.fucking* hands off me!"

"Ooh, she's swearing, Joe," Jimmy said sarcastically, stepping back a few inches to avoid a punch, and landing his fat foot right on the spine of my English notebook. "We're just having fun, Carracino. Messing around with you."

"She's still my girl," Joe said a little too seriously. He pulled me closer to the hedge and tried to plant a slobbery kiss on my neck.

Hot tears began to prick my eyes as I clawed at him. *"Stop!"*

From the corner of my eye I saw someone behind them and sucked in a breath.

"*Get off my sister*," my brother warned in as deep a voice as he could muster. He stood there in his hooded sweatshirt looking fierce.

Jimmy laughed. "Well, look at you, little man. All pumped for a fight." He put up his fists and shadow boxed at my brother.

Tony was furious. He glared at Joe as I wrenched myself free. "Don't you touch my sister again. I'm warning you."

Joe hiked up his jeans. "What are you going to do, huh, shortcake? Beat me up?"

I grabbed Tony around the shoulders to hold him back. He was about six inches smaller than me, but he was much faster on his feet than they could be half drunk. Enough to worry me about what might happen if I let him go.

"Come on, Tony. Let's just go home."

Tony and Joe were deadlocked in a stare, and I didn't like the look in Joe's eyes. He was far too serious.

Jimmy laughed and started walking away. "She's not worth the trouble, Sanderson. Let's get out of here."

Joe spit on the ground at Tony's feet and my brother tensed.

I yanked Tony by the shirt. "Come on. We need to get home."

My brother finally broke the stare and looked away from Joe. A flicker of concern cut through the anger on his young face. "Are you okay? Did they hurt you?"

This was beyond humiliating. I bent to pick up my books and homework papers, gathering them into a leafy pile, not daring to look my brother in the eye. "No. Let's just go, okay?"

Joe finally ran to catch up with Jimmy while my brother watched.

I spun on my heels toward our house and tried to calm my erratic heartbeat.

Tony ran to walk by my side. “Why do you let them treat you that way?”

My words got stuck in my throat.

A cool wind blew across me and I shivered. How could I explain what they continued to do to me? That they’d picked me at the pool this summer, over all the other girls at Middleton, to torture with their undivided attention? As tough as he might be, my little brother would never understand. He just wasn’t old enough.

I gave him a shrug. “I don’t know, Tony. They just do it."

He sighed. “Well, they’re both jerks.”

I loved my brother sometimes. “Yeah. I know.”

Tony shook his head and walked up the driveway to shoot baskets.

I saw my grandmother watching us from the window and thought then about what she’d written to me.

A lady carries herself with dignity and pride.

From somewhere deep inside myself, I found my one remaining morsel of strength to lift my chin and walk toward her.

I even tried to smile.

20.

Two hours later, Grand-mère gave me the perfect excuse to stop uselessly trying to memorize the fundamental differences between eukaryotes and prokaryotes.

While my brain was still functioning on low-normal after my run-in with Jimmy and Joe, we ended up going out to dinner at Artie's Pizza on Main. The place was jam-packed post-baseball and filled with players from my school and their parents. I was glad, because thinking about the continuous decline of my once good grades was almost as bad as worrying about what had happened to me this afternoon.

Grand-mère wanted to surprise my brother and me with an American meal, and she'd taken us to the most popular place in town. So here we sat. Me trying to disappear by wrapping my cardigan up to my neck and slumping into the corner, and my grandmother looking far too elegant in this cramped red vinyl booth at the middle of the restaurant. Her fitted apricot wool dress and gold bangles stood out amid the tee shirts and baseball caps in the crowd around us. Every time her golden hair caught the light, I shrank a little more.

In the back corner, three girls from the football cheer squad kept eyeing us, whispering behind their hands every time they looked my way. Maybe I was paranoid, but I could swear they were talking about me. They kept staring at us.

Tony, who seemed to have forgotten what he'd witnessed earlier in the day, thought it was cool to be surrounded by older kids and chatted with my grandmother nonstop.

I tried to hide behind my hair and my bulky cardigan as I polished my spoon until it shone.

When the deluxe thick crust pizza was delivered, my brother grabbed a cheesy piece and immediately started to stuff his face.

He let out a strangled gasp, dropped the mouthful onto his plate and let the pizza slice fly. "Holy schmoly! That's blazing!"

"My darling, do not be in such a hurry," Grand-mère scolded with a little laugh as she brushed back his hair. "Good food should take much time to enjoy."

Beside him, my grandmother glowed. In the dim light she leaned toward me and spoke in such a quiet voice I had to strain to hear.

"Liliana, let us have, how you say . . . an adventure? Would you take me out for Saturday?" Grand-mère asked while hovering over the big red plastic basket of garlic bread the waiter had put on the table. She glanced at the toasted ciabatta more than once, inhaling deeply, but never taking a single bite of the savory treat or dipping even a crumb to the plate of balsamic and olive oil.

This woman had more restraint than anyone I knew, but the fresh-baked bread smelled far too good for me to resist.

"Take you out?" I asked, ripping off a hunk of the delicious greasy bread. I dragged the piece through the oil and stuffed it into my mouth. I felt oil dribble onto my chin, and took a second to wipe it away. "Where do you want to go? Tony's football practice?"

She shrugged and refolded her paper napkin into a neat triangle, pressing it smooth with her fingertips. "Perhaps. But you would take me somewhere *you* like to go?"

Tony blew on his pizza like he was blowing out candles then dared another huge bite. When the cheese didn't scald him, he dove in.

I picked a piece of pepperoni off my slice and popped it into my mouth. "Like where?"

"I do not know," she said with a delicate gesture of her hands. "Where do you go without school?"

"With her grades, it ain't the library. So give me some cheese," Tony demanded, motioning with greasy fingers.

"Isn't."

When I glared at him, he rolled his eyes and reluctantly added, "Please."

I slid the plate holding the Parmesan grater toward him and turned back to my grandmother. For some reason, with rowdy kids and clanging dishes dulling my voice it seemed easier to talk to her amid the chaos of the noisy restaurant. "Sometimes I like to shop yard sales or thrift shops."

She looked confused as she shook her head and put a finger to her lips. "I do not understand. Explain this to me."

Chewing my pizza, I thought about how to phrase it. "When people have stuff they don't want, they sell it. You know like clothes and jewelry. Stuff."

A smile brightened her face. "*Comme le flea market à Paris*?"

I nodded as I chewed. "Exactly like the flea market, except in different places every week all over town. But I only go to ones I can ride my bike to."

"Ah." Her eyebrows pulled together in question. "But do you not shop in *les boutiques*?"

I shook my head. "Naw. I like things with history."

Grand-mère made the French equivalent of my father's clucking noise, sort of a whoosh of air between her teeth with a little clicking of the tongue. "*C'est parfait*. I will drive us and you and I will visit . . . how you call it . . . yard sales?"

Her accent made bargain hunting sound so exotic.

"Cool." Squeaking chairs and a rush of laughter distracted me, and I looked toward the group of baseball players getting up to walk past our table.

I dropped my napkin on purpose and ducked to retrieve it under the table to avoid them.

But when I popped back up with my hair covering half my face, Billy Martin was staring at me.

"Hey, Carracino," he said.

He paused just for a second, looked at my brother and grandmother, then back at me.

Then Billy Martin smiled, nodded and walked away.

"Who was that?" my brother asked nastily.

I shrugged and avoided my grandmother's inquisitive stare. "Just a kid from my gym class."

Tony kind of glared at me, then over my shoulder at Billy as he and his friends opened the front door and left.

I tried to reassure him. "I hardly know him."

While my grandmother nibbled on her second slice of mushroom and looked at me curiously, I let out a sigh and pushed away my plate.

"Can we go soon? *Please?*"

21.

After dinner I attempted to create flow charts for both aerobic and anaerobic respiration – without cheating –for my impossibly hard biology class. I wasn't really succeeding, but I worked away on my laptop at the dining room table while my brother watched television in the next room with my grandmother.

My internet phone rang with a call from my dad. I debated ignoring the call, but knew he'd just call the house phone a few seconds later if I didn't answer.

Punching the button to accept, I waited until his handsome face appeared to fill my screen.

"*Cara*!" he said with a big smile. "So good to see your face! We miss you!"

I smiled. "Hi, Daddy. How's it going?"

"Busy, busy," he said.

My brother perked up when he heard my dad's voice. "Is that Dad? I want to talk to him!"

"So how are you with your Grand-mère? Are you having much fun together?" he asked.

My brother shoved me aside and nearly knocked me off my chair. "Hey Dad! Guess what? Coach is putting me in first string from now on! Isn't that awesome?"

I pinched my brother to move over and he squealed.

"Cut it out!" he said as he whacked me in the arm. "I need to tell him! It's really important!"

My father laughed. "I see nothing has changed."

"Nothing at all, Daddy," I said, pushing my brother out of the way so I could be in front of the camera. "He's still the same brat you left."

"Am not!" Tony complained. He shoved me again and this time I really did fall off the chair onto the floor. Tony monopolized the conversation in a flash.

They rambled on and on about football, the plays the coach was running and how Tony was supposed to perform in next week's big game against New Canaan. My brother was ecstatic to talk football again, and I didn't want to interfere with their manly-man chat session.

The perfect excuse to leave.

"'Night, Daddy," I said, poking my head in front of the camera one last time.

He started to respond, but Tony wouldn't let him. He was on a football rant again by the time I left the room.

"Goodnight, Grand-mère," I said as I passed through the living room.

She was in her reading chair again, smiling at me. "*Bon nuit*, my sweet."

My grandmother looked up at me with so much expectation.

"Thanks. For dinner," I said. I tucked a hunk of my hair behind my ear.

She nodded.

I'm not sure why I decided to, but I crossed the room and gave her a quick hug. "It was . . . nice."

Her smile of appreciation warmed me and she kissed both my cheeks.

"Faix de beaux rêves, Liliana."

I pulled back, gave her a quick smile and went upstairs to my room.

Outside my bedroom door sat my hatbox from Worthington's topped by the bag of sewing scraps Kerry had given me. I carried them both into my room and moved toward my work table. When I moved the bag to my project basket, I noticed the cream envelope.

Just like the last one, with my name in her beautiful script across the front.

I opened it quickly and read the note.

My dearest Liliana,
A lady is always tidy.
Je t'aime,
Grand-mère Camille

I sat in my chair and stared at her words. Muttering, I tossed the note onto my desk with the rest of the magazine clippings, fabric swatches and drawings covering test papers marked with big red Ds and Fs.

Shaking my head, I complained out loud to the note. “Well, if you wanted me to pick up my stuff, why didn’t you just say so?”

22.

"Lili, I must talk to you," Margaux pleaded into my voicemail. "Please call me."

I erased the message on my cell phone without thinking twice about it. Margaux's dismissal of me still ached, and I didn't want to talk to her.

Besides, I felt really fat today, and her voice reminded me of exactly how jiggly my body was. This morning, with my favorite jeans in the wash I'd been forced to wear the tighter ones, and the button-down shirt I'd put on was stretched across me like my chest had grown overnight. Yanking on the front to loosen the fabric across my straining buttons, I was about to turn around and go home to change when Sophie caught up with me.

"Got a project for you," she said as she fell into step and pulled me toward school.

Giving up on my hopeless shirt, I sighed. "What's up?"

She handed me a magazine and I took it, but not without staring at her first.

"Are your eyes . . . *violet*?"

She smiled. "Trying new contacts again. Like them? Thought I'd change up my boring eyes."

"Your blue eyes are not boring. They're beautiful." I shook my head. "And those are kind of creepy, if you must know."

"Let's get to the important stuff."

She tapped the magazine page with a willowy model wearing an ankle length gown and draped across a stone wall. The pale pink dress she wore was clinging to her shape beneath the diaphanous fabric. But I knew that if she'd been standing, the dress would have rippled with every breeze like some of the costumes Sophie wore on stage. It was pretty, but the straps were all wrong.

"So?"

Sophie leaned close. "He called again. Last night. We talked for over an hour," she said with a huge smile.

"Really?" I asked. I was happy for my friend, who'd secretly pined for Adam Brock since she'd moved here and found he shared her love for all things extraterrestrial.

Rubbing her nails across her chest then blowing on them, Sophie grinned. "We're going out Saturday night!"

"That's great!" I held up the magazine. "But don't you think this is a bit dressy?"

She laughed. "It's not for that. I just want to give you plenty of time to finish before the after party."

"Finish what?" I asked. My foot skittered across a pine cone and I stumbled.

Sophie righted me. "Making my dress for the after party on opening night. I have to look *fan-freakin-tastic!*"

My friend could not look anything but. "Did Adam ask you?"

"He hasn't." She shrugged then pirouetted ahead of me. "But he will!"

I hurried to keep up with her, shifting the magazine onto my books.

Sophie laughed. "Come on. We've got planning to do before homeroom!"

Five hours later, Tyler Jackson started following me between classes as I was on my way to Family Life Skills with Mrs. Russell.

He started in on me, whistling through his cupped hands toward me.

Then, in a too-loud voice, he announced, "Hey, Carracino. Heard you hooked up with Barnett and Sanderson in the bushes."

I spun around to face him and felt my face redden as half a dozen kids stared at me, mouths hanging open. Two sophomore girls I vaguely knew by name started laughing as they looked back and forth from him to me.

"Leave me alone, Tyler," I told him. "You don't know what you're talking about."

The girls moved closer to hear better.

I turned fast to get away from them, but Tyler was right behind me.

"You just let me know when it's my turn," he said in my ear.

My hand connected with his face before I could stop it. It was automatic, not a slap exactly, but close. I hit him in the mouth and he kind of groaned in surprise.

I felt his slimy lips against my skin and pulled away fast, wiping my hand on my jeans.

The two girls gasped.

My classroom was up ahead and I hurried.

Tyler had other ideas. He grabbed the back of my shirt and pulled me toward him.

"Hey!" I shouted, nearly dropping my books.

Just as I got a good look at the girls' gossip-loving faces, I felt him pull my shirt by the tail again. Too hard. I looked at my chest just in time to see three of my already strained buttons give way and fly toward the lockers.

A half a second later, I was standing in the hallway of my school, surrounded by a dozen slack-mouthed kids who couldn't take their eyes off my ugly bra or my boobs.

Time froze in a truly awful way.

I was totally exposed.

And Billy Martin was standing five feet in front of me, staring.

When Tyler got a good look and started laughing, he finally let go.

Heart racing and tears burning in my eyes, I clutched my tattered shirt to my chest as I bolted past Billy toward the safety zone of Mrs. Russell's classroom.

As I swept by him on my run of shame, his low voice resonated in my ear. But he wasn't talking to me. He was talking to Tyler.

All he said was, "You're a real asshole, Jackson."

23.

The classroom was filling as I dumped my books on a table and rushed to the back corner facing the supply wall. My hand trembled as I tried to search for replacement buttons and a needle and thread. I knocked a tray of bobbins to the floor with a crash, and flinched as they scattered.

At the whiteboard at the front of the class, Mrs. Russell clapped her hands. "All right, let's settle down and get to your machines. We've got a busy sewing day ahead of us and we need to start wrapping up. Today I'll be checking your progress on how you've set your sleeves. Only two more days and we'll move onto our unit on machine embroidery."

The dozen girls in the class murmured amongst themselves and shuffled toward their seats. None of them paid much attention to me. Somebody flipped on the stereo and music quickly drowned out the talking.

But I still couldn't turn around. Not until I made myself decent again.

I clutched my shirt across my chest. Snatching a box of random buttons from the cabinet, I pulled it toward me with my free hand. The buttons rattled against the plastic box as my hand shook.

This was so unfair. Tyler had gone way too far.

Shaking my head to fight back the tears, I set the buttons on the work counter and pushed at them with my fingertips until I found a few I thought would work.

Footsteps sounded behind me and I closed my eyes and sighed.

"Lili, I asked you to get started on your work," Mrs. Russell said as she approached. She bent at the waist to scoop up a handful of bobbins.

I shook my head. "I'm sorry. I can't."

She spilled the bobbins back into their bin and put a hand on my shoulder. “Why not?"

One look at my face, and concern settled on hers. She touched my arm and whispered. “Lili, what’s wrong? Are you sick?"

I clutched my shirt tighter. “I just need a few buttons, Mrs. Russell. I’ll be fine when I get them sewed on.”

She waited a measure before she spoke.

“Well, that’s no problem. Let’s see what we can do,” she said kindly. She put a hand on mine and smiled. “What are we working with here? I’m pretty handy, you know.”

Staring up at her, I tried not to cry. Out of the corner of my eye, I saw Susi Nichols stand up. I cringed.

It wasn’t hard for Mrs. Russell to figure out how upset I was, and her voice was gentle. “Let go of your shirt, Lili. I can help you, but I have to see.”

Footsteps sounded behind us. Susi Nichols clicked over to where we were standing, her heels tapping even noises across the linoleum as she walked. She was a girly girl, all prim and proper. The original Miss Goody Two Shoes with corkscrew blonde curls.

My body immediately tensed.

“’Scuse me, ladies,” she said, edging between us. “Need a spool of red thread for my topstitching.”

She stared at me with her big blue eyes, glanced at the shirt I was clutching, then over to my teacher.

“Am I . . . interrupting something?” she asked with a bit too much curiosity.

Mrs. Russell handed her the thread. “Just go on back to your sewing, Susi, and I’ll be over to check your progress in just a few minutes.”

“Sure." She gaped at me and I looked away.

My teacher sympathized. “All right, Lili. We’re alone.”

My voice was really quiet. “I *can’t* show you. It’s too embarrassing.”

Somebody laughed behind me and I shut my eyes.

Mrs. Russell smiled and gave me a quick hug. “Okay, okay. I understand. Now why don’t you go in the changing room and slip your shirt out to me? When it's all fixed, I'll give it back to you. Nobody will know."

"Nobody else, you mean," I said as I pulled the curtain closed.

In the mirror, the sight of me in my torn shirt was even more humiliating than I'd imagined. I stripped off the cause of my latest problem and pushed it through the curtain. Inside the small space, I was confronted by my own shirtless reflection.

I had no choice but to look at it, seeing nothing on my body but the big, lumpy breasts packed into an ugly bra that spawned all my troubles.

Some days I wish I could just rip them off.

Turning to face the changing room curtain instead, I closed my eyes, breathed through my nose to keep from losing it, and waited for what felt like an eternity as cold air slithered over my naked skin.

"Here you go, Lili." Mrs. Russell handed me my shirt, the rips and missing buttons nicely repaired. I buttoned without looking at myself again and slipped back into the classroom to go directly to my table.

"Come on out in the hall with me, Lili," she said. "We'll only take a minute."

Susi Nichols shot me a look then whispered something to the girl sitting at the machine next to her.

My sewing machine was just a few feet away. "But –"

Mrs. Russell spoke firmly in her teacher voice. "We need to talk. Now."

She gave me a look that told me I couldn't possibly argue with her, so I nodded and reluctantly followed her outside. In the deserted hallway, we stood by the lockers.

I crossed my arms and stared at a poster that screamed *Choose Abstinence, not STDs.*

She sighed. "Want to tell me about it?"

Shrugging my shoulders, I said, "It was just a stupid accident."

"Come on, now. We've known each other for a long time. You can be honest with me." She spoke gently. "Losing one button is an accident. Three is something entirely different. What happened, Lili?"

If I told her what Tyler had done to me this time, he'd get in big trouble, and his friends would make a huge deal out of it, and then those guys would never let me forget it. They'd find a way to make this whole incident *my* fault, like I'd asked for it or something. They'd flip the tables on me.

No. I couldn't tell.

But she persisted.

She prodded. "Is somebody bothering you here at school? Is it a boy?"

Try three. I looked up at her then and gave her the biggest fake smile I could manufacture. "Nothing I can't handle, really. No worries."

Mrs. Russell came closer and lowered her voice. "You know you can talk to me. Anytime." She took a measured breath. "If someone isn't treating you right, and I can help, you know I will. I care about you, Lili."

As she brushed my hair back over my shoulders, I gave her a nod. "Yes, ma'am."

"How are your grades?" she asked, folding her arms over her chest. "I know you're fine in my class, but what about the others? Any problems?"

I started to panic. "My . . . my grades? Why . . . why do you want to know that?"

"I'm your teacher, Lili, and you've always been a good student. I can tell by your tone and the way you're acting that something's really wrong here, and I'm concerned. Officially. Do we need to schedule a session with your counselor?"

I shook my head. "No, ma'am. I can handle it. I promise."

I could tell my teacher wasn't entirely satisfied with my answers, but she paused for a moment then decided to stop pushing.

"Now go on back inside and concentrate on that gorgeous coat you're making. You'll feel much better."

I took her escape clause and ran with it.

24.

By the end of this miserable day, the Middleton rumor mill was in full swing. I'd taken more critical stares and verbal jabs from kids I didn't even know in just a few hours than in all my years being alive. And it pretty much sucked.

She hooked up with Jimmy and Joe at the same time.

Tyler took off her shirt in the hall.

She's a slut.

Truth had no bearing on the words and whispers coming out of these kids' mouths.

Truth couldn't change the way they were looking at me now, like I was somehow different than the girl who walked through the school doors this morning. That by some amazing feat between classes I'd transformed into exactly the kind of girl who'd go down on the boys in the bathroom before lunch and wrap up the day with a hand job at the back of the bus.

They'd invented a reputation for me, and I hadn't done a thing to earn it.

They didn't know me, but they spread the lies.

Sophie caught up with me as I skirted along the far side of the parking lot to avoid Jimmy's truck, my head down to avoid any looks.

"Hey, wait up, Lil!" she said, rushing to my side and grabbing my arm. "What the hell's going on with you? I'm hearing all sorts of things, and they're not good."

I glanced up at my friend as we walked. Her face was pulled into a frown that bordered on anger.

"Which rumor? That I'm failing biology *and* math? Or the sex in the bushes kind, or maybe the stripping in the hall kind? Or perhaps you heard the plain old she's a slut kind?"

Sophie shook her head and tucked a strand of hair behind her ear. "It's not funny, Lil."

I sighed. "You don't have to tell me that. I'm well aware."

"I don't understand what happened," she said quietly, pulling me onto a side street that would let us avoid the sidewalk crowds. "What set this off?"

We sat on a stone wall beneath a shady oak.

"I refuse to talk to you and your fake purple eyes. You don't look like my friend," I said with a sigh. "Put on your glasses. Please."

"Oh, fine. Be a killjoy," she said. She reached into each eye and plucked out the contacts. When she flicked them into the bushes and put on her glasses, she nudged me hard. "Satisfied?"

"Mucho."

"So spill."

With as little emotion as I could manage, I explained my latest humiliation, right down to Billy Martin's eyeful of my chest.

"I'll kick Tyler's ass next time I see him," she seethed, toeing the stones beneath our feet. "He's such a loser."

I sighed. "And it only took four hours for that to become what you heard. I got to tell you, Sophie, kids have killed themselves over this kind of bullying. And I understand why."

"Maybe, but you don't have to be one of them." She wrapped her arm around my shoulders and pulled me toward her. "It'll be okay, Lil. We'll make this better."

I leaned against her as the cool breeze blew and wondered out loud. "How?"

25.

Saturday morning was sunny and bright, but the temperature had dropped into the fifties for scrounging morning with Grand-mère. With a map in hand and the first address plugged into the GPS, we set out in my mother's beloved silver Mercedes for four separate yard and barn sales in Greenwich and Stamford.

After a sleepless night of replaying the day's events, I was ready to think about anything other than my mid-section display.

My grandmother had dressed casually for the occasion, with just enough makeup to look elegant but natural. Crisp black pants tucked into sleek boots fitted her long legs to perfection. She wore a cream-colored turtleneck, tucked in with a really wide leather belt that made her waist look impossibly small. And she'd draped her shoulders with a nubby mohair wrap.

She amazed me with how perfectly put together she looked, even so early on a Saturday morning.

On the other hand, I looked too ordinary for description, hidden beneath my favorite cable knit sweater that hung almost to my knees.

The GPS computer voice told us to turn left onto Deerfield Road and we did, a little too abruptly. Grand-mère cut off an approaching car in the process. To the sound of screeching brakes, she gave a tiny wave and a smile to the angry driver, and then carried on as if she hadn't broken any number of traffic laws.

The Mercedes hugged the shoulder. I ducked reflexively when she came too close to an overhanging tree limb and branches and leaves scraped the window. The tires bit into the gravel before she got us back on track and holding our lane.

I thought I detected a note of tension on her face, a subtle tightening of the muscles that betrayed she was anything but perfectly calm.

And when she took a major pothole head-on and the car jolted, the situation became crystal clear. My grandmother was not used to driving. Probably hadn't done it in years. When she wasn't on planes working with Christophe, she lived in Paris, where she rode in taxis or on the Metro or in his private limousine wherever she went.

"Are you okay driving?"

She sucked in a breath, ran a stop sign and clutched the steering wheel until her knuckles were white. "*Mais oui*," she exhaled."So what do you search for at these *événements* when you visit?"

I blew on my paper cup of double espresso and shrugged. "Never have a plan, really. I just look for things to inspire me."

We followed the GPS directions again, turning onto a long, winding road of rolling farms and fading summer gardens with rows of heavy-headed sunflowers dipping in the breeze. We were deep in horse country now, and split-rail fences edged pastures where quarter horses and paints grazed and roamed.

"*Regardez*. So magnificent, no?"

Alongside us, a group of riders cantered with their horses along a rough trail. Grand-mère got distracted when the lead rider in a grey jacket and white jodhpurs led his huge chestnut horse into an effortless jump over a fallen tree. It surprised her so much she almost swerved our car off the road and into the nearest fence, but corrected at the last minute and got us back on track.

"They have so much control," I said as I watched the other horses in the line take similar jumps.

Up ahead, cars clogged the roadside.

"Looks like we found the spot."

Grand-mère visibly relaxed her posture. "When you shop, what inspires you, my darling?"

I breathed in and caught the subtle scent of her perfume. "I don't know. Fabrics. Vintage shoes. Cool clothes. Just details, I guess."

We arrived at the house with silver balloons on the mailbox and a chalkboard announcing the sale leaning against a bushy evergreen. She parked the car on the street, sort of. The front end nosed toward the yard's fence at a weird angle like a fallen domino among the row of neatly parked vehicles.

"*Nous sommes arrive*," she said with a sigh as she shut off the car and we got out.

26.

I felt that little thrill I always got when I first arrived at a sale, the adrenaline rush of needing to run ahead and explore and dig up treasures before anyone else got to them. The money stuffed in my jeans pocket made me itch to spend it.

A crowd picked through tables out by the barn and we walked along the chipped stone drive toward a spinning wheel and pair of old boat oars. "Looks like they have lots of antiques."

My grandmother nodded and shifted her cognac-colored leather satchel from one arm to the other. The purse was one of my mother's newest designs, sculpted with detailed leather work and her signature buckles in burnished bronze. This handbag was from her fall line. I knew because she'd given one to me, too. The purse sat in my closet on the shelf, still in its protective sheath next to the last four she'd given me that I'd never used.

Grand-mère's face lit up. "Let us explore *dans* the barn first. Looks intriguing, does it not? All dark and dusty."

I smiled. "Okay."

This was a strange experience, being with my proper grandmother and digging through other people's castoffs. We'd never done anything like this together before. In fact, I don't remember ever doing much of anything with her that didn't involve me consuming mass quantities of food or coffee.

She wandered away to examine a table piled high with old Tupperware and canning jars. I heard her mumble with a shake of her head. "*Très bizarre.*"

People milled about, inspecting the sets of china and odd crystal glasses or rummaging through stacks of old record albums and magazines. But none of those items interested me.

In a dusty shaft of light from the hayloft doors, a basket of fabrics on a picnic bench caught my eye and I moved toward them. In the basket, I bypassed the dull checks and stripes, skipped over a paisley and let my fingers drift over a faded pink brocade. But when I came to a length of silky red Chinese satin, I pulled out the weave to inspect and found it was almost as long as I was tall.

My grandmother came up behind me. “It is very beautiful. Red is your color.”

I drifted my fingers over the smooth fabric and studied the intricate embroidered pattern. “I just love the texture.”

She gave me an impromptu hug and kissed me on the forehead. “You are your mother’s daughter after all, my love.”

I looked up at her and took in her radiant smile. “I’m not like Mother at all.”

“Ah, but you are, *chérie*." She spotted a full-length mirror leaning against the barn wall and gestured toward it. “Come with me.”

We walked to the walnut framed mirror and she stood behind me as she turned me to face it.

“Do you wear a shirt beneath this?” she asked, tugging on the sleeve of my oversized sweater.

“Just a tee-shirt,” I said. She had me curious now. “Why?”

She smiled and set her handbag on an old milk can. “Take off the sweater. Please.”

I tossed my sweater onto an old trestle table. I stood there in my long-sleeved super-faded Lucky Charms tee with the dancing leprechaun that used to be bright green. Now the only feature that retained any sort of color was the lucky shamrock on his hat.

Grand-mère gathered and wrapped my hair into a loose knot at the nape of my neck.

“Such gorgeous cheekbones you have, Liliana” she said as she ran her fingers along them. “You should show them more often.”

Cheekbones? I'd never thought about them one way or another.

My grandmother smoothed my shirt across my shoulders with her long fingers and pushed up my sleeves. She draped the Chinese fabric across my front, then tugged on the fabric below my chin and spread the folds evenly across my shoulders.

I stared at my reflection, amazed by the luxurious shawl she'd created with a few simple folds and tugs. I looked more grown up. Sophisticated, almost. "How did you do that?"

A middle-aged woman with a coat rack in one hand and a picnic basket in the other stopped to watch. She was plain and frumpy, with drab hair, barn clothes and muddy boots. Her face was lined and leathery from years of hard work. She nodded. "Great color on you."

I smiled at the lady.

Grand-mère continued. "Fabric is your friend, Lili. You must allow its fibers to speak to you and work with them on your body."

She wrapped the cloth around my waist from front to back and back again, tucking the ends into delicate ripples. "The right fabric can accent a small waist and the wrong can make your middle look larger."

"Wow." The lady next to my grandmother let out a low whistle and set down her bulky purchases. "I think I need to take you home with me."

In the mirror, I admired the silhouette. For some reason, with the fabric twisted and tucked just so around my waist, I didn't look so fat.

With a smile, my grandmother worked her magic on the satin again, shifting it over one shoulder and gathering slightly. "Finish the hem, add a brooch at the shoulder, and you have an elegant drape for any outfit, day or evening."

I turned to get a better look at the effect she'd created. "I really like that."

She gathered the slippery fabric into her fingers again and draped it around the back of my neck. Looping one end over the other at the front, she gave it a twist and joined the fabric again at the back of my neck. "And now you have a glorious . . . how you say . . . *collar*?"

"I call it a cowl neck," the lady interjected, nodding. "I tell you. You French ladies sure do know how to work a scarf. You should give lessons."

My grandmother laughed. "*C'est naturel, madame.*"

I touched the twist and smiled. "That is too cool."

With fast hands, my grandmother unfastened the fabric, straightened then crossed the length around my neck and pulled it taut against my breasts. She reached behind me then crossed the fabric again and pulled back around to the front. With a final flourish, she knotted the ends into a soft rose.

When I looked at my reflection, I let out a tiny gasp.

If I hadn't been wearing the leprechaun shirt, I'd look, I don't know, *glamorous*. With my hair up and off my face, my throat looked almost graceful. And my body . . . the parts all looked different somehow.

"Now that's really something," the lady said, nodding in approval. "Oh, what I wouldn't give to be a teenager again." She grabbed a hunk of her belly and laughed. "But this old body couldn't pull off that look in a million years. No ma'am. Not in a million."

With a sigh, she picked up her coat rack and basket again and leaned toward me until our eyes met in the mirror. "You're a lucky girl to have someone teach you like this. My mom dressed like a farmer's wife always ready to muck the horses' stalls. Not a lick of fashion sense in my house."

I smiled at her, not sure what to say.

She sighed and shifted the heavy coat rack to lean against her shoulder. "Want my two cents? Wear what you want now because before you know it you'll be married with three messy kids, a hairy dog and a bunch of noisy good-for-nothing hamsters. And if you don't watch out," she said, hitching a thumb at her chest, "you'll end up looking as worn out as this old shoe here."

With that pronouncement and a self-deprecating laugh, she walked away and left us alone at the mirror.

"Well. That was *intéressant,"* my grandmother whispered.

"I'll say," I said, running my fingers over the rose at my waist and studying my reflection. I'd never be brave enough to wear a top like this with bare shoulders. So . . . fitted.

My grandmother smoothed a strand of my hair and let her hands come to rest on my shoulders. "You *are* a true beauty, my love."

She smiled and shook her head. "Just a beautiful, beautiful girl, Liliana."

27.

"Schedule a haircut, Liliana," my mother scolded during our transatlantic video call that had set me on edge in less than 30 seconds. She was in full-on businesswoman mode, issuing orders and directives. "You know how I do not like when your hair hangs in your face and I cannot see you."

I grit my teeth and tucked my hair behind my ears and tried to focus on the sketch of a high-heeled sandal she had posted on the wall behind her worktable in their rented flat. It was quite pretty. "Yes, Mother. You've told me you hate my hair a thousand times."

"I don't hate your –"

"Whatever, Mother." She was grating on my nerves.

"How is school? Do you have tests this week?"

Now she was really pushing my buttons. I snapped at her and lied. "School's fine. No tests."

"My, you are disagreeable this evening." She sighed then tried to lighten the mood as she took a sip of her wine. "Where are your grandmother and Tony?"

"Football practice," I said. "I'm home alone."

"Ah. Did you get the package I sent you?" she asked.

I heard a tone on her end and I could see her surreptitiously check her iPhone. She began texting someone before she even waited for me to answer her question. I knew it was midnight in Italy, but the time didn't stop her from working 'round the clock. My mother was a workaholic with colleagues the world over. Clocks did not matter to her.

"If you're too busy, Mother, we can talk later."

Please.

Glancing at her phone and typing two-handed, she finally looked up at the camera again. "No, I am perfect just now. I am between meetings."

Between meetings. At midnight. I sighed. "No package yet."

A smile graced my mother's face. "I have sent *une surprise* for you and Grand-mère."

Lord only knows what she sent. Italian clothes in impossibly small sizes. Belts that would never fit around my waist. More purses I'd never use.

Trying to conjure up some enthusiasm, I gave her a half smile. "Goody. Can I go now?"

She tsked. "I hope you are behaving for your Grand-mère and not being so very rude to her. You have a terrible attitude, Liliana. Is everything all right?"

No. Not by a long shot.

"Of course," I said, looking at my watch. "But I have an English paper to finish, Mom. It's due first period in the morning. Do you need anything?"

She looked miffed. "Just for you to be happy. Are you preparing for the recital with Margaux? I must call her but I have been too busy."

I froze. Then I lied seamlessly. "She's fine. Aunt Nina's fine. Tony's fine. We're all fine. I'll tell them you called."

She was back to the phone in her hand, running her thumbs across the keypad as she typed. "Good, good."

I prepared for more questions, but they never came. Talking to my mother was hit or miss. Sometimes she grilled me with 20 questions. Other time she went through the motions of mothering, saying what she thought she should, asking just enough questions to seem concerned. She might have been, actually, but she didn't stop long enough to actually listen to the answers. Tonight was one of those times. She barely looked up from her phone, and the expression on her face told me that this conversation was a lost cause.

I gave her the out she needed.

"I'll tell Grand-mère and Tony you called, and you tell Daddy I love him. Gotta go, Mom. Homework calls."

"Good girl, Liliana," she said. "*Au revoir, ma chérie.*"

With a push of a button, I zapped her preoccupied CEO image into cyberspace and went upstairs.

I was telling her the truth. I did have an English paper to write, but I didn't want to think about crafting sentences without dangling participles and misplaced modifiers. So I diverted to the bathroom instead.

In the bathroom I shared with my brother, a cream-colored envelope addressed to me was propped against my hairbrush. I knew exactly who it was from.

I opened the envelope and a handful of bobby pins spilled out with the card. The note in her flowing script read:

My dearest Liliana,
A soft chignon will complement every lady's face.
Je t'aime,
Grand-mère Camille

I smiled and remembered what she'd done with my hair earlier.

Then I took a long hard look at myself in the mirror. My thick, dark hair was clean but lackluster, hanging in long shapeless hanks from a center part to either side of my face. Nothing horrible, just nothing special either.

I brushed it straight back into a ponytail and gave a twist. Only this time, I fixed the knot at my nape with a few pins to hold it in place. The chignon was kind of lopsided, but it looked okay.

Turning to one side and then the other, I examined my face.

Maybe Grand-mère was right.

I did have cheekbones after all.

28.

After learning she'd officially been crowned Cinderella, Sophie stayed home with a strained muscle on Monday, and I was forced to walk to school alone. While she iced her calf and recuperated in the comfort of her plush bedroom to guarantee a perfect performance on stage, I endured the hell that was the high school parking lot.

Despite my extreme efforts at subterfuge, Jimmy Barnett spotted me on my way in, latched on like a leech and wouldn't leave my side.

He wasn't saying anything to me. He was just there, shuffling along next to me, leering. At me, at my butt, at my chest. And he didn't even make any attempt to hide his stalking.

A couple of kids smoking a joint by their car laughed as he swaggered by, stole a free hit, then went back to bothering me.

I did my best to ignore him, but when he got right in front of me and exhaled the sweet smoke into my face, I stopped. Fanning the fumes, I pleaded.

"Will you just leave me alone, Jimmy. Please? I'm not in the mood."

"I'm not doing anything to you," he said, hands raised. "I'm just walking into school, same as you. It's a free country."

I shook my head and turned to my right. "Suit yourself."

Two girls passed us, and one of them fake coughed while the other called me a skank.

I cringed at the name and felt my heart squeeze.

Jimmy followed too close, tailing me by just a few inches. When he started panting and faking an orgasm in my ears, I stopped short and locked my knees. He smashed into me and I elbowed him right in the gut.

He groaned.

"Grow up, Barnett. I mean it. You're not six anymore."

He leered at my breasts. "Neither are you."

I stepped around him and he choked out a laugh.

"Just having some fun with ya, Carracino. No harm, no foul."

I stared at him, my pulse racing. "You're an idiot."

He grinned. "But I know you still want me."

He repulsed me. "Is that all you think about? Sex?"

He came closer.

Susi Nichols was getting out of her car two spaces over. I clutched at the lifeline and called out to her. Anything to avoid being so close to him.

"Susi, wait up!" I shouted, ducking out of his path. "Got a question for you."

She waved vigorously at me and smiled, her blonde curls bouncing. "Oh hey, Lili."

Thankfully, Jimmy turned the other way.

And I was left behind to invent a conversation with Susi.

"What'd you need to ask me?" She shifted her bejeweled pink backpack onto her shoulder and smiled at me.

My mind drew a blank as we walked toward the entrance to D Wing. We only shared one class together, and I hardly knew anything about her other than that she was on student council, she lived for *Glee* and she liked sparkly things. She reminded me of a wind-up doll.

She laughed. "Cat got your tongue this morning?"

"Actually, it has. Can't remember what I was going to say," I fibbed. I stepped over a puddle shimmering with a streak of motor oil. "How's your jacket coming along?"

She shrugged and hiked up her backpack. "Crappy. I don't know how you sew so well. I keep screwing up." She paused. "Hey, speaking of which, what happened to you the other day? You looked so, like . . . upset in class, you know?"

The tone of her voice had changed subtly enough that I knew the rumors about me had reached her. She was fishing for information to back up the gossip, but I wouldn't cave.

I shook it off. "Nothing. I was just having a really bad day."

29.

Three hours later, I understood just how bad a day I really could have. My nightmare happened in social studies with the bored substitute who abandoned any semblance of a lesson plan. He handed back last week's test and took roll, but that was the extent of his official duties.

So with a blazing D- to add to the growing collection in my backpack, I learned he was giving the class a free period. He lay down the only rules to follow while he read *Hitchhiker's Guide to the Galaxy*.

No phone calls in or out. Keep the noise to a dull roar.

Within a minute, the cliques took sides and the cell phones came out and web surfing began. I put on my headphones and tried to tune out while I attempted a math problem that didn't make sense. I hated Euclidean geometry, and Pythagorean's Theorem was confusing the hell out of me.

But the noise two tables in front of me wrecked my focus.

"Oh my God, will you look at this," Tara cried out, shoving her phone in Ashley's face. They laughed hysterically . . . then stared straight at me.

A chill ran up my spine.

Ashley's and Tara's thumbs worked double time as they laughed. About 15 seconds later, Chip Sunningdale let out a whoop and a "Yeah, baby! That's what I'm talkin' about!" He showed his phone to Mark Underwood and Sam Reimer, then they stared over at me and high fived.

I began to sweat as I shrank in my seat.

The cell phone in my pocket vibrated and I took it out with trembling hands. The screen flashed a new message and I opened my email program.

Gavin Meyers gave me a pat on the back from behind my desk. "Good going, Carracino. I *like* it."

I stared at him then back at my phone. The message was a text from Sophie marked "Urgent 9-1-1."I shot to my feet and grabbed a bathroom pass off the sub's desk.

"Be right back," I said, not waiting for permission.

A couple of people laughed as I hit the hallway in a run.

In the stall of the bathroom that smelled like a block of industrial disinfectant, I dialed Sophie and spoke softly.

"What's wrong?" I asked, sitting as soon as she answered. "Are you okay?"

She stifled a cry. "Oh, Lil. I don't know how to tell you. It's just so awful. I . . . I--"

Leaning my head against the cool metal side wall, I clenched my fingers into a tight fist. "Did something happen to my parents? Or Tony?" Panic began to rise. "Is it Grand-mère?"

"No! It's nothing like that," Sophie wailed. "Nobody's hurt."

"Then quit with the dramatics already!" I said, slamming my fist into the wall so hard the paper holder fell to the floor and skidded into the next stall. My tension sizzled. "You scared the hell out of me."

I relaxed a little until Sophie sucked in a ragged breath and said, "It's about . . . you."

I sat up straighter and the toilet seat beneath my jeans rocked. "Me? I'm fine."

She sighed heavily. "No, Lil. You're not."

My breathing quickened. "What are you saying, Sophie?"

"Hang on," she said. "Okay, go ahead. Check your email. I forwarded the message to you."

"Forwarded what?" I opened my email program and waited for the message to download. Putting the phone back to my ear, I said, "Just tell me, Sophie."

"I can't explain. You have to see," she said. "Four different people I hardly know just sent this to me in about five minutes."

"It's really bad, isn't it?" I whispered. "Something was going on in class."

Sophie was blunt. "Yeah. I wish I could lie."

My hands shook as I opened the email.

The message said, "*Just ask and she's all yours.*"

Below the single line was a picture far worse than the first one someone sent me.

This one was a close-up of my face to my chest in the wet pink leotard. The pale cloth was sheer, and my nipples were standing out clear as day. With my half-closed eyes and the surprised expression on my face that could have been mistaken for another feeling, I looked like a porn star in mid-act.

I couldn't manage to speak.

"You still there, Lil?" Sophie asked quietly. "You okay?"

I cleared my throat. "No. I'm not."

I closed my eyes and tried to breathe normally.

Pictures had flown around last year, even to the middle school, of a junior named Zoe Graham, too drunk at a Saturday night party to know they were being shot of her naked on somebody's bed. Some girls said her beer had been dosed. Nobody ever found out who took the pictures, but everybody got them. For almost six months, she lived with the constant teasing, the comments, the unwanted attention from guys, shrinking deeper and deeper into her own world. Finally, after she had a serious meltdown with lots of screaming and breaking of glassware at a Stamford shopping mall, her mom pulled her from Middleton and transferred her to a boarding school where she could get "special" attention. No one had heard from her since, but most people assumed she'd been shipped off to a mental institution.

I wanted to cry, but I had to think, had to figure this out. "I've turned into Zoe overnight."

Sophie sighed. "Who would do this to you?"

"I'll give you three guesses."

I didn't have to guess. Tyler, Jimmy or Joe. Always them.

She clucked her tongue. "But you never did anything to those guys. I don't get why they've got this vendetta for you."

"Me neither," I wondered aloud. "And I don't know how to undo this, either."

Someone walked into the bathroom and slammed open the door of the stall next to me.

"Gotta go, Soph." I hung up the phone, waited for the girl next to me to get busy, and walked straight into the deserted hallway and through the nearest door to go home.

30.

Grand-mère was in the garden pulling the weeds choking the flame-red chrysanthemums when I walked up the driveway. Her hair was long and smooth beneath a wide-brimmed hat, and she wore a loose sweater and jeans. My mother's back-of-the-closet clothes most likely.

I'd ditched my books in social studies, refusing to go back to retrieve them. With a quick call to the front office, I asked them to pick up my stuff and told them I'd gone home too sick to stay in class. After a stern lecture, they assigned me a week of detention for cutting class and leaving school without permission. But I didn't care. I couldn't stay there and face the stares.

Now all I had with me was my phone, and I clung to it like a security blanket.

"Lili!" my grandmother said with a smile. "*Quelle surprise!* You are home so early! I did not expect you."

I shrugged and moved closer to the bed of mums, where half of the groundcover was well-groomed and the other frowsy with leafy invaders. "I'm not feeling very well, Grand-mère."

She got to her feet and dropped her trowel in the dirt. "What is wrong? Are you ill?"

"Yeah." It wasn't a lie. I really did feel sick as I rubbed my temple. "Don't know. I just have a really bad headache. *J'ai un mal à la tête*. I think I need to lie down for awhile."

My grandmother stripped off a garden glove and lay a cool hand against my forehead. "You are not warm, so that is good. Shall I get you some medicine for the head?"

"No. I can get it. I'm just going to my room and take a nap. I'll come down for dinner in a bit."

Worry lines creased her beautiful face. "If you are certain I cannot help you then?"

I shook my head. “I think I’m coming down with something.”

Confusion tightened her expression.

“I might be getting a cold,” I explained, opening the front door. “But I should be fine after I sleep.”

She clucked her tongue. “You will call if you need me? I will not be long here in the outdoors with *les mauvaises herbes*." She gestured to the mound of scraggly weeds she’d already pulled. “They are everywhere, these bad boys.”

My parents cared nothing for gardening. I gave her a tired smile. “I’ll be okay. Thanks.”

Every part of my body ached with the reality I’d yet to face, my half-naked image screaming along the broadband all over town. Just the thought made me want to throw up.

No amount of aspirin would help this. I was way beyond that.

When I went into the kitchen to get a diet soda from the pantry, I passed the wine bar. Something made me stop, turn around, and grab the first bottle within reach. Burgundy wine, the kind my parents served in the huge glasses as big as bowls.

I stared at the label and felt the heavy bottle in my hand.

Why the hell not?

Maybe having a few drinks would help ease the pain I was feeling right now. I hadn’t had more than half a glass at once yet, but there was always a first time. Plenty of kids I knew drank all the time and told me how great it was to get trashed and just let go. Maybe it would make me feel better to get plastered for once. I was overdue.

I glanced out the window toward my grandmother. She was back to her digging, looking serene and elegant, even in the garden sunshine and dirt.

So with a bottle opener and crystal wine glass in one hand, and the big green bottle of *Pommard Premier Cru Les Épenots* in the other, I slipped up the stairs to my room and closed the door.

My parents drank wine like this by the bottle every night, with a slice of bread and cheese or a steaming platter of grilled meats and vegetables. My grandmother did too, and so did my aunts and Nonna Lena. It was a French and Italian family tradition, to have wine with the evening meal, and I'd been given small glasses for as long as I could remember. But on its own, every time I'd had more than a sip or two of the dark wines, they tasted sour and biting to my tongue.

Today was different though. I wanted to feel something, anything other than the misery I was experiencing right now. Bitter would be good.

My grades sucked. My life was ruined.

I twisted the corkscrew and pulled out the cork, loving the hollow "blonk" sound as the seal broke and released the grapy vapors. With a big splash, I poured a glass and picked up the stem. Lifting it to my nose as I'd been taught, I breathed the familiar smell deeply. The drink smelled earthy and rich and sweet and I tried not to grimace as I took my first swallow. With each sip, the heavy acidity of the burgundy grapes coated my throat, numbing just a little bit more.

The first glass went down really rough, burning my taste buds and making the insides of my cheeks feel all puckery and dry. I poured another glass and walked over to my mirror, wine in hand like I did this all the time.

I stared at my reflection while I drank greedily. I needed the alcohol to kick in, faster.

In this ugly bright blue sweatshirt, I looked like a gumball, all round and fat and unappealing. I turned to the right and to the left, looking backward over my shoulder into the mirror. There wasn't a single good angle to look at . . . *me.*

I drained my glass with a few hard gulps and shook my head.

My body was my enemy.

If I didn't look the way I did, none of this would be happening to me. But no matter how many ugly sweatshirts I wore, I'd never be able to escape the truth.

I had the body of a slut.

I poured another glass of the wine, taking a huge swallow that dribbled off my lips and onto my chin. My head was feeling sort of drowsy and light, kind of loose like when I was just about ready to fall asleep.

But tension settled deep in my belly as I inspected myself. The sweatshirt was too big for me to see anything, to see the parts I hated up close. Clinking the glass on the edge of my desk, I stripped off the sweatshirt and threw it on the floor next to my sewing machine.

With uneven steps, I pushed off one of my mannequins to steady myself. The faceless woman toppled to the floor, knocking into the others and making them all fall like soldiers on a battlefield.

The noise made me wince, but I didn't care. I left them and made my way back to the mirror. Standing there in my bra and jeans, the tears I'd been fighting came and began to spill. I drank long, hard swallows of the wine until a fuzzy feeling took hold of my brain.

I cried silently, rocking with disgust.

My reflection taunted me. From the side, my breasts stuck out a good four inches, maybe five. They were squeezed into a sports bra that smashed them into a lumpy shelf.

I wish I'd never been born with them.

By the fourth glass I was feeling no pain, but I could barely catch my breath either. My bra was too tight and cut off my air. I wanted to take it off, but I was too tired to fight stretching it over my head.

I slammed my glass onto my desk and watched it fall, spilling what was left of the red wine all over the carpet.

I blinked hard and gripped my desk. Shook my head. I didn't care about the purple stain seeping into the rug. I just wanted to get rid of this stupid bra.

Rocking forward and trying to focus, I grabbed the sewing scissors from my animal crackers tin. Stumbling back to the bed, I sat hard and swayed. The cold metal felt heavy in my hands.

The scissors glinted in the light. I lifted them up to my chest and slipped one of the blades beneath my strap.

My thoughts twisted as I tried to stay upright.

I knew what to do.

Just cut them off.

Just a few big cuts and they'd be gone.

Everything would be fine.

My head swam as the wine gripped me in its strength and I opened the scissors as wide as they would go.

I shook my head to clear it and failed. Rubbed my eyes with the back of my hand. Wiped my watering mouth. I felt sick. I pressed the blades against the bra and cut hard until white heat and a flash of pain scorched through me.

I sucked in a breath. When I saw the blood seeping into the cotton of my bra, little dots of woozy blackness pricked my sight.

I dropped the scissors onto the carpet and lay back against my pillow, closing my eyes to what I'd done.

Pain throbbed through me as I pressed my hand over the cut.

Blood seeped between my fingers.

But it didn't matter. Nothing mattered.

Even if I died today, right here and now, my naked picture would still be out there, spreading like a disease, making people sick every time they looked at it.

I blinked. Tried to focus on just the pain. To forget. Couldn't.

The bed spun as I closed my eyes and spiraled into darkness. I flipped onto my stomach for relief and let my arm hang over the side, suddenly too drunk to walk this off. I swung my arm to find my balance. Rolled my head. Groaned.

Nothing helped. The spins wouldn't stop.

Eyes open. Eyes closed.

Spinning. Twisting. Reeling.

My stomach lurched, my throat tightened, and I heaved my breakfast and a bottle of good red wine all over the floor.

Sometime later, with puke in my teeth and my face smashed to the pillow, I finally fell asleep to my life spinning out of control.

31.

Someone was shaking me by the shoulders. And shouting. In French.

"Liliana!"

My grandmother held up the empty wine bottle and spoke harshly as she tried to get a reaction out of me.

I just wanted her to stop yelling. I tried to lift my head toward her and let out a groan.

"You are drunk!" she said, poking me to look at her. "Tell me you are not drunk. It is only three o'clock in the afternoon! And you are a child!"

I blinked. Hard. Couldn't focus on her face. Felt pain. Lots of pain. Let my head fall back face-down on the pillow. Closed my eyes.

"Just so tired. . . . Need to sleep. Tired . . . ."

"Merde," she swore as she hurled the bottle into my trash can.

The crash made me flinch.

A second or five minutes later, I couldn't tell, she wiped the edges of my mouth with a wet cloth and uttered something harsh I didn't understand.

I pushed at the cloth with a floppy hand. *"Quit it!"*

She sighed, swore again, and finally left me alone to suffer in peace.

I drifted back into a drunken sleep.

32.

When I woke some time later, everything hurt.

I opened one sticky-feeling eye and spotted my dignified grandmother sitting in a chair by my bed, holding a book. But she wasn't reading. She was just waiting for me to wake up. And staring.

My head pounded and my chest throbbed. I slowly rolled onto my back and blew out an unsteady breath.

"*Mon Dieu!"* my grandmother shrieked. She dropped her book and rushed to my side. "Liliana, what have you done to yourself?"

I heard the fear in her voice and started to get scared myself. "*Grand-mère?"*

She was motioning toward my chest. I looked down and saw the blood. Dizziness hit me hard and I fought to keep from passing out. "*What—*"

She grabbed at my blood-soaked bra strap and pulled it back.

We stared at the horrible gash in my skin, reddened and seeping with my own blood.

She pressed at my flesh.

"Thank God, it is not deep, just broad," she said, shaking her head. "It does not look like it needs the stitches."

A wave of nausea rolled over me as a memory of the scissors in my hand crashed into my thoughts.

I felt the blade cutting me all over again and began to shake.

"How—"I tried to touch the wound with trembling fingers, but she held them back.

The pain magnified the more I stared at my chest.

"*No*. Do not make what you have done worse," she said nervously. "I will be right back. Do not move, Liliana. Do not touch *la blessure* or it will bleed more."

She hurried into the hallway and left the door ajar.

I lay back, tears flooding my eyes.

What had I done?

My brother stuck his head in the door. “Hey Lil—“

I tried to wave him off. “Go!”

“Holy cow! *What’d you do?"* He rushed in, concerned. He came next to the bed and stared at my chest. “You’re bleeding. It looks bad. You need a hospital, Lili.”

I wiped at my tears when I saw how scared he looked. I didn’t even care that I was laying there in my bra. I just wanted him not to worry. “Just go, Tony. I’ll be okay, buddy. It’s just a stupid cut. Promise.”

My grandmother whisked him out of the room. “Wait downstairs, Tony.”

“But she’s hurt,” I heard him say in a high voice. “Maybe we should call an ambulance? Get her a doctor or something. That’s a whole lot of blood.”

Grand-mère whispered quietly to him and smiled. “No need. She had a simple accident and she just needs a bandage. She will be fine, *mon chére*." She kissed him on both cheeks and gave him a big hug. “Now, do not worry. I will explain everything to you later. Be a good boy and go watch television, hmm?”

He waved a hand in front of his nose. “Stinks in here. Did she puke or something?”

My grandmother nodded. “Her stomach is upset. Now *allez mon chére*. I will be with you shortly.”

He stared at me again, but I couldn’t keep looking into his confused face. I turned my head toward the wall and started to sob.

The door clicked shut and Grand-mère came to sit beside me on the bed.

She didn’t ask questions while I sniffled and wiped my runny nose with the back of my hand. She simply found my scissors on the floor, wiped off the dried blood, then cut through the straps on my bra until the elastic snapped behind my shoulders. I didn’t move. When she cut the center line, the strained elastic held strong until the very last second and hit the mattress while my breasts sprung loose and out into the open air.

My humiliation was so deep I wanted to die. I was almost completely naked in front of my grandmother.

She set the scissors on my night table and pushed aside the scraps of the bra. With delicate hands and a folded towel, Grand-mère covered me and patted my shoulders.

"We will make you better, Liliana," she said tenderly.

I breathed in and got a whiff of peroxide.

She dabbed at my chest around the wound with a cold cotton ball. "We will clean this, and bandage you. I will take you to see the doctor. And then later we will talk."

"I don't want the doctor and I don't want to talk," I cried. I couldn't look into her beautiful face and not feel deeply, horribly ashamed. "I just want to make this go away."

She pressed a fresh cotton ball to the peroxide bottle again and sighed. "Whatever makes you so sad, we will determine an answer. Together." She put a hand on my arm and squeezed. "*Ma chérie,* this will hurt I am afraid."

As she pressed the wet cotton ball against my throbbing wound, I clenched my teeth and covered my mouth to keep from screaming.

"You are a brave girl, Liliana," she murmured as she tried to repair the damage I caused. "Do not ever forget you have a kind heart and a good soul, *ma chérie.*"

She sighed. "And you are brave enough to handle even the most frightening things."

33.

Thankfully, we skipped the horror of a doctor's visit when Grand-mère called and found out my shots were all up to date. I wouldn't die of tetanus or blood poisoning. Not this week at least. And if I took care of the cut with the antibiotic ointment the office prescribed, I might not have a permanent scar to remind me of how stupid I'd been.

But morning came way too soon for me. My grandmother was ready and waiting at the bottom of the stairs, dressed to the nines in designer clothes with her hair perfectly coiffed in an elegant twist.

I, on the other hand, was a walking disaster in one of my father's old white shirts and someone else's old sweat pants. I couldn't raise my arms high enough to brush my hair without wanting to cry, my head ached, the cut on my chest throbbed like a son of a bitch, and I dreaded with every fiber of my being what the day would bring.

"We'll talk later, okay, Tony?"

He shrugged but didn't respond.

She'd sent Tony off to school and asked me to stay behind. I still hadn't been able to face my brother yet, to explain what had happened. He gave me a wary look over his shoulder as he walked out the door, and I dropped my gaze to the ground. I couldn't meet his eyes.

Truth is I didn't even really know how to explain it myself. And I had no idea how to put it into words that he'd understand.

My life was a mess on so many levels.

"Are you ready?" she asked, steering me toward the kitchen. "I have made us a very special breakfast to share."

I held back. "I have to get to school, Grand-mère. I'll be late."

She shook her head. "No. You do not, Liliana. You are not attending school today, *or* for as long as it takes. You are at home."

Uncertainty cut through my pain. "Why?"

She brushed her hands together. "You and I need time, *ma chérie*. To talk."

I stood in the foyer, dropped my coat to the floor and crossed my arms. All of a sudden, a frightening thought crossed my mind.

She told.

"Did Mother tell you to do this? Sounds like her."

"No. Your Mother knows nothing of this, nor does your Papa. And they will not unless you do not talk to me now. Then I will ask you to call your parents and tell them everything."

"Is this some kind of weird French punishment?"

She gave me one of her most beautiful smiles and a chill raced along my skin. I did not like this, not one little bit.

She swept her hand toward the kitchen. "Shall we?"

Taking a few steps forward, I felt my heart begin to race. What was my strict grandmother going to do to me? Could she possibly make me feel any worse than I already did?

I walked into the kitchen and glanced toward the table, where a bottle of red wine sat surrounded by filled balloon glasses.

My stomach heaved at the sight.

"Come, come," she said as she linked arms and tugged me toward the liquor. She gave a creepy little laugh. "We have drinking to do, you and I. Never too early to start, do not you agree?"

"But I don't want any," I protested, trying to hold back.

She pulled and sat me down hard on a chair, then pushed a glass toward me. The wine sloshed, leaving translucent ruby rings on the crystal as the liquid resettled into the bowl of the glass.

"But why do you not want a drink? You were in such a hurry to grow up last afternoon and begin drinking so early in the day . . . *alone*. I thought perhaps you would prefer this special . . . meal . . . instead of *une omelette et café au lait.*"

This was too much.

I shook my head. "Grand-mère, I know what I did was wrong. You don't have to remind me how stupid I was." I paused to catch my breath. "I feel horrible. I won't do it again."

"Ah, but you are," she said. She pointed to the stomach-turning red wine. "*Drink.*"

I pushed back from the nauseating smell and slid the glass across the table to her. "*No.* I don't want to."

She stared me down and wouldn't relent. "*Drink it now!*"

My anger flared. "*I said no!*"

We'd reached an uncomfortable stalemate of sorts, sitting in tense silence for more than a minute with the wine between us.

Finally, I tossed her an olive branch. "I'm sorry."

She smiled. "*Bien.* We will save the wine for a more appropriate occasion. Now perhaps you should explain to me why you cut yourself and got drunk in the middle of the school day."

34.

How could I begin? The stress running through my body was monumental. While she put away the wine, I got up to get a glass of orange juice. My hands were shaky as I poured. Grabbing the aspirin bottle, I shook out three and popped them into my mouth. She waited for me to take a few gulps and come back to the table, juice glass in hand and aspirin in my belly.

When I sat, she was patient. But not for long.

"So?" she probed with eyebrows raised.

I buried my head in my hands. "I don't even know what to say."

She sighed, and folded her hands across her lap. "Begin with why you left school so . . . so *brusquement.*"

My unannounced departure had indeed been abrupt. Brought on by sheer embarrassment and panic in the middle of a laughing class. I still couldn't find the words to express the sinking feeling in my stomach when I saw the email Sophie had sent.

Forget grades, my life was just . . . *over*.

She spoke softly. "Just *talk* to me, Liliana."

When I thought of the disgusting image I'd seen of myself on my phone, my nose prickled and tears clogged my throat.

My grandmother gave a little cough to remind me she was still there, waiting for an explanation.

"You may forget I raised three impetuous daughters all without a husband by my side. You think I do not know drama? We experienced a crisis at home every single day of our lives. And we all survived," she said with gentle persistence. "Nothing you can tell me will be a surprise." She waited a measure. "So why did you cut yourself, Liliana?"

My wound throbbed, reminding me of just how reckless I'd been. I leaned on my hands and massaged my temples. "I wasn't trying to . . . . Maybe I was . . . I don't know. I just wanted that bra off and I couldn't breathe and I wasn't . . . thinking straight."

She tapped the table and clucked. "Ah, *oui*. Your *bra*, if that is what you wish to call it, is a discussion for another moment." She shook her head.

I looked up at her and she reached for my hand. Her eyes were sincere.

"You can trust me with your troubles, *ma petite chérie*. I will listen."

As she stroked my hand with her fingers and I looked into her eyes, I believed I could. I drew a breath and took the plunge into full disclosure.

My voice was barely a whisper. "Someone is trying to ruin me."

She smiled and I frowned.

"How can you smile?" I asked, appalled.

"Because, my dear, someone less will *always* try to ruin you," she declared. "Such is the way of a woman's life."

I sat back. "But it's not fair."

She leaned forward and patted my hand. "Ah, *mais oui*. Life is never really fair." She shook a finger at me. "But you can always learn to make it *feel* so."

I crossed my arms. Her attitude pissed me off. "Okay. Let's play 'what if.' What would you do if someone posted a practically nude picture of you in an email and you didn't say they could? Then they sent it to everyone you knew?"

"On the . . . internet?" My grandmother blanched slightly, stiffened in her chair and sat back. She gave a shrug then she pursed her lips. "That all depends. Was *le visage* flattering?"

Now I was really mad. "Flattering? What possible difference could it make if it was? They had no right to post that without my permission!"

She motioned with her hand. "Show me the photo. I want to see it."

"Too embarrassing," I whispered.

"Ah, show me, Liliana," she said with impatience. "It is just a photo. Nothing I have not seen, I am certain. I have had much experience with this."

I closed my eyes. That much was true. She'd posed nude for artistic reasons, and my bare breasts had been on full display for her when I was too hysterical to stop it.

Reluctantly, I took the phone from my pocket and opened the email.

She tsk-tsked. "Unkind, for certain, with the words they write. But you should not be embarrassed of your body. It is all yours and you should embrace it."

I grabbed the phone from her and stuffed it back into my pocket. "I didn't get the beautiful gene, Grand-mère. I'm not you."

She pondered my response for a moment, considering. "*Non*. You are not."

Then she smiled at me.

"Liliana, there will always be people who dislike you and wish to make you look bad. It is the way of a woman's life. *C'est destinée*." She breathed deeply. "Struggle is often the price of great beauty."

"And I have to pay that price?"

"We all do, in some way." She nodded. "But your strength and power *as a woman* will come from how well you deal with *des adversaires*."

"Do you know what it feels like to wake up every day and know that when you go to school people will screw with you? Do you have any idea how horrible it makes me feel, every single hour of every single day?"

She smiled. "The boys called me *la cigogne*. How you say . . . the stork? I was all arms and legs with a neck far too long. Their words and their gestures were so very cruel. So in some small way, I do understand. But only you can let your *adversaires* make you feel unworthy."

My opponents. I sipped my juice, thinking. "And what if there are too many? What if it feels like everyone's against you?"

She pushed aside the glasses of wine. "That is *simple*. Then you must be brave, and very strong, and know *exactly* who you are." She tapped my chest. "In here. *Votre confiance* will be your guide."

My confidence.

Not possible when you couldn't stand the sight of yourself.

35.

I wallowed in self-pity for the rest of the day, hibernating in my father's library with a few magazines, my phone and the television playing some random talk show about long lost friends. With no books at home, I couldn't even think about catching up on homework. Not that I could concentrate on it anyway, even if I wanted to.

While I stuffed my face on extra salty pretzels with mustard dip, Grand-mère was in the kitchen making calls. She promised she wouldn't tell my parents about what I'd done.

I almost believed her.

My father had stockpiled his texts to me, sending them all in one batch through some fluke of technology. I opened one at random and read.

As I look around the streets of my Roma, I am reminded of you in every gorgeous Italian woman I see. My beautiful daughter, my cara mia. I miss you.

Are you keeping the boys on their toes?

My father's texts to me were all the same. He meant well. He really did. He wanted me to be happy, but he never dug too deeply into my problems because that would mean he would be forced to admit something was actually wrong with our perfect life.

I was used to his white lies about my looks.

He always thought guys would be dropping like flies to take me out. Little did he know they were plastering my practically nude image all over the internet instead, doing God knows what to the picture in the privacy of their bedrooms.

Despite the rumors and the lies, the sad truth was that at 14, I'd never even been kissed by anyone other than relatives, and that would never count in the grand scheme of romance.

But Sophie had. When I called to tell her I was majorly hung-over and feeling sorry for myself, she'd yelled at me hard then told me her good news.

"Adam kissed me last night!" she said giddily. "Right as we sat in our seats to watch *Avatar*. You know, last night, when you were shit-faced and puking because you're a *stupid* dumbass."

I ate another dip-covered pretzel and crunched in her ear. "You're such a nudge. Thanks for rubbing it in."

I didn't have the heart to tell her about how I'd cut myself. As I felt the edges of the bandage, I didn't know if I'd ever be able to confess that.

"Hey. What are friends for if not to show you the error of your ways?" She laughed. "Anyway, Adam just leaned over, pulled off my three-D glasses, and planted a kiss right on my lips. Just like that. Like it was no big deal at all!"

"What'd you do?" I asked, pulling a knitted blanket around my shoulders. I tried not to feel jealous that she'd been the first of us to experience a real kiss, though deep down I'd always expected she would be. She was the pretty one. The girl with personality and *chutzpah*.

Nestling deeper into the corner of the sofa, I stared up at the ceiling. "Was it . . . nice?"

She sighed deeply. "Yeah. It was. Really nice."

I had to ask. "Did you . . . you know . . . *French*?"

Sophie laughed. "Absolutely, baby! He just stuck that tongue in my mouth and it was like my tongue knew exactly what to do," she explained. "You'll get it, too. It just kind of happens and you don't even think about it. You just do it, Lil, and damn it feels nice. Just like they say. It makes you feel kind of tingly inside."

I wondered if I'd ever get the chance to learn. "I should already be an expert, right? You know, since I'm a skanky ho slut and all."

I threw my half-eaten pretzel back onto the bag while Sophie scolded me.

"Stop that right now before I come over and wallop you. I don't want to hear that crap."

Rolling onto my side, I draped my arm over my eyes. "I can't. My life sucks. And I'm going to fail freshman year."

She sighed. "You won't fail because I won't let you do that to yourself. You'll get your act together. And they're jerks, Lil, the lot of them. It just feels rotten this week. Next week no one will even remember that picture."

"I wish."

"So when you coming back to school?" she whined. "I miss you already."

I could tell by her even breathing that she was stretching. "Soon. Never. I don't know exactly. I may skip the rest of high school and move to a convent. Maybe on Raratonga, or up in the North Pole. They don't have internet there, do they?"

"Nice try. You can't avoid this forever, so here's the plan. I'm not gonna leave your side in the halls and I don't care if I'm late to class. They'll live without me for a few minutes," she vowed. "And we'll stick real close before and after school. They won't get to you again."

I groaned and grabbed another pretzel. "Sophie, I appreciate it. But you can't do that. It's not realistic."

Sophie protested. "Well, I'm coming over tomorrow. Tell French Grandma to be on the lookout. You can sneak me in even if she says no. I'm a good climber."

The thought of my ballerina friend scaling my roof made me laugh.

I lifted a pretzel to my mouth and took a huge bite.

My grandmother came into the den and put her hands on her hips. "It is time to go, Liliana. Please put down the food and hang up the phone."

"Where are we going?" I asked, my mouth full.

Sophie whispered into the phone. "You're going somewhere? Now?"

"We have an appointment," my grandmother said, looking at her watch. "And you have mustard on your chin."

"We have an appointment," I repeated to Sophie, watching my grandmother.

Grand-mère raised her eyebrows and pursed her lips.

I wiped my chin and said my goodbyes.

Wherever we were going had to be better than facing my teachers' disappointed stares and listening to taunts all day.

36.

Thirty minutes later, we walked into the white-walled Stamford photo studio of Richard Ranesford, where soft jazz music played through invisible speakers.

Bold portraits of famous models lined the walls, some in black and white, and others in dramatic color with moody lighting. I identified Tyra Banks strutting in her underwear, and Gisele Bundchen in a bikini up to her knees in aquamarine water on a Caribbean beach, and Ashton Kutcher wearing only his muscles and his Calvin Kleins.

Richard Ranesford was apparently a very talented man behind the camera with well-heeled clientele, but his receptionist had obviously stepped out to lunch. The desk was empty save for a lone crimson Gerbera daisy in a slender vase and a closed appointment book.

"Tell me why we're here again?" I asked quietly, afraid to disturb the reverent hush in the deserted reception area designed in Italian modern leathers with a gleaming black marble floor.

"We have an appointment," she repeated cryptically.

"Who, we?" I moved across the room toward something I recognized, a picture of my grandmother, taken years ago, wearing only a streak of body lotion, a cleverly bunched towel, and a magnificent smile. "Wow. You always looked so happy in that shot."

She stopped admiring an image of a young black girl I didn't know whose face seemed to glow beneath the shadows of a flowering dogwood tree. Grand-mère stared straight at me. She smiled. "We are here for you."

"Me?" I asked when I realized she'd answered my question. Flutters of panic made me suck in a jagged breath. *"I* have an appointment? *Me? With this guy here? Are you mental?"*

Footsteps approached and a man with shaggy gray hair came closer. He wore faded jeans, scuffed cowboy boots and a huge turquoise ring weighing heavy on his hand. His Ed Hardy tee-shirt blazed with an attacking hawk, an open-mouthed skull and a crowned heart bearing the banner New York City. The shirt's snake fangs curved out to bite his paunch.

His voice boomed. "Camille! So good to see you. What's it been? Ten years since the last *Vogue* shoot? Is it possible you are even more beautiful now?"

"Richard," she said warmly. My grandmother lit up and extended her face to him. "Thank you for seeing us. You are so very kind."

"It is my absolute pleasure. I cleared the decks today." He kissed her on both cheeks and gave her a hug. "It's been far too long, my darling. You look fabulous, as always."

"Ah, but you always did know how to flatter me," she said with a gentle French lilt. "Lovely to see you as well. I have followed your success with great admiration."

He winked at her. "I owe it all to you, Camille. You know I do."

She gave him a coy smile and looked away.

I stood there like a mute, quivering in my sneakers.

"Richard Ranesford, please make the acquaintance of my granddaughter, Liliana Carracino," she said sweetly, extending a gracious hand in my direction.

He put his hand on my arm and gave a squeeze. "So nice to meet you. Can I call you Lili?"

I nodded. My legs wobbled.

He hitched a thumb over his shoulder. "Come on. Let's go on back and get started. We're all set up."

I yanked on my grandmother's indigo St. Pierre jacket as she followed him into the cavernous studio beyond reception. "*What are we doing?*"

She smoothed her jacket and her necklaces pinged together. "You will see, *ma chérie*. Let us go."

I had no real choice but to tag along. One way or another, she would make me do this eventually, and I was too tired out for another battle.

Inside, a white seamless backdrop draped the floor and back wall of the studio. Stand lights, umbrellas, reflectors, two computer screens, a digital printer and a fancy camera on a tripod formed a ring around an empty stool. Some of the equipment was so technical looking I couldn't even name what it was.

"I'm working solo today," he explained to Camille. "Sent my assistants out to lunch so we could concentrate and keep this low-key."

This man intended to take photographs.

Of me.

My stomach clenched and I felt the sheen of a cold sweat beginning to break out on my body as he flipped on bright lights.

"Just take a seat over here, Lili," he said, motioning to the stool in front of the camera.

"Oh, that's okay. Just take pictures of Grand-mère," I suggested. "She's the model. I'm nothing."

He just smiled at me and shared a glance with her. I could tell they'd been plotting against me. My heart raced.

"Sit, Liliana," she said in that voice that had dared me to drink more wine.

"But I'm a mess! Models are supposed to have fancy makeup and clothes and stuff. I'm wearing dad's old shirt!"

"*C'est parfait*, she said. "*Sit.*"

I knew when I was beaten. We'd get home sooner if I made it easy on everyone and cooperated.

Richard moved to stand behind the camera and make adjustments while my grandmother took a seat at a round table set with a crystal chiller of champagne and strawberries. She poured a flute, allowed the bubbles to settle, and lifted it to her lips.

Jazz music piped through the space while my heart pounded and my hands got all sweaty.

I walked past the light stands and cameras and perched uncomfortably on the edge of the hard stool.

"Looks good," he said.

I didn't know what to do with myself. Didn't know where to put my hands or how to hold my feet or where to look.

Didn't have any idea how I could hide with that lens pointed right at me.

He pressed a button and a bright flash went off, momentarily blinding me.

I blinked hard.

"Just taking a couple of test shots, okay? Today we'll be working in black and white. Going for a raw look. Nice and natural."

I blinked away the white spots and tried not to squint as I crossed my arms over my stomach and held on for dear life. "Why are we doing this exactly? I hate having my picture taken."

My grandmother let out a silvery laugh. "Precisely."

I stared at her to my right, and the camera started clicking away.

"Look toward me, Lili," Richard said. "In a few minutes, you'll find the camera doesn't lie. It doesn't know how."

"*Great*. Just what I need."

With a turn of my chin, I looked over at him, at the camera searing into me. All I could think about was the truly awful pictures of me someone had circulated.

"The lens only picks up what's real," he explained while staring at his computer monitor. He gave us a wave to join him. "Now both of you come on over here and let's take a look at our baseline."

He fiddled with the keyboard, tapping in a sequence of commands. Grand-mère and I stood behind him, watching. Within a few seconds, my picture filled one of the screens.

I cringed at the sight. "Oh, God."

He nodded. "Okay. It's natural. Lighting's a little stark." Richard dragged an image to the right screen so that my face filled both monitors. "Pretty girl . . .

"Are you blind?"

". . . but really bad body language," he continued.

"What do *you* see, Liliana?" Grand-mère asked.

In each picture he revealed, my arms were crossed against my mid-section. I looked like I had a stomachache, or diarrhea. My shirt pulled tight. My head hung forward and my hair fell in thick clumps onto my chest. Deep shadows darkened my eyes. "Nothing special, that's for sure."

He clicked on an image and opened the print command. With a punch of a button, my picture began to appear on a sheet of glossy paper.

"*I* see great promise," my grandmother said quietly, nodding. She sipped her champagne again.

I looked up at her while Richard made a few adjustments to his camera.

"Okay, go on back to the stool now, Lili. Only this time I want you to leave your arms by your sides. And unbutton that top button, will you?"

"You're not going to make me get naked are you? I don't want to do that. I won't."

He laughed. "No, nothing like that. You just look a little too stiff. We're tweaking what we've got to work with here."

Reluctantly, I opened the button and spread the collar slightly. I sat on the stool and gripped the sides while I propped my feet on the bottom rung. My sneakers slid forward. "You want me like this?"

He smiled at me and the camera flashed. "Good. Now lean back a little."

As I sat there holding my pose in my dad's old white shirt, he shifted umbrellas, lit light banks and bounced the beams off reflectors, made all sorts of miniscule adjustments to his equipment.

I closed my eyes and tried to tune out.

Think happy thoughts.

Ignore your life.

With another series of clicks, he continued photographing me.

He flipped a switch and a breeze blew across my face, rippling my hair behind me.

I breathed deeply, closing my eyes and leaning my head even farther back to work out a kink in my neck.

His voice instructed. "Arch your back just a touch."

Why was my grandmother torturing me like this? It was cruel to force me to do what she and her daughters did as naturally as breathing. I wasn't beautiful like them. Not by a long shot. And I'd never wanted to be a model and live that life, always being inspected and evaluated and picked apart.

"You've got to loosen up a bit, Lili," Richard coached.

I looked over at my grandmother nibbling on a strawberry while I smoothed my sweaty palms on the thighs of my jeans.

"Let's try this. Roll up your sleeves a few turns and shake out your hands."

Then he gave me more advice. "Stop thinking so much. Just get into the music. Concentrate on breathing and let go."

I looked away from my coolly elegant grandmother and up again at the tracks of lights overhead, stretching my neck into the breeze and trying to unwind my stiff body as I forced myself to concentrate on distinguishing the notes of the jazz piano. But tension settled in my muscles and held me tight.

Still, sound and light and camera clicks hit me from all angles.

"It's okay to relax, Lili," he said quietly. "Just take a few deep breaths."

I didn't want to be here right now any more than I wanted to be in school. I didn't want to see myself in more bad pictures. Hadn't I had enough photographic traumas for one week?

But I forced myself to roll my shoulders and let my hair fall behind me.

Richard did whatever fashion photographers do. He moved around, giving me subtle directions to shift my legs to the right, look down just an inch, thrust my chin forward ever so slightly or open my eyes wider. I never knew when he would take a picture or when the lights would change.

"Breathe, Lili," he'd say as he clipped up my hair. "Just breathe and don't worry so much. You're doing great."

Eventually, fatigue alone helped me relax.

After forty minutes of me sucking in studio air and him moving like a cat on quiet feet, he declared that we were done.

"Give me about fifteen minutes to wrap up, Camille," he said, sitting in a rolling chair behind the computer. "Why don't you go on in the conference room and flip through the books?"

"Très bien," she said, whisking me away with a satisfied smile.

37.

The conference room, much like the reception area, was decorated with framed photographs of beautiful people I recognized from magazines. Perfect skin, bones with absolute symmetry, shimmering cascades of hair.

As I studied them, I spotted one of the images that had haunted my childhood.

There she was.

My grandmother, looking spectacular and golden, lay against a swath of black velvet in her rope of Balcroix diamonds.

The image was perfection in every way, and so was this woman.

And I thought I couldn't feel worse. I was so intimidated by these polished images of fashion's icons that I slid into the first seat I came to and buried my head in my hands.

Across from me, Grand-mère opened a black portfolio on the table and flipped the pages until she found one she liked.

"Tired?" she asked.

I nodded. "Yeah. Why'd you make me do that? That was really mean. I'm not a model, Grand-mère. I should be in English right now anyway."

Ignoring the question, she pushed the portfolio toward me. "What do you think of this girl?"

I leaned back and rubbed the edges of my bandage beneath my shirt. My cut had that itchy starting-to-heal feeling and throbbed like a toothache.

She clucked her tongue against her teeth. "Liliana, I asked you a question."

Sighing, I stared at the image that captured a smooth-skinned Nordic girl with a serene expression and sea-green eyes. Her wheat-colored hair was blown back away from her face, and her chin jutted forward. "Her jaw looks strong. Good. Like she knows who she is."

My grandmother smiled and slid another portfolio my way. "And this one? What does she look like?"

In the head-on shot, I noticed that the model's dark eyes were kind of mysterious, her brows subtly arched, her mouth slightly parted. "She looks like she has a secret, like she wants to say something but she won't."

Grand-mère turned the pages in a third book and motioned toward a portrait of a sleek young woman, standing tall in an outrageous outfit, shoulders back, looking up at something far off in the distance.

"Strong," I said easily. "She looks powerful."

My grandmother smiled at me. "*C'est sa confiance*, my darling."

Yeah. Confidence. Mine was in short supply.

Richard hustled into the room carrying a big package he set on a chair. He popped a thumb drive into the computer at the end of the table, pushed a few buttons and a wall screen lit along the far wall. When he dimmed the lights, he asked us, "Ready?"

They exchanged glances and nods, conspiring against me one more time.

I shrugged and sat back, crossing my arms and wishing I were home.

A blink later and my first picture filled the screen. More than six feet of me right there big and huge in glaring black and white. I looked horrible and fat, all hunched and sunken in bunched up clothes like a reject.

"God, help me," I said, sliding lower on my seat. "I could show you plenty of bad pictures of me at home. Do we really have to do this? I did what you want and played your game. I want to go home now. I need more aspirin."

"Be patient." My grandmother was annoyingly insistent as she pointed to my picture. "What does that image say about the girl?"

"That she's completely *miserable*?"

Richard laughed out loud. "Right on the money, Lili." He put up another image, only slightly better than the last. "But in this shot we're starting to see the girl, not just her insecurities."

I stared at the image of me with my hands clenched to the sides of the stool. With the button at the neck open, my shirt looked looser. My muscles were still tight, but my face looked brighter, my body somehow longer and leaner. Surprisingly, I didn't look so top heavy.

He advanced the frames and I couldn't help but shift forward in my seat and stare at my changing image. My dark hair looked somehow thick and luxurious in his trick studio lights. And the pictures captured something in me I'd never seen.

"What did you do to these shots?" I asked Richard. "That . . . that doesn't even look like me! You Photoshopped the hell out of it, didn't you? Made me look thinner?"

"Nope. I just shed light on what was already there," Richard said. "I didn't retouch anything at all."

Grand-mère smiled. "But it *does* look like you, Liliana. This is the *real* you. *La vraie nature."*

My true nature.

A new shot filled the screen and I let out a little gasp. "*Wow*. That can't be me. I look so different."

"Bingo! That's my favorite," Richard said, sitting back in his chair. "You were absolutely right to trust your instincts, Camille. Lili's got it."

"Got what?" I said.

Richard stared at me and smiled. "You're a natural beauty, Lili."

I shook my head. "No. You're wrong. Just –"

"Look," he said, pointing at the screen. "It's right there in front of you. Listen to the professional, here."

I turned and found I couldn't stop staring at my picture.

In this frame, he'd captured a fleeting moment, an essence of something intangible that seemed to come from within. With my hair clipped back behind me, my jaw line and cheekbones were edged with quiet shadows, sculpting my face with a drama I'd never imagined I possessed.

I'd been transformed by a little wind and lighting.

"*She* knows who she is," my grandmother announced.

I studied the eyes, deep and luminous. Mysterious.

"*She* holds something back. Keeps a secret."

My gaze swept along the soft lines of my body draped casually over the stool. I looked relaxed. Comfortable. Graceful.

"*She* is a strong woman."

In this image, I didn't look like a social reject.

I glanced at Richard. He was nodding his head as he hitched his thumb toward my image on the screen. "No doubt about it, Lili. In my professional opinion, I'd say *she's* a beautiful girl, through and through. I'm proud of that shot, and I wouldn't change a single thing. It's completely honest."

"But –"

Richard stood and removed one of the framed photos from his wall.

My grandmother gave me a smile. "*Ma chérie*. You must accept this undeniable truth about yourself."

She paused. *"The camera does not lie."*

Richard slid another framed photo from the package he'd carried in with him, and mounted it on the wall.

After he'd straightened the image and stepped back, I gasped.

In the frame was the last shot he'd taken of me.

My image was up there on *his* wall . . . right next to my grandmother's most famous portrait.

He smiled. "This is where your image belongs, Lili. And this is where it's going to stay."

My grandmother gestured toward my portrait. She spoke tenderly.

"My dear Liliana, she *is* beautiful. And *she* is you."

38.

When he got home from school, I was waiting for my brother on the sofa, flipping through a magazine I wasn't actually reading. Grand-mère had left me alone to think. She was in my mother's room taking a hot bath, and the light scent of her bubbles and candles drifted down the stairs.

I didn't know what to make of the experience with Richard Ranesford. That face up on the screen was me, but it wasn't. What he'd captured was all an illusion, lens trickery photographers like him were so good at. I wasn't buying it.

A shiver rippled through me and I pulled on a sweatshirt. The weather was cold this afternoon, a brisk bite of the coming winter.

Tony pushed through the door with his usual show of force, and a gust of chilly wind and dried leaves blew into the room. He stood there as the door banged against the wall and the picture frames rattled like they did every day.

"Hey," I said, rubbing my arms to get warm. "How was your day?"

He stared at me and quickly started walking away.

"Tony, I'm taking you to practice today," I said as he strode past me. "Go get ready, okay? I made you a snack and left it on the kitchen table."

He shrugged and tossed his backpack to the floor. "Whatever."

Fifteen minutes later, after he'd chugged a huge glass of milk and scarfed down two PB&J sandwiches with his favorite seedless raspberry jam, he'd dressed in his football gear and we headed out the front door. His cleats made scraping noises on the sidewalk as we steered our path toward the rec field at the center of town.

My little brother was giving me the silent treatment, and he was good at it. He'd had plenty of practice lately.

I shoved him with my shoulder and connected with his pads. "Quit being so noisy, will ya? You're driving me crazy."

He punched me in the arm. "I got nothing to say to you."

I swallowed hard and tugged open the pockets on my winter jacket. "Well that's too bad. I need talk to you."

He frowned and swung his football helmet at his side.

My voice was shaky. "I'm sorry I scared you. I didn't mean to, Tony."

He sighed. "Yeah, well, you did."

I put my arm around his padded shoulders and tried to give him a squeeze. "I'm really sorry. I mean it."

He pulled away, angry. "How'd you cut yourself like that? It's not like it was your finger or something. That was just . . . weird."

His curiosity was tinged with fear, and my heart felt like it would break into a million pieces. He was only ten. As much as my brother annoyed me, I loved him. He was part of who I am, and when he was hurting, so was I.

"It was an accident, Tony," I tried to explain. "It's so embarrassing. I just wanted my stupid bra off, and I guess . . . I sort of slipped when I went to cut it with the scissors."

My admission sounded hollow even to my ears.

Had my cut been an accident, or had I done it on purpose? Part of me wasn't so sure.

"I found your wine bottle when I took the trash out," he said quietly. "I didn't know you cut school and got drunk. When'd you start doing that?"

Shame rippled through me. "I don't. That was the first time I have, and I don't plan to do it again. Trust me."

Whether or not my words were a lie didn't matter. Someday I'm sure I would drink again, but not for the same reasons. To forget. To obliterate my misery. To wipe out my reality with an alcohol-induced haze. That just made more angst and misery, which made you feel worse. And the hangover, not to mention the guilt, was absolutely the worst sort of punishment.

He chastised me. "Really dumb, Lil."

"Yeah." I nodded. "Don't tell Mom and Dad, okay?"

He shook his head. "You should."

"I will. Eventually."

We approached the football field, where dozens of orange-shirted kids in white pants did synchronized jumping jacks in neat little rows.

"Looks like you're late," I said, motioning toward the team and stuffing my hands into my pockets.

He kicked a pine cone into the bushes and hung his head. "I don't care. What's going on with you, Lil? You've been acting really schizo lately. It's like I don't even know who you are anymore."

The photo of me in that email flashed through my mind, and I prayed he'd never see it.

I had to be honest with him. "I'm in a bad spot, Tony. My grades stink, and some kids have been really giving me a hard time at school."

He turned to me as we walked into the end zone. "Those boys from the other day?"

"Yeah." I nodded. "And a bunch of others, too. It's a really long story."

"I hate those guys." He looked fierce, determined. Tony stopped walking and faced me. "Why are they picking on you?"

I shrugged. "It's because of the way I look."

Confusion settled on his face. "But you look like you. Nothing's changed."

I stared into my brother's big brown eyes. "Yeah. I know."

A sigh escaped me. "And that's the whole problem."

Pretty pictures made no difference.

39.

A biting wind whipped across the Tigers' football field, slicing through my coat like tiny needles pricking at my skin. The temperature had dropped a few degrees while I sat here watching my brother run plays and scrimmage with the other orange shirts against his teammates in blue jerseys.

The metal bleachers had turned to ice, and my butt was quickly going numb. The parents here had been smart enough to bring stadium blankets and thermoses of coffee to keep warm, but I was freezing. And to make matters worse, my coat's zipper was stuck open.

I stood and jumped off the risers onto the hard ground. I needed to move to get the circulation going again.

Hoping to get my blood flowing, I jogged along the sidelines past a row of over-eager corporate dads shouting orders at the players and behind them the wannabe littlest brothers pretending to be Peyton Manning or Lawrence Taylor as they tossed a foam football.

When I hit the opposite end zone away from the action, I stopped and jogged in place. My cell phone rang in my pocket.

I pushed the button to take the call. Breathlessly, I answered. "Hello?"

Heavy breathing met my ears.

"Who is this?" I asked. "Sophie, is that you?"

The breathing turned into full-scale panting and groaning.

"Not funny, asshole."

In a screechy whisper, the female caller made an accusation. "*You're such a freakin' slut.*"

I sucked in a breath.

When a few girls burst into laughter on their end and hung up the phone, I stared at the incoming number.

Unknown caller.

Billy Martin walked over to me and I must have looked shell-shocked staring at my phone.

"Seen a ghost?" he said with a laugh. "You look kind of creeped out."

I shoved the phone back into my pocket. "Hi."

What was he doing here?

"You weren't in school today."

He'd noticed? "No. Wasn't feeling great."

He nodded toward the field, hands in his pockets. "Little brother?"

"Yeah. He plays quarterback."

Billy nodded and moved closer to me. "Mine's a tight end. Number twenty-seven."

We stood there beside each other in awkward silence for a minute. I didn't know what to say to Billy Martin. I'd never had an actual conversation with him before, other than about volleyball shots in gym class.

"You look really cold," he said with a laugh as he pulled deeper into his varsity baseball jacket. "You should zip up your coat."

Embarrassed, I shrugged. "Can't. Zipper's stuck."

Billy reached over and tugged my coat by the zipper toward him. "Let me see if I can fix –"

We were standing close enough that I could feel his warmth, a body block in the chill of the evening.

Out of nowhere, an orange blur crashed into Billy's middle and sent him flying toward the ground. He yanked my coat with him as he fell. On the way down, he let out a solid "*whoomph*" of air.

I let out a garbled scream, stumbled and landed on my knees on the hard dirt just a foot away.

Tony was on top of Billy, pounding him with his fists and making horrible angry noises.

I scrambled to my feet and pulled hard on my brother's jersey. *"Tony! Stop!"*

"Get off me, kid" Billy said, throwing up his hands to block the blows. He rolled quickly and got to his feet, knocking my brother to the side. "What the hell's your problem?"

Tony's dark eyes blazed with fury. "You leave my sister alone."

I gasped. "Tony, oh, *no*! Billy's not--"

From somewhere on the field, a whistle blew sharply three times and the thunder of footsteps came closer.

"Fight!" a boy yelled.

Tony clenched his fists again and snapped at Billy as the crowd of players gathered 'round. He bounced in place. "Get out of here before I hit you again!"

"You should have been a defensive tackle, kid. That's some sack you've got there," Billy said, brushing off dried leaves and grass. He tilted his head to the side and rubbed his neck. "Didn't even see it coming."

"We got a problem here?" the coach said, reaching our sides with his whistle at the ready. He confronted my brother. "What's going on, Carracino? You causing trouble with these kids?"

"This guy was attacking my sister!" Tony said, glaring at Billy. "He had his hands all over her!"

In the glow of the field lights, I could see the coach flush.

Billy laughed and stepped back, hands up. "Whoa, there! You got the wrong idea, partner."

I shrank into my coat and offered an explanation to the bewildered coach. "No, he wasn't doing anything, Coach Connors. It's okay, really. Just a big misunderstanding."

The coach took off his cap and scratched his head. "Well –"

"I'm outta here," Billy said as he backed away. "I don't need this shit."

I stared straight into my brother's eyes and wondered if the confusion would ever leave their dark depths.

Then, as my brows tightened and tears pricked at my own eyes, I wondered if that same confusion would ever leave mine.

I had no idea what was happening to my life.

40.

Later that night, I found another note tucked in between my pillows.

My dearest Liliana,
A lady works with her assets.
Je t'aime,
Grand-mère Camille

I didn't want to work with my assets. I wanted to forget.

But I held onto the note, lay back against my bed and willed sleep to take me far, far away.

41.

She knew I was still struggling. It was the second day she'd let me stay home from school, and I'd locked myself in the safe haven of my cluttered room to think all morning. One of the things I did not want to think about was how far behind I was in my classes, and it was getting worse every day.

Sophie confirmed that my obscene picture had indeed spread throughout school. People were talking about it everywhere she went. If my guess was correct, my chest had made an appearance on virtually every cell phone and computer belonging to the town's entire teenaged population. And deep in my gut, I was absolutely sure there was not one person at Middleton who *hadn't* seen my nipples flashing the camera like high beams.

My grandmother didn't seem to think it was any big deal – she'd been nude countless times in photos and on purpose – but how was I, the one with the not perfect body, supposed to cope with the reality that everyone I knew had seen me at my most vulnerable? By going back to school, trying to fake caring in the slightest about grammar and pretending everything was fine with my life? No. Thank you very much, but I'd rather not.

The jagged cut across my breast was healing, pinching my skin as it came back together. I rubbed the cream into the wound, feeling the sting with every touch. The hangover was long gone and my appetite was back, but this . . . this right here was the worst sort of punishment. To feel the pain of what I'd done every time I slipped a bra over my head and manipulated the elastic just right so it wouldn't cause me a stab of pain. It was the pits to try to make sense of how I'd sunk so low and let this happen. I couldn't look at myself in the mirror.

Grabbing a fresh bandage, I covered my self-inflicted flaw and sighed.

After getting dressed in my oldest sweatshirt and jeans and swallowing two aspirin and half a diet soda, I was rubbing my eyes to rid the weariness when someone knocked on my bedroom door.

"May I come in?" Grand-mère asked politely.

Moving toward my mannequins, I grabbed a box of pins from my work table and told her it was okay. Some of my work had torn when I'd knocked them over the other day, and I was in the process of making repairs and alterations. I kneeled on the floor and shoved a few pins in my mouth to hold them.

She entered my room carrying an empty wicker laundry basket and took in her surroundings.

She moved a few steps while I pinned. I noticed her studying my inspiration wall, where clips of great designs from fashion magazines and swatches of fabric were thumb-tacked alongside bits of decorative trim and buttons. I'd pinned up the patchwork piece I'd made in Mrs. Russell's sewing room. Aunt Nina's face was there, gazing intently into the camera to sell a shade of her lipstick that was the perfect blend of coral and rose. And Margaux, too, had made my board, a snapshot from her early days as a prima ballerina with the Paris Ballet, the image faded and curled at the edges but beautiful nonetheless. Snapshots of two of Kerry London's fabulous quilts added brilliant color to the display.

Grand-mère leaned forward for a closer look at one of my mother's advertisements for last year's spring collection of buttery leather mini-bags. I liked the pale Easter-egg colors she'd chosen, so the ad graced my wall next to a watercolor painting of a blue Chinese urn filled with bright red poppies.

My grandmother turned toward me. "I will do the wash now. Where are your soiled clothes?"

Her do-the-laundry outfit was expectedly sleek yet casual, an off-the-shoulder black sweater that accented her collar bone, and curve-hugging leggings and ballet flats that made her legs look five feet long. Her gorgeous mane of hair was long and loose and tucked beneath a wide velvet band.

"The laundry's in the closet on the floor," I said through my pins, motioning toward the double doors next to my bed. "But I can do it later. You don't have to. I've done it since I was eight."

"No bother, *ma chérie*."

I turned back to assess my work. Behind me, she shuffled through the clothes and made quiet noises, clucking her tongue almost imperceptibly now and then.

Trying to concentrate, I smoothed an embroidered cutwork panel at the hem of a linen skirt and began to pin. After I secured all of the panels in position by basting with a few quick stitches, I'd get down to work evaluating their placement. More often than not, I added too much embellishment on the first round then ended up taking away for a more dramatic effect. This was good therapy for me, to focus on a project.

But she was watching me. I could feel it as surely as the scratchy carpet beneath my bare knees.

I turned around to find her staring, the filled laundry basket on my bed.

"Did you make all of these clothes?" she asked in a steady tone.

I shrugged as I studied the row of partially clad seamstress mannequins. "Well . . . yeah."

"Ah." Her face lit with a smile. "And why do you not wear these creations?"

I shook my head, fast. "Oh, no. They're kind of like, I don't know, like art. I'd never actually wear them. They mean too much to me." I glanced at the intricate jackets with textured trim and swirling skirts with subtle embroidery hidden in the folds. "Besides, they're not really my kind of clothes."

I lifted the hem of the cutwork skirt and released, watching it fall and realign with gentle undulating waves.

My grandmother gave me a big smile and ventured toward my closet. She pulled out an old nubby green sweater, one of my favorites. Despite a few barely noticeable moth holes, it was comforting and hung practically to my knees.

"But am I right? You would wear . . . *this*?"

I nodded. "I love that sweater. It's super comfortable."

"I see," she said with a nod. She tossed the sweater onto the bed and pulled out a pair of black jeans folded haphazardly over a wire hanger. They were faded to the color of newspaper ink and baggy enough to disappear in. "And these?"

I didn't want her to comment on my jeans. I'd bought that pair in Worthington's Wonders when Brian had picked up ten garbage bags of clothes from a dead rapper's house.

"What's your point, Grand-mère?"

She gave me that mysterious smile again, but wouldn't tell me. She just walked over to the bed, picked up the laundry basket and moved toward the door.

"Please finish your work and join me downstairs in thirty minutes. We have an appointment."

I folded my arms across my chest and whined. "Another one?"

"*Mais oui, ma chérie.*"

With a nod, she was gone.

42.

I had nothing to say. Not as we drove on the Merritt Parkway, cars screeching to get out of my grandmother's crooked path, not as we cut off a plumbing repair truck to take the exit at the last minute, not as we whirled diagonally into two parking spaces and jerked to a stop in front of the *très chic* Bebi's.

"Why are we here?" I asked.

As if I didn't know.

I might be a wardrobe troll, but even I knew that Bebiane Knudsen was the Scandinavian wunderkind of the fashion world, snagging all the best young celebs to dress for the MTV music awards and Grammies. Her lingerie was the stuff boys' wet dreams were made of, her evening wear sublime. She'd done up Demi Lovato and Taylor Swift, and I'd seen one of her dresses on Elle Fanning at some other awards ceremony. Her clothes were hip, stylish and rich with unexpected details, and more than one look had made my own inspiration wall.

But Sophie should be here enjoying this instead of me. This was definitely her scene, and she would be star-struck.

My grandmother smiled and got out of the car with a gentle swoosh of her stunning black cashmere coat.

She didn't say a word on her grand exit.

I punched the dashboard a few times to get the frustration out of my system and reluctantly followed.

I was being manipulated in a major way. It was French payback time.

This shop was a lot like Sophie's closet, only about five times the size, with funky black crystal chandeliers and stark but striking floral arrangements in neon brights. The clothes were orderly on identical black hangers perfectly spaced two inches apart. They were made of exquisite fabrics. And they looked far too elegant to touch – or wear.

I was instantly intimidated in this palace of high fashion where I felt every bit the ninth grader.

"Bebiane! Look at you!" my grandmother said warmly, kissing both of the young designer's cheeks when she rushed over to greet us.

Bebi wrapped her in a big hug. "It's so good to see you, Aunt Camille." Her accent was very Scandinavian, but strangely Americanized. "I'm glad you finally came to the shop!"

They were a picture in contrast. Grand-mère tall, elegant and French, and Bebi, short, pink-haired and shouting edgy style from her strappy shoes to her bustier.

With a gesture to her surroundings, Bebi gave a great turn and her fuchsia skirt swirled around her like a blooming flower. "What do you think, Godmother? Have I done you proud?"

Godmother? To Bebiane Knudsen?!

There was so much about my grandmother's life I didn't know.

My grandmother pressed her hands together. "*C'est magnifique*! You have done a splendid job. And thank you for this glorious coat." She gestured to the sleek cut of cashmere draping her frame. "*Absolutement parfait* for autumn in Connecticut. *C'est merveilleux.*"

Bebi blushed. "I'm glad you like it. You know I'd do anything for you, Aunt Camille. You wear it very well."

Bebiane was clearly another in my grandmother's vast legion of admirers. What had she done for all of them?

My grandmother nodded. They shared a conspiratorial look, and Bebi gave a miniscule nod. At the back of the shop, a curtained area lay waiting beyond the spotlighted mannequin in pumpkin-colored tweed.

"Are you ready to have some fun, Lili?" Bebi asked me.

I sighed and stuffed my hands into the pockets of my boxy pea jacket. I didn't have it in me to feel enthused. "Whatever. I guess. I'm not sure why I'm here."

Bebi smiled anyway and led the way.

Through the curtain, I stepped into another world. Rolling racks of clothes lined the walls of the room, while tables of scarves and jewelry and gloves and purses filled the spaces between them. Again, a chilled bottle of champagne was at the ready, this time paired with a crystal bowl of lush black cherries and a platter of sugar-glazed *petit fours.*

I shuddered, dreading what was coming next. I felt ready to cry. "No offense, Bebi, but do we really have to do this? I detest trying on clothes."

My grandmother simply held up a hand to Bebi and arched one perfect eyebrow. "Why?"

Running my hand across the hanging garments on the closest rack, I watched them swish softly back into place. I shrugged. "I can't explain, really. Clothes never work on me."

My grandmother clasped her hands in front of her. "Liliana, let me ask you a very, very important question." While I took off my coat, she paused to make sure I was paying attention. "Why do you try with all your might to resist fashion and beauty when examples are all around you every day?"

"I don't know," I said quietly. But I knew the real reason. And one-fourth of it was standing not six feet away.

"Your parents both have beautiful style."

My parents. Yes, they were always impeccably dressed. And busy. And oblivious. Or worse yet, completely absent. I didn't want to go there, not now.

I had to give her some sort of answer. "It's not like . . . I mean . . . I *like* fashion. A lot, actually. Just not for me."

"But you design such lovely clothes." She gestured toward my ancient sweatshirt and jeans, but she didn't need to say much. "And yet you wear . . . *this.*"

Bebi took notice and interrupted. "You are a designer? You should show me your pieces sometime. I'd love to see them, Lili. Perhaps I could help you."

Show my work to Bebiane Knudsen? No way. That'd be like handing Michelangelo a finger painting and saying "what do you think, Mikey?" I sighed and stared at my insistent grandmother. "I told you. The clothes I make are like art to me. Call it my therapy to embroider and do appliqué, if you want to. It's just something I *do*, not wear."

Her lips curved in a smile. "Yes, but there is a reason you chose clothes for artistic expression, ah? You *understand* a woman's style."

I met her gaze head on. She wasn't being critical. But she just stood there, genuinely wanting to understand my reasoning for the way I dressed.

She and Bebi waited me out until the silence grew so thick that I had to say something.

"If you really must know, I wear clothes I can hide in, all right? I don't want people staring at my disgusting body," I said finally, looking straight into my grandmother's eyes and blurting out my deepest insecurity as I crossed my arms over my chest. "Because no matter how hard I try, I know I can never be a legend like *you*, or gorgeous like Aunt Nina, or successful and talented like Mother and Aunt Margaux. You're all superstars."

"But you are only fourteen–"

"And do I have to remind you that you became world famous at the same age?!" My voice edged to a higher pitch as I clenched my fingers into fists. "Do you know how hard it is to live in your shadows? I'm the ugly duckling in a family of glittering freaking swans! I'll *never* grow up to be as good as any of you!" I pounded a fist against my thigh. "It's so unfair to think I could ever compete!"

Bebi shook her head sympathetically, but my grandmother sighed.

"We put you under a great deal of pressure, ah?" Grand-mère asked, sadness in her voice.

I rubbed the weariness from my eyes. My voice was thick. "You have no idea. It really sucks sometimes."

For a moment, she looked like she might cry. Her brows pulled tight and her mouth fell into a frown. "*C'est tragique* you feel this way, *ma chérie,* but we cannot change *who* we are."

Shrugging my shoulders, I looked up at her and tried to apologize for my hurtful words. "I don't want you to change,

Grand-mère. You shouldn't have to just to make me feel better."

Bebi cleared her throat and stepped back.

Grand-mère smiled and walked to me to wrap me in an uncharacteristic hug. She kissed both of my cheeks and held them between her hands as she looked into my eyes. "But *you* can change, *for you*. Take what you deserve. To feel better. We are not in competition, Liliana. In France, we use the phrase *avoir sa dignité*. To have pride in yourself. And you must do just that, to feel good on the inside. Here."

She touched my heart, and for the first time in a long while, I didn't feel the sharpness of my wound.

"And here," she said, tapping a finger to my temple.

I leaned against her, breathing in the scent of her delicate perfume.

Bebi smiled and nodded, glanced at me and my grandmother. "Camille, I'll keep busy out front. Call if you need me. In a few minutes, I'll send in Mrs. Knox."

"Merci, Bebi."My grandmother cleared her throat, stepped away from me and clapped her hands like the efficient taskmaster I knew her to be."Now. Step into the dressing room, Liliana."

I did as I was told, and sat on the pink striped bench, hard, and closed my eyes. It was emotionally exhausting having to navigate building a relationship with the grandmother I'd just started to know, and I kept making stupid mistakes, telling her things I shouldn't and being irresponsible and foolish.

Deep down, I didn't want to disappoint her, like I always did my mother.

Grand-mère noticed me. And she cared.

Her voice was firm. "Now please undress and come out here."

She snapped me out of my funk in a hurry. "*Undress?* Why take off my clothes? It's so freaking humiliating. Haven't I been through enough?"

My grandmother ducked her head into the dressing room and saw me scowling, so I kicked off my shoes to make her happy.

"Please. Just leave your panties and bra on and join me. No one will see. We are alone, and we are just girls."

She smiled, but I wasn't convinced . . . and I knew I was wearing my ugliest flowered underwear.

"*Please,*" she said again. "I must show you something."

At this point, I'd already been as embarrassed as I'd ever be in front of my grandmother, laying in my own puke and blood with my boobs exposed. Standing in front of her in my underwear was just another slightly less horrible event I'd endure.

Just get it over with.

I stripped as fast as I could, and nervously opened the curtain. Cold air hit my skin as I leaned into the room. "You're sure no one will see me?"

My grandmother smiled and beckoned with her slender fingers. "Come here, *ma chérie.*"

Nervously, I walked forward on tender steps, hugging my middle and glancing around like someone would burst through the curtain at any minute and take my picture. A breeze blew across my bandage and made me shiver.

My grandmother took me by the shoulders and led me toward the octagonal platform in front of the mirror.

"I don't want to look," I whined back at her, closing my eyes.

"But you must. You must see the whole truth," she said firmly, turning me to face my own reflection. "Open your eyes and put your hands at your sides. *Relax.*"

I lowered my arms and held my breath as I inspected.

"You are not trying, Liliana," she said calmly. "Do not be afraid of your body. Each of us has our own natural gifts. Yours are your lovely curves."

I grunted then sucked in my stomach. "You don't have to remind me."

"*Ah.*" She nodded and gave my shoulders a reassuring squeeze. "See your shape and its lines. *Regardez.* Really *look* at yourself."

I shut my eyes. Drew a deep breath. Then opened my eyes to stare at my reflection. I frowned when I saw my wide hips in the ugly underwear with the faded pink flowers. Grimaced when I took in the bandage above my breast.

"I'm pale. Too squishy." I sighed. "Overall, I'm not much to look at. Can I stop now?"

"Did you not learn anything from your photos yesterday?" She sighed. My grandmother leaned her cheek against my shoulder. "Oh, my Liliana. You are so very, very wrong about yourself. You do not *see.*"

She shook her head and ran her hands down my arms. "Your skin glows from within. You have been blessed with a woman's figure, with curves that many will always envy." She paused and gave me a nod. "And that includes me, *ma chérie.*"

"You?" I asked in disbelief. "Why would you possibly ever envy *me*?"

She smiled. "I will never wear clothes the way you can. My body is what the designers call a clothes hanger. Boring. Thin and with straight lines," she explained dryly. "I hang clothes well, but your body is *voluptueuse.*" Her fingers cupped my narrow waist. "And you should know you are *absolutement* lovely."

She paused and stepped back. "I would not lie to you, Liliana."

I met her eyes in the mirror and forgot for a moment that I was standing in front of her in my granny panties and stretched-out sports bra. "If that's true, then why don't I ever *feel* lovely?"

She gave me the tenderest of smiles. "You feel badly about yourself because you have trained yourself to look only for the flaws. The time has come for us to undo all that bad training."

43.

I tried to convince myself it was just like wearing a bathing suit to a day at the beach. I wasn't almost nude. The embarrassing parts of me were still covered. Models did this all the time, and my leotard hadn't been much bigger.

But Mrs. Knox, Bebiane's professional bra fitter, was a formidable ex-New Yorker. Short, solid and well-shaped, she assessed my body with a trained eye before taking out her tape measure and wrapping it under and around my breasts.

She shook her head and reassured me as I trembled under the lights.

"Honey, I've seen probably ten thousand boobs in my day, and every one of them is a different shape and size, even in the pairs," Mrs. Knox explained. "Busty or flat, big nipples or small, they're all normal. Now let me see what we've got to work with on you so we can figure out what we need in a bra."

I swallowed hard and tried to relax. "Okay."

She spotted my bandage, glanced at it curiously and gave me a funny look. But she had the grace not to mention it. Instead, she went to work and tugged on the heavy elastic strap over my other breast.

Her voice was gravelly. "Have you ever been properly fitted?"

She looked over at my grandmother. "*This* is unconscionable. A sports bra on a girl like this." She flicked my waistband. "And these panties . . . don't get me started. It's an absolute crime."

She turned back to me. "Where did you buy these?"

I was extremely self-conscious and getting a tad bit defensive. "I don't know. The grocery store maybe. What does it matter?"

"Doesn't anymore," Mrs. Knox said. "They're history."

The ladies at my side shared a wise look while I stood between them next to naked with my chest oozing out of the bra from all directions.

My grandmother nodded in agreement. "I shall have a very harsh talk with my daughter for allowing this. I taught her far, far better than that." She tsk-tsked. "*Quel dommage!*"

It *was* a pity. I can't remember the last time my mother had noticed, or cared, about my underwear. I always did my own laundry. She gave me money to buy clothes, but never paid much attention to what I wore unless she hated it, and then she was sure to correct me. And unless I was out with Sophie spending her father's money, I always shopped alone wherever I could reach with my bike.

"Have you ever worn underwire?" Mrs. Knox asked. She stuck a finger in the bottom of my bra and I flinched. "You need really good support."

"No kidding," I said sarcastically, feeling the weight of my breasts with every breath.

She looked at Grand-mère. "I'd say she's a thirty-two E."

"*E?*" I shrieked. "Are you kidding me? That's, like, circus freak size!"

Mrs. Knox laughed. "Nine out of ten women wear the wrong size, so don't get hung up on the letters." Mrs. Knox cupped her hands around my boobs and gave them a lift. "Go for style and proper fit. Thirty-two E oughta do it. I'll be back with some for you to try on."

I pressed my hands over my eyes. Never in my wildest dreams did I think I'd be getting felt up in my underwear in Bebiane Knudsen's prestigious boutique. My first time to second base had been by a graying New Yorker with a huge emerald ring and arthritic knuckles.

My grandmother handed me a robe to cover myself.

I slipped it on gratefully, tied the waist and sat on a bright orange velvet chair next to the sweets. Shoving a cherry into my mouth, I stifled a sigh.

"The worst is over, *ma chérie*," Grand-mère said with a smile. "Now we will build your foundation."

"Huh?" I spit a pit into my hand.

She stood and aligned her body into one of her signature poses, right foot forward, left shoulder back, chin tilted to elongate her throat. Just like that she metamorphosed into the legendary Camille Le Jeune, *haute couture* icon.

I marveled at the sight. “How do you do that so fast?”

She curved her lips in a knowing smile and relaxed her stance. “A woman’s true beauty emanates from within.”

“So you’ve told me,” I said. I spit out another pit and watched them stain my palm red.

My grandmother fluttered her hands along the lines of her body. “Without the proper foundation, clothes will never look right.”

I found a napkin to bury the pits and wiped the juice from my palm. “What are you talking about? Visible panty lines?”

She relaxed her pose and smiled. “Do you know why French women always carry themselves with such confidence?”

I shrugged. “Because they’re born beautiful?”

“Do not be silly. That is just not so." She shook her head. “Beneath their clothes, they always wear the finest. They choose the most beautiful delicates to feel sleek and smooth, those that provide a foundation of strength from which they build.”

Nodding, I set my sights on a table of Bebiane’s scanty lingerie. “To feel . . . sexy?”

“*Peut-être*. But it is not about *sexy*." My grandmother whispered as she picked up a silk camisole by a slender strap. “You must wear silk and satin and lace to treat yourself well. You are free to choose this to feel feminine.”

I was starting to get what she was talking about. “To build confidence?”

She let the silk flutter to the table. “*Exactement*. Live for *yourself*." She smiled and threw up her hands. “And have fun!"

So, for the next three hours she and Bebiane invited me into their secret fashion world. I was astounded how little I’d understood before now.

But when I got back home to recharge my dead cell phone and wait for Sophie, none of what I'd learned mattered.

My whole world collapsed in on itself.

44.

While Grand-mère made dinner, I sat at my messy desk to turn on my computer and open my inbox. 232 new messages sat waiting. I'd never had so many emails in my life, not even from online drug and penis enlargement spammers.

Something was seriously wrong.

The first one at the top of the lists was from my dad, telling me he was sending me money to go out and buy myself something pretty. The next was from my mother, reminding me to get a haircut.

But the other 230 emails made my stomach turn. Most of them contained my picture, or neatly cropped sections of my select body parts. But their message was loud and clear.

Subject: SLUT!

Subject: Whorebag tease

Subject: Let's go out Saturday

Subject: Nice one, skank! Two guys at once?

Subject: Wanna fuck, wild thing?

Tears of frustration started spilling by the fifth email, where people called me such horrible names and made such bone-chilling accusations that I couldn't go on to read whole messages. Whoever sent them didn't even have the guts to sign their real names. The senders were Daffy Duck, The Wicked Witch of the West, Hannah Montana and other names I recognized from childhood movies and cartoons. Whoever was behind this onslaught of hatred and disrespect, someone, or several someones were clearly out to get me.

I traded my tears for anger as I scanned through one subject line after another, checking the extent of the fall of my reputation.

Didn't take long to realize it was below rock bottom.

My grandmother's words echoed in my head. *"Life is never really fair. But you can learn to make it feel so."*

Try though I might, I just couldn't make this feel fair. This attack felt like they were trying to slaughter me, one nasty insult and one lie at a time, to see just how much they could push me before I snapped like Zoe had.

I knew exactly how she felt, and I was a fragile thread away from snapping my own high tension wires.

Everything good I'd felt about myself today dissipated when I'd first clicked my keyboard. These people hiding behind the made-up names reminded me of how far I'd fallen in their judgmental eyes, even if they weren't courageous enough to reveal themselves.

And what was it all for? A few crappy pictures someone else had taken of me on a really bad day? Lies they'd help spread without knowing any facts? A reputation they'd invented for me?

My stomach clenched as I buried my head in my hands and closed my eyes. I needed a plan.

Life is never really fair.

I had to do something. Be productive.

Take charge.

Without even turning it off, I unplugged my computer from the wall, not caring that I might damage the hard drive. Maybe I would destroy the evidence. What difference would it make, anyway, when I never wanted to look at my email and see any of it again?

Counting to ten, I drew a huge breath and exhaled slowly to wash away some of the gnawing tension in my body. My muscles were clenched, my teeth grit together. I breathed again and again until the bitter ache began to leave me and I felt like I'd regained at least a touch of my equilibrium.

The aroma of simmering *coq au vin* drifted up the stairs, reminding me that there were other elements to focus on in life besides my harassment, good things worth savoring. And Sophie was coming over for dinner, too.

Staring at my cluttered desktop, I reached for the closest pile of papers and began to organize. While I sorted old homework papers, it dawned on me how badly I'd let my life slide out of control. I'd never been more than a B+ student making the occasional A, but this past month and a half . . . well, lately my grades barely ranked above failing. It depressed me intensely on a whole other level, and I knew I had to do something about it before I got into serious academic trouble that couldn't be remedied. Tucking the papers into a folder, I set them aside to deal with when I was in the right frame of mind to make a concrete plan.

I tackled the newspaper and magazine clippings on my desk next and knew the sad truth was I might never recover from this character bashing I'd taken.

My fall from grace was complete.

Here at the bottom, I didn't have many options. Report all 229 of my email assailants to the FCC and police and let them figure out what to do about it? But that would require identifying who actually sent these emails, and for all I knew, they could have come from one person using different screen names. Just the thought of playing detective with such a volume of email overwhelmed me.

So, my choices were slim. I could move to another town and start over. Or run away. Or kill myself.

Since moving wasn't really an option, and I didn't have the guts to run away and live on the streets, I considered the final scenario.

Suicide.

I couldn't even imagine.

In the past year, I'd heard news of other kids who had tragically done just that. Killed themselves, left their grief-stricken family and friends behind wondering what they could have done to help. These kids chose suicide to end their lives over bullying, and school harassment, and daily teasing in person and online that had escalated to truly unbearable levels. I understood exactly how they felt. I intimately knew the gut-twisting desperation and the self-hate, the skin-crawling sensation that you'd been violated and torn to shreds just for the pleasure of the crowd. Those poor kids, like me, were just like the gladiators who unwillingly sacrificed their lives for sport, letting themselves be ripped apart by the lions while the crowd applauded and cheered.

I might feel like one of those gladiators now with my flesh and spirit flayed, but there was a huge difference between me and the kids who couldn't endure it any longer.

I may have been put in this position and held against my will, but I didn't want . . . *no* . . . I *refused* to cave under the pressure and let my attackers win.

And that left me only two choices.

Keep the *status quo* and take it like a wimp, or figure out how to change.

Change. Sounded so simple.

I'd have to reinvent myself. Celebrities did it all the time.

My hand brushed across one of my grandmother's notes. I opened the flap of the envelope and slid it out to reread.

A lady carries herself with dignity and pride.

I pushed through the stacks and found another of her notes.

A lady is always tidy.

And another and another.

A soft chignon will complement every lady's face.

A lady works with her assets.

By the time I read the last note again, I knew exactly what she was trying to do by writing them.

My grandmother was teaching me everything she'd learned in more than 50 years of fashion and beauty.

She was giving me a roadmap for change.

45.

In the kitchen, I saw her standing by the stove stirring a pot and wearing a white cooking apron. She'd pushed her hair back, and she was in perfect profile, the picture of natural beauty in soft light.

I walked over to her and wrapped her in a hug, leaning my face against her back. This woman I felt like I'd barely known weeks ago had opened her heart and become something I never knew I needed until this very minute.

"Thank you," I said softly.

She turned to face me as she put her arms around my neck. "Why do you thank me, *ma chérie*? For the lingerie?"

"No. For being here." I smiled up at her. "For being you."

Grand-mère, the woman with more control than any other woman on the face of the earth, got tears in her eyes as she stared at me.

"I love you," I whispered, giving her a kiss on both cheeks.

She wrapped me in a tight hug then and pulled me close. *"Je t'aime, ma chérie. Je t'aime aussi."*

We stood together until she cleared her throat and shooed me away. "Now go set the table before your little friend arrives. We must always be ready for our company, ah?"

She was back in control and teaching me, and I loved her for it.

The phone rang while Grand-mère was cooking and I'd loaded my hands with silverware. To answer it, I transferred the cutlery to one hand.

"Hello?"

"Hey, Lili," a boy said.

He didn't say anything else. Just breathed. I started to get nervous and I glanced at the Caller ID.

Unknown.

The silverware clanked as I tightened my grip. "Who is this?"

"Aw, you know who this is. You see me every day," he said, teasing. "Go ahead. Guess."

The voice didn't sound familiar. Deep, and a little bit scratchy, but like no one's I recognized from school. Not even Tyler, Jimmy or Joe. "Whoever this is, quit playing games. I don't have time."

"I've got some games we can play at my house," he said in a sing-song voice. "How about let's fuck each other's brains out? That'll be fun, won't it?"

My stomach clenched as I gasped and the silverware fell from my hands to the tile floor.

"Lili!" Grand-mère shouted from the stove as she wiped her hands on an apron. "Are you alright?"

"Yeah. Wrong number." I slammed the phone and bent to pick up the silverware. My hands shook and the cutlery rattled.

Who would say such obscene things to me?

The back door pushed open and banged into the bench, and Sophie walked in carrying a huge box. "Special delivery just in time for dinner!"

I shuddered to push back the sound of the boy's voice daring me to react. I couldn't let him get to me.

Sophie set the box onto the floor and sighed. "It was on the porch."

When I went to close the door, Margaux stopped me.

I hadn't anticipated her and she caught me off guard.

"Hello, Lili."

She stood there under the porch light, wrapped in her dancer's sweater and pants and still wearing her leotard from class. Our eyes met and I knew there would be no avoiding this confrontation. Not any longer.

I looked down, embarrassed. "Hi, Aunt Margaux."

"Lili." She leaned forward, kissed me on both cheeks, and closed the door behind her. "Are you still angry with me?"

"No. It's okay." I shrugged. "So, I'm not a dancer. There are worse things, right?"

She shook her head. "*Bien, bien.* But I must ask you to do something for me."

"After dinner." Still rattled from the phone call, I needed an immediate diversion, and Margaux's favors weren't it. I turned toward Sophie. "You get new glasses again?"

She straightened her slim pale pink frames. "I convinced Ma to get a whole bunch in lots of styles and colors. Adam even likes these."

I smiled. "Those are good on you, don't you think, Grand-mère?"

She and Margaux exchanged greetings. My grandmother turned to look at Sophie. "*Certainement.* And you should keep many styles to complement your fashions. *Les lunettes* are quite attractive, indeed."

Margaux agreed with her assessment. "They look splendid, Sophie."

"I'm even thinking about wearing them to school," my friend said hesitantly. "I'm not holding out hopes for the contacts. They just make my eyes hurt."

I gestured. "That package from my mom?"

"Yup. All the way from Italy." She jumped up onto the counter and grabbed a ripe pear from the fruit bowl. One bite and juice was dribbling down her chin and onto her leotard. She swiped at the stickiness and frowned.

"Open the box before we eat, Lili," Grand-mère suggested.

"Will do." I knelt down and tore at the tape wrapping the cardboard. Inside, a note in my mother's handwriting on corporate letterhead lay atop crumpled packing paper.

"What's it say?" Sophie asked, polishing off her pear. She tossed the core into the trash can and reached sideways for a dishtowel to wipe her hands.

I read aloud. "A sneak preview for all of my girls. Wear them well!"

Shoving aside the paper, I uncovered five neatly wrapped rectangular boxes. I pulled out the first one and read the label.

"This one's for Aunt Nina," I said. Pushing the box behind me, I grabbed the others and gave one to Grand-mère and Aunt Margaux, then found mine. The last box was marked "For Cinderella Sophie."

"For me?" she said in surprise, hopping off the countertop. "Your mother never gives me presents!"

"I wrote to her and bragged you got the role," I said with a smile.

"And what did you say about your own dancing?" Margaux asked pointedly.

"I didn't." Shrugging, I shifted my gaze to the box in my hands and refused to admit I was a wimp. So I changed the subject quickly. "I think I know what these are."

Sophie rattled the box. "Shoes?"

"Shoes! She's going to start making them," I said, lifting the lid. I extracted a sandal with four-inch narrow heels and delicate straps of ivory leather trimmed in curved slivers of mother of pearl. "These are . . . wow!"

I unlaced my sneakers and peeled off my striped socks.

"Mine are the color of rose petals. She knows I love pink, doesn't she? They even match my glasses!" Sophie shrieked. She flipped off her flats and slipped her feet into the sandals. Bending over to fasten them and admire the sparkling pink crystals edging the straps, she couldn't contain her excitement. "This is the softest leather I've ever felt! Feels like ribbon. And look how they catch the light!"

Margaux took a seat at the table and unwrapped her gift. From her fingers, she dangled a pair of sandals the color of sea glass with sparks of citrine stones. "Ah, these are exquisite. Adrienne knows how I love fresh colors."

Grand-mère's shoes were the color of buffed pewter, with strands of brushed silver beads waterfalling from the ankle strap. She set them aside to try on later. Instead, she watched us while she tended to the *coq au vin* bubbling in its Dutch oven and filling the air with a stomach-rumbling aroma.

I rubbed my toes before slipping my foot into the beautiful shoe. "I've never worn heels like this. I hope I don't break my ankle."

"Remember to be graceful and you will not."

Margaux's comment irked me and I turned away.

She clucked when she couldn't squeeze her foot into the sandal. "Ah, *zut!* Mine are too small."

My grandmother laughed. "You have big feet, *ma chérie."*

Tony walked into the kitchen and took in the sight of girls and shoes scattered everywhere. He snagged a slice of warm bread from the basket near the stove. "What's going on? You opening a shoe store?"

"Mom sent presents," I said, looking up at him.

"Where's mine?" he asked excitedly. He dug into the box and came up empty-handed.

I laughed. "Unless you want high heels, you're outta luck."

"What a gyp!" He scowled. "I'm watching wrestling until we eat."

Tossing his bread crust into the shipping box, he stormed out.

Margaux sat back in her chair and stared longingly at the elegant shoe in her hand. "*Maman*, why did you make me with such big feet? I wish they were *mignon*."

Grand-mère smiled at me. "Ah, Margaux. You will never be dainty. We can change many attributes about ourselves, but I am afraid the size of your feet is not one of them."

I took a few steps and teetered on my new shoes while I tried to balance.

Margaux huffed. "The Chinese used to bind and arch their girls' feet for centuries. To make them smaller and more desirable," she explained to Sophie. "They would wrap them tighter and tighter so they could wear beautiful embroidered shoes and sway when they walked. Some of their feet were only four inches long!" She turned to glare at her mother. "Yet still -- they danced!"

Grand-mère tsk-tsked. "And the practice was abandoned for a reason. It is barbaric to torture a woman in the name of beauty."

"Yes, but I can never wear beautiful tiny shoes with . . . *these.*"Margaux held up her own dancer's feet to her mother. "Perhaps I should bind *my* feet to make them smaller."

Sophie snickered, but I couldn't.

Binding was a technique I'd actually tried.

Before I could stop myself, I blurted out what I knew.

"Did you know Catholic nuns used to be *required* to bind their breasts under their habits right up to the nineteen thirties?" I asked my grandmother. "And Joan of Arc did it too, to pretend she was a boy so she could fight in the war."

"I don't think I want to know why you know that," Sophie said.

I'd bound my breasts to flatten them just a few months ago when all this started, wrapped them so tightly in gauze strips that it was hard to take a full breath. In the end, Jimmy Barnett still tried to grab a squeeze when I walked past him on the way to last period science. And by then I was out of breath *and* angry and I had more problems than at the beginning of the day.

"I tried binding," I admitted matter-of-factly. "Doesn't work."

Margaux gasped and stared at me. "Lili! You did not do that!"

My grandmother shook her head. "*No, Lili.* Tell me you did not resort to such foolishness."

"I did. It really hurt," I said softly. "And when I took the bandages off, I was exactly the same. None of it mattered."

"That's kind of twisted," Sophie said, eyeing me with disapproval. "What made you do something so incredibly dumb? And why didn't you tell me?"

I shrugged as I stared at my feet in the new sandals. "Desperate times call for desperate measures."

Grand-mère stepped in and stopped the conversation. "We all have our challenges, girls," she said, looking at me. "Margaux, without your dancing feet, you would not be *you.*

Sophie, your eyesight will always require glasses. And Lili, your curves *belong* to you."

Grand-mère and I shared a knowing glance while the others nodded. I practiced walking in my new shoes and felt the sway in my hips with each step. This gift from my mother made me feel grown up, and feminine.

Sophie stood up to inspect her long legs. "Not bad, hmm? Think Adam will like them?"

I nodded and gave her a big smile. "It's a given. Your legs look amazing."

The phone rang and I reached behind me to answer it. "Hello?"

"*SLUT! SLUT! SLUT!*"a girl screamed in my ear.

I panicked.

"Stop calling here!" I slammed the phone and everyone in the kitchen stared at me.

"Who the hell was that?" Sophie said, hands on her hips.

A blush crept up my cheeks as I tried to backpedal. "Another telemarketer. Is dinner ready, Grand-mère?"

We ate together, oohing and ahhing over the delicious meal, but I couldn't stop staring at the phone. Sophie noticed and spiked me under the table with one of her new heels. She gave me a weird look, and I shook my head.

My nervous energy escalated with every bite.

The phone rang again and I flew to my feet, knocking over my empty juice glass and almost twisting my ankle in my new shoes. By the time I grabbed the receiver, my built-up tension exploded.

"Will you stop calling here! *Just leave me alone already!"*

Stunned silence descended on the kitchen and my mother's voice filled my ear.

"Lili? What is the matter with you?"

It took me a second to process the stares and register that my mother was talking to me.

My nerves were getting way out of hand, and even Cinderella's glass slipper couldn't take me away from this mess I was in.

I struggled to explain.

"I thought you were another prank caller." I sucked in a breath and sighed. "I'm sorry, Mother. I'll be just fine."

But with the way they were looking at me, nobody in the room seemed so sure.

46.

Dozens of lame excuses could not reassure Sophie that I was, in fact, okay. She could read me too well, and she was pissed I wasn't telling her.

By 7:00 the next morning when I was still deeply snuggled under my covers to avoid the day, she'd climbed my roof and broken into my bedroom. She scared me half to death when the window opened and she launched her backpack over the sill.

I sat up fast and clutched my heart when I saw her platinum head coming toward me. "Sophie?"

"I'm not going to school until you tell me everything, *bubeleh,*" she demanded as she slid the window shut. "You owe me explanations. You're all freaked and it's freaking me out, too."

"Nice cat burglar clothes," I said with a yawn, motioning to her all black ensemble. "Very *To Catch a Thief*, I must say."

"You like this? I thought it would be appropriate for breaking and entering," she said. Then she smiled. "Kind of fun climbing that tree. Haven't done that since I put on *pointe* shoes. Ma would have a cow."

"You could have rung the doorbell. Nobody would have cared. They're all up." I shifted in bed, untangling my tee shirt and pulling my knees to my chest. Rubbing the sleep from my eyes, I sighed.

She flopped onto the bed next to me. "So why are you acting all *meshugeneh*? Is French Grandma making you that crazy?"

I shook my head. "No. Actually, she's pretty great. She's trying really hard. It's . . . good."

She shoved me. "Then what gives?" She spotted the lingerie bag from Bebi's and shrieked as she pulled out a bra in cherry red. "*Aaghh!* You went to Bebi's without me, you bitch! And you didn't even tell me?"

"Bebi's a nice person. Wait 'til I introduce you."

She whacked me with the bra. "*Ughh!* You met her! I can't believe you!"

I nodded. "Soph, there's way too much to tell. A lot's been going on while you rehearsed. I don't even know where to start."

She tossed the bra back into the bag. "*Spill it!* And don't tell me more about Bebi now or I'll kick you. I want to know what's really going on with you."

"Did anyone ever tell you you're a really pushy broad?"

She smiled. "It's probably why you're my only real friend. Now talk."

I bit my lip and tried to sound nonchalant. "Well. After I got more than two hundred hate and smut emails last night –"

"*What?*"

I continued, unfazed. "After dinner, I did some research in my dad's library, looking through his law books, you know? The legal term for what whoever did is cyber-bullying, but it might be just plain old stalking. I'm not exactly sure." I shrugged. "But the bummer is that it takes a whole lot of proof to punish it, and Connecticut's laws are still pretty lame. They're supposed to get better, but not soon enough."

"What do you mean?"

"The law protects kids from regular beat-you-up bullies in school, but the schools can't really do anything about online stuff since it's beyond their jurisdiction," I explained. "I just know it sucks to be me right now."

Sophie shook her head. "I knew these guys were bothering you, but this. . . . This is so wrong," she said softly. "This has gone way beyond teasing, hasn't it?"

"Way. Now it's not just the guys. Some girls are in on it, too, but I don't know who yet. My reputation's trashed. Everyone thinks I'm a slut . . . and you know what the worst thing is? The sad truth is I haven't even had sex yet."

I tried to stay calm but my body was jittery and I felt my face pull into an ugly grimace. "I haven't even been kissed by a boy, Sophie. And now I'll never be. They all think I'm a skank."

By the time I finished telling her all that had happened, Sophie was crying, but I couldn't. Not anymore. She slid over next to me and wrapped her arm around my shoulders. "It's so unfair, Lil. You never did anything wrong."

"Yes, *I did.*" I jumped to my feet and grabbed my braless breasts in my sleep shirt. "I grew these."

Sophie wiped her tears and shook her head. "*No, Lil.*"

"*Yes,*" I said with a nod. "Tyler and Joe may have started all of this because I had the biggest tits at the pool, but Jimmy tagged along and the rest is history. Now the whole freakin' school's in on it, and I'm their punching bag."

She grimaced. "How can you sound so . . . passive?"

"I'm done being emotional, Sophie. I'm spent. I don't sleep more than an hour at a time. My insides feel like jelly. I may never check my email again. The phone rang about fifty times last night until I finally turned the ringers off and let the calls go straight to voicemail."

She showed every bit of her concern as she sat up straighter. "What can I do, Lil?"

"I don't know."

I moved toward my inspiration wall and stared at a picture of an art quilt Kerry had made last spring. The scene was abstract, with a field of flowers just coming into bloom and opening their petals to the sun with its promise of something new to come. I tried to focus on each tiny stitch pulling the pieces of the quilt together to create a beautiful image, to combine the individual elements into something greater, a fulfillment of her artistic vision.

The promise of something new. Sounded so hopeful. Sounded like a solution.

I had to believe that all of this was happening to me for a greater purpose. If I didn't, I'd drive myself crazy.

"Just don't ever stop being my friend," I told Sophie.

I breathed, breathed, breathed.

Her voice was gentle. "Lil—"

Finally, I exhaled a deep breath. "I just have to learn to deal. Somehow."

Aunt Nina's picture on my wall caught my eye. I studied the flawless image she'd cultivated so carefully and read her company name.

Splendor.

To be splendid was to be impressive and magnificent, to be absolutely brilliant.

How appropriate. I wanted to be splendid, to transcend my troubles. I needed a heavy dose of splendid if I ever hoped to beat the people keeping me down.

A lady carries herself with dignity and pride.

"I need to do something major, Soph. I can't keep letting these guys trample me. We've got three more years at Middleton and I'll never survive if I don't do something."

A lady works with her assets.

Sophie was on her feet and rubbing her hands together. "So what's the game plan? How do you want me to help? Hire a few hit men? Call the feds?"

I laughed and turned to her. "Just cut school with me today."

She whipped out her cell phone. "I'll call Ma and tell her. What are we doing?"

A smile crept onto my face. "We have an appointment."

Her eyebrows arched. "We do?"

"But first," I nodded, "I need to deal."

Sophie stood behind me and waited as I rebooted my computer and reopened my crashed email program. When it finished sending and receiving, 138 new emails clogged my inbox.

"Wow," she said as she let out a low whistle. "You weren't making this up."

"Nope." I opened the first note, we skimmed the disturbing content and I hit reply.

"That's disgusting," Sophie said.

I glanced up at her. "And illegal."

She watched while I typed the response I'd been debating all night and drafting in my head with the help of some of my dad's law books and the research I did online.

Cyber bullying will not be tolerated.

Your emails are a violation of service provider terms and conditions and will be traced. I have forwarded each email to my ISP and will contact the appropriate authorities if you attempt to communicate with me again.

I sighed. "Haven't done all that yet, but I intend to." I pressed print and send while Sophie gave me a high five.

"Think it will work?" she asked.

"I'll keep copies of everything for my file." I breathed a sigh of relief. "If this doesn't stop whoever's harassing me, I'll show these emails to my dad and we'll go to the cops to investigate and press charges. In the meantime, I'm getting a new super secret email address."

"You know Adam's a total genius on the computer," Sophie said proudly. "He's into all kinds of programming and forums and stuff, and he's always online. We should talk to him about this."

I turned to her, curious. "Think he'll help me find out who's sending me these notes? If I need to go to the cops with my dad, it will make it a lot easier if I've got actual ammunition."

Sophie grinned."Yeah. I'm sure he'd do that for you. Or, for me, anyway. I'll text him and ask him to come over here."

I nodded. "That'd be great, Soph. Thanks."

Her thumbs got busy on the keyboard of her phone. "Okay, I'm texting *my man* now."

I sighed. "Don't gloat just because you have one and I never will."

"No gloating. Got it." She laughed. "Ignoring your self-deprecating comment and eating a huge slice of humble pie now. Whoa, yes, filling my belly with it. Yes, ma'am."

I heard a chime and Sophie jumped up and down. "He said he'll do it! Adam will come over on Monday night!"

"Cool," I said with a nod.

Standing up, I gave her a huge smile as I pulled my hair up into a chignon and fixed it with a few pins.

I clung to my goal. I would not go back to Middleton High on Monday and be the girl in that picture that had spread through school.

I would not let them beat me.

I laughed. "Now let's go get fancy and play with makeup! My mother and my Aunt Nina have been dying to make me over for years."

As we walked toward the hall, I repeated something my grandmother told me on the way home from Bebiane's.

"Inner beauty is power, *ma chérie*. You need to learn how to use it."

47.

Meyer's Grocery was packed on Saturday when we walked in to restock the refrigerator and pantry, which had fallen to war ration level. We were left with carrots - Tony's least favorite vegetable – some random yet suspect leftovers and unidentifiable freezer packets, and a few bottles of fancy vinegars that nobody liked. The cupboards were pitifully bare.

For the outing to the grocery store, Grand-mère looked stunning, as usual, in pewter colored slacks with a matching sweater. She'd wrapped her shoulders in a burnout velvet scarf that added just enough texture and movement to draw focus up to her face. And her jewelry was indeed classic – three brushed silver bangles and an enormous smoky quartz ring.

I remembered the last note I'd received from her just this afternoon.

A lady's clothing endures the test of time.

What did it matter that this French lady in my life bumper-parked and hit curbs every time she turned a corner in the car? Done deal. Driving would never be her strength, but fashion and beauty were. The more I studied her, the more I learned, and the more I could kick myself for not paying attention sooner.

I'd wasted so much time. And not just for learning about clothes and makeup, which was nice, but not nearly as important as the other things I'd missed. I'd wasted precious years robbing myself of the relationship I could have had with my grandmother, even from afar. And now I was trying to make up for all that lost time.

As I fought to steer the cart with the wonky wheel and tossed my brother's favorite chocolate cereal onto the other food in the basket, I caught sight of myself in the round security mirror hanging over the aisle. The slim leggings and big turtleneck I'd worn to Splendor were okay on their own. But when I'd started to experiment and I'd taken that length of Chinese silk we'd bought at the yard sale and wrapped my waist like an obi sash, the clothes had become an actual outfit, and they looked kinda cool. My curves were definitely still there, but a whole lot less objectionable. With my hair pulled back into a loose chignon and Aunt Nina's makeup smoothing my spots and flaws, I almost didn't recognize myself.

Camouflage, my grandmother had called it, the elegant art of concealment and manipulating perceptions with illusion.

Sounded good to me. If I could change my appearance until nobody recognized me, so much the better.

"I want rocky road," Tony said excitedly, tugging on Grand-mère's sleeve. "And chocolate chip. Ooh – and maybe some strawberry shortcake. And can we get hot fudge sauce, too? And marshmallows?"

Grand-mère smiled at him and smoothed his hair. "Let us go choose a sweet together, ah? But only one, so it must be very special."

Always respect your body, she'd said. *Indulge, but never overdo.*

I listened, and I'd already lost three pounds.

"I'll go get some fruit. Meet you at the registers."

The store was crowded with housewives lost in thought as they stared at coupons and lists, and mothers battling willful toddlers who reached with sticky outstretched hands and cried for a cookie or some other sweet they absolutely positively had to have right now.

When I turned the corner into the aisle with the bright displays of butternut squash and late summer zucchini and ruby red pie apples, I did not expect to see Tyler Jackson poking through the cantaloupes in his green striped Meyer's Grocery vest and nametag.

Seeing him here was so out of context, but it was too late to turn back without looking like a fool. He'd spotted me and he was only five feet away.

I tilted my chin, sucked in a breath and headed straight for the oranges. But he stopped me.

"Carracino," he said, nodding. "Looking mighty good tonight."

I grit my teeth. "Leave me alone, Tyler. I have nothing to say to you."

"Hey, we're just talking here," he said, blocking my cart to sidle up closer.

I shoved the cart forward and tried to move him. "I need to get by. Please let go."

Amazingly, he did. He stepped aside and went back to his cantaloupes and I breathed a sigh of relief as I passed him.

An older woman in a blue raincoat tapped him on the arm. "Young man, can you help me find the Belgian endive? I'm probably staring right at it and can't even see it. I left my glasses at home on the coffee table."

The jerk was uncharacteristically polite as he nodded down the aisle and smiled like an extra helpful boy-next-door store clerk. "Sure thing, ma'am. The endive's right there, next to the parsley and the other herbs."

What a scam artist he was.

He turned away from the woman and hurried in front of my cart. He groped my breasts again with his eyes, then gave the two cantaloupes in his hands a few hard squeezes and licked his lips.

"Nice and ripe," he said.

Squeeze. Squeeze.

Sweat prickled my skin. If my cart weren't nearly full, I would have abandoned it, just walked away from him and right out the front door of the store. I wanted to throw up right on him, but I stood my ground and clutched the shopping cart until my knuckles were white.

"Tyler, seriously. I just need fruit. Can you give it a rest for once?"

He leered at me, devoured me with his eyes as he leaned forward. My cart was within range of his essential parts and it took all my strength to hold back from crushing them into infertility.

I glanced up at the security mirror and saw what we looked like. To anyone else, we were just two kids hanging out. But to me, it was yet another in the long line of endless confrontations I was forced to endure.

One of my brother's football friends entered the aisle from the other end, shopping with his dad. He glanced over at me and gave me a little wave. I tried to smile but it kind of died before it reached my lips.

This was pathetic, constantly feeling this ambushed.

But Tyler's voice was low, more menacing than it needed to be. "I said we're just talking, Carracino."

Not here. Not out in public with my brother's friend watching.

Please don't let him humiliate me now.

My breathing was tight and my jaw clenched. "I'm really tired, Tyler," I said as firmly as I could. "I don't want you to keep harassing me. Just let go of my cart. *Please.*"

"Young man," the woman said impatiently while she poked through a mound of leafy greens. "I still can't find the endive. Are you sure you have it?"

Tyler focused his sights on my chest and licked those lips again like a depraved delinquent.

"I'm *coming,*" he said with too much intent. And then, the pig thrust his hips forward and dropped the cantaloupes into my cart. "Yes, ma'am, I'm coming right now."

Thoroughly disgusted, I watched him snap back to good employee mode while I grabbed a bag of oranges.

Without looking back, I fled to the safety of my grandmother's shadow.

48.

Sophie and I met at the corner and I handed her a cup of espresso.

"Who are you?" she said with a laugh. "And what have you done with my *shlumpy* friend?"

"*Shlumpy*?" I repeated. "Is that what I looked like before?"

She shrugged and got busy sipping her coffee.

"Nice way to dodge my question." I gave her a shove as we walked.

She smiled. "Seriously, Lil, you look amazing. Where'd you get the new duds?"

"Presents from Grand-mère. She bought me a whole new wardrobe from Bebiane's, and they delivered it last night." I shook my head. "I tried to refuse, but she insisted."

"Whoa! That's huge," Sophie said happily. "It's about time."

"If I looked so bad, why didn't you ever say anything?"

Sophie shrugged. "Because you're my friend, and I love you for *you*. Not your clothes or your makeup. But you need to be a better friend and tell me what you're going through. You've kept stuff from me, and it kinda hurts."

"I'm really sorry, Sophie."

Suddenly emotional, I changed the subject, pointing at my face. "I tried to remember Nina's rules. Nourish my skin. Conceal my flaws. Accent my best feature."

Sophie laughed and boldly imitated my aunt's French accent. "Strong lips or eyes, but never both." She gave me a nudge. "You did good, Lil."

We were avoiding the obvious subject, but I needed to. I glanced at my new clothes. I was wearing jeans with a white shirt and black jacket, and I'd thrown on one of the wide, chunky leather belts my mother designed and had given me ages ago. On a whim, I'd wrapped one of my embroidered charmeuse scarves around my neck. It was rosy red, but when the light hit the fabric it glimmered with soft gold.

"I know what we should do. Let's get our ears pierced after school today," Sophie said excitedly. "My treat. They'll do it downtown at the jewelry shop. And then we can buy a buttload of crystal earrings and hoops. Murray gave me my own credit card last night."

"Big move for your dad." I sipped my espresso. "What about your Ma?"

Sophie snorted. "She'll live if I want to get holes in my head. And then she'll have something else to shop for *ad nauseum*. She's already ordered like a dozen pairs of glasses for me."

I stared at her frame-free face. "And why aren't you wearing them to school?"

She shook her head. "I just can't give up hope. Not yet. I've got two more kinds of lenses to try."

I pulled the jacket around me as a breeze picked up. "Don't you have to rehearse this afternoon?"

She shrugged. "Margaux postponed our class a half an hour. She's got a major problem with the costumes, and she's all freaked out that we'll be naked on stage when *Cinderella* opens."

"Costume trouble?" I wondered why she hadn't mentioned it the other night. "I thought she had a great seamstress."

"Think the woman had a breakdown and quit. Mags even begged Kerry to take over, but she's too busy designing another quilt for someone. We're kinda stuck."

Sophie stood taller as we approached the school, and my mood visibly shifted. One look at the pre-homeroom crowd was all it took to send tension rippling through me.

"God, I am so far behind in my classes. I'm in serious trouble, Sophie. And I have to start serving detention this week for cutting the other day." I sighed. "I don't want to do this."

"You'll deal, I have no doubt. Do your homework in detention." She nudged me forward. "So, ready to take on the whack jobs for another week?"

"*No freakin' way*," I said.

When I saw a few people already staring at me, I drew a deep breath, scrambled to find some shred of self-confidence, and forged ahead through the double doors to fight another round.

As we walked the hall toward our lockers, I could tell something big was going on. The air felt charged like right before lightning strikes. That kind of hair-standing-on-end sensation that made you feel like sparks would fly out of your fingertips if you touched something.

Kids I didn't even know kept staring then ducking behind their hands to whisper.

A chill raced along my spine. "This isnot good, Soph."

She strutted. "Walk it off. Act like you don't care."

I took longer strides and someone grabbed my butt and squeezed. When I spun around, three guys I didn't know were smiling at me with their hands in the air.

One of them said, "Nice ass, babe." The others laughed and stared at my breasts.

I couldn't bring myself to respond, and tried not to feel dirty and used. Instead, I turned on my heels and just kept moving toward homeroom.

The chatter and trying-to-be-subtle pointing got worse.

"Do I have a 'gossip about me' sticker on my back or something?" I asked Sophie quietly as I shifted my books from one hand to another. "Everyone is staring."

"Maybe it's because you look so good today. Killer jeans," Sophie said, holding her head high and poking me. "Just keep walking, Lil. Put on your game face."

"God, Sophie, they all know. Don't they?"

She shook her head. "Those emails and phone calls will blow over in a few days. Ya just gotta survive a little while longer. You'll need major league balls of steel."

When we rounded the bend to another hallway, a noisy crowd was gathered around my locker. Someone saw me coming, whispered, and the kids moved silently to the side.

When my locker came into view, I felt like I'd been zapped by ten thousand volts.

I literally couldn't move.

"Wow. That sucks." Sophie got out her phone and took a picture. She sighed deeply. "I guess now you've got more proof, hmm?"

I didn't care about piling up the proof right now. I just wanted to disappear.

On my locker, someone had taped a lacy black thong.

But that wasn't the worst of it, by far.

Spray-painted in bright red letters below the underwear was a single word.

WHORE.

49.

"Snap out of it," Sophie hissed. "They're all staring at you."

I blinked hard, shook my head and turned around. "Gotta go."

"Where are you going?" she asked as I walked away.

I didn't answer, but I held my head high as I zipped past the snickers and glares.

This was my last straw.

The front office bustled with activity as I walked in and dumped my backpack on the main counter. "I need to see Principal Dailey. Now."

"Please wait your turn, Miss Carracino," the secretary said as she peered at me over her reading glasses. "Miss Redding was here first."

The snooty senior girl in her boyfriend's varsity letter jacket stared and let out a sigh as she shook her agenda at me. "We're a little busy here."

I put my hands on the countertop and leaned forward to stare into the older woman's eyes. "I don't care. This is an emergency."

The girl huffed and crossed her arms. "Really?"

I ignored her sarcasm. "This can't wait."

The secretary took off her glasses. "I'm afraid it must. The administration is at an off-site planning meeting until Wednesday. What do you need?"

The girl raised her eyebrows and something in her brain clicked.

She figured out where she'd seen me before. Her smug smile said it all.

I grabbed my backpack and headed for the office doors. "Just forget it."

A snarky laugh hit my back on the way out.

First bell rang and I ignored it, veering off into the art hall instead. The janitors hung out there by the loading dock with their equipment carts sometimes.

I walked past classes in session and headed for the door open to the outside at the end of the hall.

The faint aroma of cigarettes drifted toward my nose and I followed it around the dumpster that reeked of sour milk.

The two old guys I knew only as Old Mo and Fat Steve were hanging out there, sitting on milk crates and smoking illegal cigarettes. When they saw me, they held the smokes behind them and waved the air.

"Help you?" Old Mo asked, exhaling a cloud.

He was nearly bald with smoke-yellow teeth and a mass of wrinkles on his leathery white face. I'd never spoken two words to him since I'd been here.

I hitched up my backpack. "One of you has to come with me. We have a big problem."

"What's that?" Fat Steve said. The big black man with the frizzy gray afro shifted forward on his crate and took a last drag on the cigarette he wasn't supposed to be smoking, before stubbing it out with his work boot.

I swallowed hard. "My locker. It's messed up. I need you to clean it, please."

Old Mo laughed and sucked on his cigarette. "That's summer work, kid. You're in the wrong season."

I bit my lip and choked back the thickness in my throat. Tears pricked my eyes and I nodded to hold them in.

"*Please.*"

The old men stared at each other then back at me. Finally, Fat Steve got to his feet. "Got nothing better to do right now. What say we take a walk, kid?"

I nodded and blinked back the tears. "Thanks."

50.

Mr. Kellerman was standing in front of my locker with a clipboard and a camera. He was an upper class physics teacher with the reputation for being a hard ass disciplinarian who gave more detentions than anyone else in spite of his laid back appearance. Right now, he looked mighty pissed off.

The maintenance cart squeaked as we moved toward him. He turned toward us and scowled when he spotted me.

I cringed and hid behind Fat Steve and Old Mo.

"Is this your locker, young lady?" he asked sharply. The lacy thong dangled from his fingertips. "Do these belong to you?"

The custodians remained mute as they studied that terrible word in red letters.

WHORE.

My voice came out in a whisper. "Yes." I shook my head fast. "I mean, no. It's my locker, but those aren't mine. I have no idea where they came from."

"Your name?"

I swallowed hard. "Lili Carracino."

He noted it on his clipboard and nodded. Then he wadded the thong into a lacy ball he clenched with a fist. With a wave of his hand to the men, he issued an order.

"Get this cleaned up, pronto." He stared at me and pointed. "*You*. Come with me."

"Yes, sir. But I didn't do anything."

He ran a hand through shaggy brown hair that needed a good cut. "Don't argue. Just follow me."

Fat Steve and Old Mo gave me a sympathetic look. "Hang in there, kid. We'll get this fixed for you in a jif. You won't have to look at it again."

I was so grateful that I wanted to hug them right then and there, but Mr. Kellerman sighed impatiently.

He barked another order. "Just come with me please."

While the janitors grabbed a bucket, some cleaner and a scrub brush, I stopped and turned to them. "I don't know what to call you."

Old Mo stared at me with a cocked up brow. "Kids just call me 'Old Mo.'"

I nodded. "I know. But that's not your real name. I thought . . . maybe you don't like the nickname so much."

He smiled. "Well, I ain't that old, really. I just look it. But it's Morris Wilbanks."

I turned to his companion. "And you?"

The older black man gave me a crinkly smile. "I'm Steve Nabors." He gave me a nod. "Thanks, kid. Thanks for asking."

"Hurry it along, Miss Carracino," Mr. Kellerman said, looking at his watch.

I gave the janitors my lock combination.

Mr. Wilbanks put a hand on my shoulder and gave it a reassuring squeeze as I turned to follow the teacher. "You're going to be okay, little lady."

Mr. Kellerman didn't say a word to me. Just looked straight ahead and kept clenching his jaw until his face muscles twitched. I left my embarrassing locker behind and echoed his sharp footsteps down the hall toward the guidance offices.

I clutched my backpack and tried to keep up. Why was this teacher making me feel like I'd done something wrong? None of this was my fault.

The whole situation felt so incredibly unfair. And I was getting tired of the refrain.

I know life isn't always fair, but damn it, I'd like it to be . . . just once.

It was my turn for some fair, wasn't it?

When we reached the guidance wing, Kellerman's jaw twitched again as he pointed toward an empty office. "Take a seat. I'll print something and be with you in a moment."

This return to Middleton was a total nightmare and it wasn't even nine o'clock yet. The chaos of the guidance office was comforting in a way, with kids bitching about their schedules and picking up college brochures.

Nobody paid much attention to me as I dropped my backpack, slumped in a chair and laid my head on the table. Behind me in the hall, I heard Mrs. Russell call my name.

"Lili? We missed you last week. Are you feeling okay?"

I spun to face her. "Yeah. I guess. I don't know."

She came into the room and sat beside me. "You're not a very good liar, you know."

"Sorry." I gave her a tiny smile. "Really rotten morning."

She put a hand on my back. "It'll get better. You look really pretty today, so that's good, hmm?"

I shrugged. "Doesn't make a difference. I feel awful."

Mr. Kellerman burst into the room and dumped a stack of papers on the table. He threw the thong in front of me and I cringed at the sight of the black lace against the scarred laminate.

Mrs. Russell stared at the panties, her mouth hanging open.

"Umm, we're about to have a meeting here, if you don't mind," he said to her as he pointed toward the door. "While Principal Dailey's out, I'm on call."

I shook my head at his lack of social graces. "No. She can stay." I glanced over to my teacher, desperately needing an ally in this cramped room. Someone I could count on to be on my side. "Can you stay with me? *Please?*"

"I think I will." Mrs. Russell furrowed her brows and gave me a hard look. "Put those . . . *things* away." She gestured angrily toward the panties. "What's going on here, Fred?"

While she closed the door, he stuffed the thong into a folder. He sighed and handed her a picture of my locker. "We've encountered a bit of trouble this morning. At her locker."

She studied the image and gasped. "Oh, Lili. Who would do this to you? You're such a good girl." She turned to her colleague. "She's never done anything wrong, Fred. It's just not in her nature. I've known her since she was ten."

"And I found this posted by the water fountain."

He slid a cut-up copy of the email across the table.

"Oh my God," I moaned when I saw it. I crossed my arms and shook my head. But my words got stuck in my throat, somewhere behind the tears I was trying incredibly hard not to spill.

Mr. Kellerman leaned back in his chair. "Well, someone apparently thinks otherwise." He clucked his tongue. "Now relationships being what they are these days, I'm not one to interfere with kids' sex lives –"

"But I'm not having sex!" I snapped, too loudly.

He held up his hands. "Okay, then, that's your business. Didn't mean to offend."

"I don't even have a boyfriend," I said, my voice softer now. "I've never had one."

This gruff male teacher was at a loss to come up with a clever retort. But Mrs. Russell stepped in to soothe me.

"Lili, I know something terrible happened to you the other day when your shirt got ripped." She took my hand. "You can tell us about it. We're here to help you, aren't we, Fred?"

She glared at him until he responded. "Absolutely. So what's the problem?"

His clueless attitude made me feel even more hopeless about my situation. "It's just . . . I tried to ignore them, but it's getting really hard," I explained. "It keeps getting more intense."

"They?" Mr. Kellerman asked, leaning forward, ready to take notes. "Who's bothering you?"

I shrugged and clutched my stomach.

"Without names, Lili, we can't do anything to make this better," Mrs. Russell said quietly.

I weighed the probability of the boys changing their behavior.

The chances were slim to none.

And if I told the school, if I spilled my guts and let the whole story leak out in all its sordid detail, I'd forever be labeled a rat, *and* a whore. I'd be the kid who turned narc and brought the wrath of the school board onto some of our school's best athletes and favored popular sons.

No one would ever talk to me again.

"I . . . *can't.*"

"Miss Carracino, are you being sexually harassed?" he asked bluntly.

Shame flooded my face, but I couldn't lie. "All the time."

Mrs. Russell sighed and shared a look with Mr. Kellerman.

"If you won't cooperate, we can only give you advice," he said with a sigh. "Try your best to ignore the boys bothering you. Turn the other cheek, as it were."

"That won't work and you know it, Fred," Mrs. Russell said harshly. She let out a sigh while she assessed the situation. "Give us a minute alone, will you?"

He pushed back from the table and stood. "We need to fill out an incident report, to document what happened today. Destruction of school property is a serious offense."

Property?

"What about trashing someone's reputation for no reason?" I snapped. "How does the school deal with that?"

Mrs. Russell snapped. "Fred, please. *Get out.*"

He walked out without another word and closed the door behind him.

Mrs. Russell took a deep breath and cleared her throat. "Okay. We're alone now. You can be honest with me." She leaned forward and took my hand. "You've got a right to feel safe at school, Lili. A legal right. It's called the Title Nine Education Act, and it protects children and preserves their right to a proper education."

I shrugged. "Thought that was just for sports."

"No, it's not." She shook her head. "School should make you feel protected, and we've got a legal obligation to do so. If you don't, then we're not doing our job."

I looked into her eyes. "And if I don't? Feel safe?"

"Then take care of this yourself, or help us catch the kids who did this and put a stop to it," she said. "Or it will only get worse."

51.

Adam Brock was what most kids might call a nerd. Actually, "might" wasn't accurate. They did call him that and a lot worse. He wasn't cool. He wasn't handsome in the classical sense. He had pimples. Yet something about his combination of crooked smile and buoyant personality made you just *like* him.

Adam was a totally likeable guy, he was my best friend's new boyfriend, and he was nice to me.

And right now, he was sitting in my bedroom with Sophie and me, drinking a soda, eating sour cream and onion chips, and staring with love-struck fascination at my quirky friend. Sophie was eating up the attention and trying her hardest not to act too silly.

They were sickeningly happy, these two.

"So, Sophie said you had big problems. With your email?" he asked. He let out a soda burp and Sophie giggled.

I tried not to roll my eyes. "Someone's been slamming my inbox with really nasty stuff. Like, hundreds of emails. And they just keep coming."

He shrugged. "Thought so."

Something about his tone tweaked my curiosity. "Why?"

He looked at my comforter and traced the pattern with his fingertip. "I saw . . . the picture. Came in an email to me a bunch of times. Kind of put two and two together."

Embarrassed to the core, I blew out a breath. "Yeah. That. The bane of my existence."

"Don't know who sent it?" he asked, stretching his long legs across the bed.

"I have my suspicions." I swept a hand across my brow. "But I was hoping you could help pinpoint it."

He motioned with his hand as he got up. "Bring it on. Let's see what we've got."

"Adam knows tons about this stuff," Sophie said adoringly as she crossed her long legs and pointed her toes. "He's incredible."

Her boyfriend actually puffed up his chest as he sat down at my keyboard and opened my email program. She immediately got up to stand behind his shoulders.

The sudden move made me smile. They were too cute together.

Adam shrugged. "Computers are kind of my thing. But go back to the beginning of all this. Square one."

I knew exactly when it started. "The first email came when I was at your house, remember Sophie?"

She tore her gaze away from his profile. "Yeah. After dinner. You know, that night you first called me, Adam."

He blushed as her hand cupped his shoulder and he looked deeply into her eyes. "How could I forget that night? It made my millennium."

My friend seriously blushed as she gave him a squeeze. "Oh, Adam. You are so romantic."

He cleared his throat and tried to concentrate. With a few clicks, he called up the emails from that day and opened the one with the "Just a Reminder" subject line.

"Wow. It's so vindictive, Lili." He shook his head then looked up at me. "So how do you want to pay them back?"

Payback? The thought had never occurred to me.

I scrunched my eyebrows. "You mean, like . . . get revenge?"

He shrugged. "Always a possibility. We could post their addresses and info on some forums and have people swarm them. You know, expose what they're doing in a major way and make the cops aware of what's really going on. People get arrested for doing stuff like they did. It can work. *Well.* Just check out Four-Chan on Wikipedia and you'll see what I mean."

I shook my head. "But that's like fighting harassment with harassment. I don't feel good about doing to them what they're doing to me. It just makes the whole situation worse, like the cycle will never end."

Sophie agreed. "Don't stoop."

Adam nodded. "Then we'll stockpile data you can use."

Now I was interested. "Okay. How?"

"We go back to the raw image in that first email. Most likely it hasn't been doctored."

I crossed my arms and watched as he right clicked on my photograph and issued the command to open it with another program. A second later, a screen completely full of letters and symbols appeared.

I stepped back. "What's that? It looks like the computer malfunctioned."

Sophie leaned closer and squinted. "Is any of that gobbledygook supposed to make sense?"

Adam kissed her on the cheek. "If you know what you're looking for it does."

She smiled and straightened, resting her hand on her cheek where his lips had touched.

Adam scrolled across the line of characters until he found what he called the identifier string. "See here. This picture was taken by an Apple iPhone." He moved the cursor a little more. "And right here . . . we've got the exact date and time it was taken."

"Wow," I said, nodding. "You *are* a genius."

He clicked a few buttons again as program windows opened and closed. "Okay. Saved a screen shot of the data to your pictures file." He pressed another button. "And now the data and image are printing for your records."

My printer whirred to life.

"I am genuinely impressed," I said, daring to get a little excited. "Any more we can do?"

He nodded enthusiastically. "Hell yeah! Now we hunt the hunter."

Sophie and I shared a smile as she placed a hand on his back.

"Isn't he so smart?" she asked me dreamily.

My ballerina was a lovesick puppy and she made me laugh. "Yeah."

Adam opened my emails one at a time, clicking keys and pushing buttons faster than I could keep up.

He was serious about the task at hand, and I admired his concentration.

"So far, I've come up with three distinct user addresses, all routed from the same ISP."

I prodded him with my index finger. "In English, please."

He looked up at me and smiled. "Sorry. Three people have emailed you using an account at the same internet service provider. But these guys aren't so smart. They may have changed the screen name to something stupid for each email, but they never bothered to disguise their actual email addresses." He laughed. "Rank amateurs."

Adam opened my computer's web browser. "We'll go to the email website and see if we can find their user profiles."

Less than a minute later, he pulled up the information.

"Oh, they're dim bulbs, for sure," he said, grinning with satisfaction. "Look at this. Everybody knows you're supposed to shield the most personal identifying info in the profile, not broadcast it to the world. There are psychos out there on the web." He hitched a thumb at the screen. "They even used their pictures. Home addresses and phone numbers, too."

Adam shook his head. Sophie and I stared as he opened each email account profile and printed them out for me.

"Idiots," he said with a laugh. "Proof positive that the emails came from them."

We read the names to be sure.

Tyler Jackson. Joe Sanderson. Jimmy Barnett.

"You got 'em, Lili," Sophie said, smiling.

I got them.

A wave of hope swept through me.

"Adam, I think I love you," I said, giving my new friend an impromptu hug.

He blushed, got to his feet, and stuffed his hands in his back pockets. "Glad to help."

When he saw the left-out look that had settled momentarily on Sophie's face, he wrapped his arm around her and pulled her close. "So are my best girl and her best friend in the mood for burgers?"

"Oh, Adam. You are the best," Sophie said, her equilibrium returned. "Isn't he the absolute best?"

I nodded and knew I had all the proof I'd need to push this legally if I decided to go that route.

I gave them both a grin. "Yeah. This *is* the best."

52.

My first negotiation to not flunk freshman year was a nightmare.

My biology teacher Mr. Saxon did not want to hear my excuses. He didn't give a flip about the stress in my life or why I'd been absent.

Asking for sympathy clearly wasn't working, so I tried a different approach.

"What can I do for extra credit?" I begged. "How about a paper? Or an extra lab, maybe? Please work with me here, Mr. Saxon. I know my grades are slipping, but I'm trying to turn it around. And I'm not asking for favors. I'll do the work."

My teacher with the fuzzy red hair and pot belly paused to consider my request. "Why should you get special treatment when I'm not giving it to the other kids?"

I swallowed my nerves. "Because I'm a good person. I've got a really decent school record. And a few months of bad performance shouldn't have to wreck the rest of my high school career."

He nodded and flipped the page on his planner. "Logical argument. What's your GPA?"

I crossed my arms. "Before now, three-point-six."

He tapped the grade sheet. "You're just one point above failing, Lili."

Nodding, I dropped my gaze. "I know. But I need to make up for it. I *will* make up for it."

"Two thousand word essay on the central nervous system. Structure, function and implications for the body. Do well, and I'll weight the effort heavily."

I gasped. "Two thousand words?"

He looked at me. "Got a problem with that?"

Quickly, I shook my head. "None whatsoever, Mr. Saxon. Thank you."

By the end of the day, I'd earned 200 extra math problems and three more research papers. Better than that, I'd earned a second chance.

At this rate, I'd never see daylight again. But I might make it to sophomore year if Jimmy, Tyler and Joe didn't do me in sooner.

53.

After school the next day, when I'd pulled my books out of my locker that had been freshly painted primer gray by Fat Steve and Old Mo – correction, Mr. Wilbanks and Mr. Nabors –I held my head high and met Sophie's expectant gaze with a smile. "Ready?"

She nodded. "As I'll ever be. Adam's in the computer lab all afternoon. What say you and I go burn in Murray's credit card and put it to good use?"

After five periods of whispered torture, I'd nearly perfected the art of staring straight ahead without flinching.

Almost.

But when Joe Sanderson swept by me and moaned in my ear, I plowed into Sophie and knocked her down.

"Joe, I am so sick of you!" I snapped. "Just keep your distance and leave me alone!"

He slapped his hand against the lockers on either side of me and a few kids stopped to watch.

Behind him, Sophie was trying to scramble to her feet.

His face was inches from mine, his breath hot on my skin and smelling of pizza.

My pulse pounded as I struggled to look unfazed.

"This is getting to be an old song," I warned as I tried to slip under his arms.

He trapped me there, lowering his arms to my waist level so I had no choice but to stay put. "Resistance is futile."

I had no choice but to stand there, with students milling by on their way to the bus and Sophie pulling herself up into a fight stance. My heart was racing and my underarms began to sweat, but I couldn't let him see my fear.

"Get your hands off her," Sophie threatened.

I sensed the volatility of this situation, but I needed to calm it down for Sophie's sake so she wouldn't get in trouble.

I held up a hand to her. "I'm okay, Sophie. I can handle this."

Joe laughed and licked his lips as he looked at mine. "You can handle me, hmm? I'd like to see you try."

As I stared into his dark brown eyes, my grandmother's words came back to me.

A lady holds back strong words and smiles.

Summoning all of my ladylike dignity, I straightened my back and gave him a weak smile. "I'd like to leave now, Joe. Are you through?"

"We've only started, Carracino," he said, laughing. He pushed off the lockers and threw his hands in the air. "We're going to have some fun, just you and me."

When he left and the whoosh of him leaving hit my face, I collapsed in a sigh and tried to shake it off.

Sophie screamed after him. "You're a pig, Joe! A real pig!"

He gave her the finger and kept walking, cutting into the crowd until I couldn't see him anymore. When I finally breathed, she touched my arm.

"You okay?"

"You know, sometimes I really hate my life. But my ears are feeling mighty naked," I said with a hysterical laugh. "How about yours?"

Sophie gave me a hug and pulled me toward the door. "I'm thinking a neat little pair of diamond studs ought to do us both for now."

54.

Zazzle Jewelry on Main was clean, expensive and dazzling under spotlights. Diamonds and gems glistened from the cases as I sat on the leatherette stool and waited. We'd picked out our starter studs – the biggest diamonds Sophie could allow her conscience to buy, and inexpensive Swarovski crystal rubies for me. Murray Fishkin liked me, but not enough to splurge for another carat, I was sure. Sophie refused to let me pay. Actually hit my hand when I took out my money.

So I let my friend spoil me just a little bit to make herself feel better.

The severe-looking store clerk with spiky black hair wore loads of black eyeliner and deep red lipstick that only accented how glaringly white her skin was. While she chewed her gum, she went through her standard lecture and handed us each a bottle of antiseptic.

"Wash your hands before you clean your ears, and swab the piercing at least three times a day, front and back," she reminded us robotically. "Check the safety catches on the posts to make sure the earrings aren't too tight, twist them now and then, and don't gunk up your ears with hairspray or make-up. In six months, you come back here and I'll hook you up with a nice selection of dangles. Posts 'til then, and don't even think about switching or you'll have all sorts of problems."

Thoroughly warned of possible reddening and infection, five minutes later Sophie was admiring herself in the round magnifying mirror they'd handed her, touching her new diamond studs. "They look amazing, don't they? Adam will love them."

She and Adam were officially an item, though they'd never be part of the in crowd. They were their own two-person sci-fi fan club of Middleton and all that.

And that made me officially a third wheel.

In my seat, I was tearing a tissue to shreds and worrying what my mother would think about my decision to pierce my ears without her permission. "I don't like pain."

The twenty-something girl with five earrings up her right ear and only two in her left smacked her gum. "You won't feel it. *Much.*"

My eyes opened wide and she grinned.

A second later I yelped when the contraption she held over my ear fired and punched a hole through my tender skin.

"One down," the girl said with a smile as she fiddled with the piercing gun.

I hissed out a breath and shut my eyes. "Do it extra fast before I change my mind."

And one big flinch later, I had pierced ears like my best friend.

I was just racking up the changes, left and right.

And while Sophie ducked into dance class and I passed by Worthington's Wonders, my old friend Brian noticed.

He actually came out of his store and flagged me down.

"Lili? Is that you, girl?"

I turned around and smiled when I saw him scratching his head.

I shrugged. "Same old, same old."

He shook his head. "Not by a long shot. The change suits you."

As the grandfatherly Yalie stood there looking at me with that wild white hair, he did something I'd never seen in all the years I'd known him. He dropped those horn-rimmed glasses from his forehead onto his nose to get a better look.

"Mighty metamorphosis, I'd say."

I crossed my arms. "Not quite a cockroach, but what the hey?"

He nodded. “Got a minute? Have something cool to show you. Picked up some really groovy stuff from a private eye.”

I paused. “Like for spying?”

“And eavesdropping,” he said. “Cameras, listening devices, the whole ball of wax.”

“Show me." I followed him into the store, an idea beginning to form.

When he displayed each piece on the counter and demonstrated the hidden microphones, microscopic digital cameras and recording devices, I was fascinated.

But when he showed me the button camera, I knew exactly what I had to do next.

Without a second’s hesitation, I used every cent of the money my dad had sent me and bought the entire lot.

55.

Across the street, Aunt Margaux stood *sur les points*, demonstrating the position she wanted Sophie to emulate while the other girls watched. From the doorway, they looked like a pair of beautiful swans with their fluttering arms and long, graceful necks.

It made me proud to know them.

A minute later, Aunt Margaux spotted me watching.

She gave me a small smile as she issued an instruction. "Girls, I must see tighter formations in your lines. Control your arms and legs, *please*."

I motioned for her and she came to my side.

"I did not expect to see you, Liliana," she said quietly. "You have avoided me. You would not even talk to me after dinner like you promised."

I looked at my feet. "I'm sorry. I've been acting really stupid and pouty."

She brushed a hand across my cheek. "You were hurt. I understand."

Glancing up at her, I asked, "Can you forgive me? I know you were only trying to do what was best for the recital."

My aunt pulled me into a hug. "We are family, and I did not mean to hurt you. But you have never let me finish what I was trying to ask you."

I scuffed my toe on the polished wood floor. "I know. That's why I came. To make it right between us. I'm sorry I was so rude."

It actually felt good to apologize to her, to make amends.

She smiled. "Then we will chat just now. And I want to say that I am sorry, too. I never meant to hurt your feelings." With a graceful turn, she called out to Sophie and clapped her hands. "Please lead the class in *pas de bourré couru*. Do not forget I expect perfection."

Sophie winked at me and nodded. "Sure thing."

With an arm around my shoulder, Margaux led me into the small workroom by her office.

In front of us on a fabric mannequin, a classical tutu had been badly stitched to a plain white bodice.

"What is *that*?" I asked.

Margaux sighed and folded her arms. "That is my disaster." She shook her head. "The seamstress, she is . . . *complètement fou.*"

"She might be crazy, but she's not a seamstress," I said with a laugh. "This is awful workmanship. It's even crooked."

"Yes, yes, I know," Margaux said. "This is not the vision I planned for our Cinderella, and I cannot sew myself. I tried but it does not work."

I approached the mannequin and gave it a spin. When I tugged on the tulle, it came off in my hand in a frothy stream.

We stared at each other and laughed.

"I need you, Liliana," Margaux said. "I need your many talents."

"What do you mean?" I asked, sitting on a swivel chair. "We both know I can't dance to save my life."

She took a seat next to me. "You may not have the gift of dance, but you are very talented, indeed."

I must have looked confused.

She smiled broadly. "I want you to design my company's dance costumes. Your mother has shown me your beautiful work, and I will hire you for a proper job.

Her words shocked me. "Wait a minute. Mother . . . showed you? When?"

"Many times while you were at school. She is very, very proud of you."

I folded my arms. "Then why doesn't she ever tell me that? If feels like all I do is disappoint her. Half the time she acts like she's sorry she ever had me."

"Do not ever say that." Margaux shook her head. "It is just her way. She cannot . . . express her love the way you might always hope for. And you are not always the most easy to talk to. But she does love you, very, very much. You just need to talk to her more, and to listen to each other."

My throat tightened as tears came to my eyes. I had stopped letting my mother into my life so very long ago when it all became so difficult.

Our breakdown was as much my fault as hers.

My aunt stroked my hair and clucked her tongue. "You have earned this chance to shine. The creative vision will be all yours. And you can finally share your talents so we all can enjoy your fine designs."

Doubt assailed me. "But it's too much pressure, Aunt Margaux. I can't do this. I don't want to let you down again."

"Ah, but you have never let me down." She smiled, taking my hand in hers. "You can do this, *ma chérie*. But you must first become Cinderella herself, and envision a bright and sparkling future."

56.

Early the next morning, when it was the end of the business day Italy time, I got dressed in my emerald-colored sweater from Bebiane, and touched up my makeup and hair.

When I was satisfied that I'd done the best I could, I drew a deep breath and called my mother from my videophone on my computer, excited to show her my new look.

A secretary I didn't know answered and I stiffened in surprise.

"Adrienne Carracino," the older Italian woman said, barely bothering to look up at the screen. "How may I help you?"

Her statement took the wind out of my sails and I frowned.

"You're not my mom." I sat back in my chair and folded my arms. "Is she there?"

In Italy the office still bustled with corporate activity, with phones ringing and people walking back and forth behind the desk on their way to somewhere I couldn't see.

The woman stared blankly at her keyboard as she typed. "Missus Carracino is very busy right now. Can I help you with something?"

I shrugged at this stranger with the sort-of professional attitude. "How about my dad?"

She finally looked up at the camera. "Are you their daughter? They didn't mention you'd be calling."

I sighed and twisted my new crystal earring. "It was supposed to be a surprise."

Someone off-camera handed her a package and she nodded. Looking back at me, she smiled. "I'll tell them you called."

And with the push of a button, I was summarily dismissed.

57.

It took me until third period to apply the most recent note slipped under my door and not miss the real meaning.

My dearest Liliana,
A lady always appreciates.
Je t'aime,
Grand-mère Camille

Grand-mère wanted me to give thanks.

But I think what she was really saying was to figure out who I was, deep inside. To know myself and be glad.

She wanted me to be the one and only Liliana Carracino, the way nobody else ever could.

Well, I'd show her that the true Lili was strong.

Liliana took charge of her own life.

And she was the one who installed the hidden camera in her locker vents that caught Tyler Jackson red-handed, spraying another disgusting word in glossy paint.

But this was only the beginning of what the true Lili would do.

58.

In detention in one of the senior history classrooms that afternoon, they put me next to Jimmy Barnett, and no amount of pleading would get the monitor to change the seat assignment at shared work tables. He was a grouchy old man named Mr. Zitzelsberger, and he had no sense of humor. At all. His lack of facial expression proved that.

Stuck in the back row together, it took Jimmy all of one minute to start in on me.

He slid me a paper and tried to grab my leg under the table.

I slapped his hand away.

He leaned too close. "My x-ray vision revealed this."

I moved away from him and made the mistake of glancing at the picture he'd drawn.

With perfect curves he'd depicted a full-frontal nude woman with long dark hair, bold nipples and pubic hair.

I let out a gasp and he laughed.

"Even with clothes on, you'll always be naked to me," he hissed.

I scooped up my books and got to my feet.

"Sit, Miss Carracino!" Mr. Zitzelsberger snapped. "You haven't been dismissed."

"I'm changing seats," I told him.

The crabby teacher came down the aisle toward me and stared. "No, you're not. Sit."

I dropped my books back onto the table, saw Jimmy snickering behind his hand, and couldn't take it one second more.

I started to clap, really loud. "Let's give Jimmy Barnett a round of applause, folks. He's quite the sketch artist!"

Kids turned in their seats to stare and started whispering. Zitzelsberger glared at me.

Jimmy froze. “Sit down before you get us both in more trouble!”

My mission to humiliate him wasn’t over. I clapped louder and let out a ferocious whoop and rally cry.

“Step right on up and get in line,” I said with a gesture toward him. “Just ask Jimmy Barnett and he’ll draw your nude portrait, too! Who wants to be first today so he can showcase his anatomy skills?”

A few people laughed.

The room monitor snatched the drawing from the tabletop, stared at it and pointed toward the door. “Get to the principal’s office, Barnett. Now! I’ll deal with you later.”

Reluctantly, Jimmy got to his feet and stormed out.

As the detention quarters fell back into a disturbed hush, I sat down, opened my notebook and started to write about the impact adrenaline has on the human central nervous system.

The stuff surged my system right now, and it made me feel like I could handle just about anything.

59.

Billy Martin tracked me down before lunch the next day. At least I think he did. He just showed up and started walking next to me as we made our way into the cafeteria, not saying a word until I felt like I had to break the ice.

"Hey," I said, hitching the strap of my backpack more firmly on my shoulder.

He nodded, but didn't actually look at me. "Hi."

Behind me, the band crowd was getting rowdy on their way to the auditorium. Somebody squeaked out a riff of clunkers on a trumpet and made me jump.

Billy laughed.

We walked another dozen steps before he finally talked. "You look nice, Lili. Really nice." He cleared his throat and adjusted his baseball cap.

I could see his Adam's apple bobbing.

He gave me a small smile. "You look different, you know?"

Out of the corner of my eye, I swear I saw him blush, and I could feel heat rise in my own cheeks. I touched the brooch on the faded antique shawl I'd embroidered in ribbon to enhance the lines of the damask pattern and played with the fabric's drape across my shoulders. He was making me nervous. "Thanks."

As the band jockeyed for hallway space and the crowd to the cafeteria thickened, our bodies were pushed together until our shoulders touched.

"Maybe . . . "

I turned to look at him walking just inches away, but he was looking at his sneakers. "Maybe what?"

He gave a nod and stole a quick glance at me. "Maybe we could go out sometime?"

A saxophone started wailing right behind me.

His voice was too quiet. "Like to a movie this weekend . . .or something?"

I stopped walking to listen to him, and the girl blaring the saxophone in my ears plowed into me.

By the time I detangled the brass instrument from my backpack strap, Billy Martin was gone.

And I wondered if I'd imagined the whole conversation.

Then I remembered I'd taped it all from the brooch pinning my shawl.

60.

“Thank God for digital recording,” I said to Sophie as we popped the device into an open USB slot in her laptop. We were killing a few minutes before her dance class began, sitting at a picnic table under the trees outside school where the stoners liked to get high at night. Sophie was busy cramming donut holes into her mouth and chugging from a carton of chocolate milk.

Nobody else was in sight.

While we waited for the files to load, I glanced up at her and noticed she was wearing yet another pair of glasses, this time with thin frames in the palest of gold. “When did you start wearing them in school?”

She nodded and put down the milk. “This afternoon, I finally caved. I need them, and that’s all she wrote. No more contacts. End of story. My eyes weren’t meant for them.”

“I’m proud of you, Soph,” I said. “They’re totally you.”

“Take it or leave it,” she said with a shrug. “It’s who I am. You’re inspiring me, Lil!”

Within minutes, I’d called up the file and we’d scanned through the footage I’d recorded until I came to Billy. “I need to listen to what he said again. I couldn’t really hear him.”

The lens was kind of wide angle, but when I had turned toward him, his full face came into view on the screen.

“He’s really cute,” Sophie said. “You should definitely go for it. Then we could double date, like in the old days.”

She burped like a boy and I laughed.

We played the recording back twice, straining to hear over the bleating brass section.

I nodded. “He definitely asked me out. Didn’t he?”

“Yeah,” she said, licking her fingers. “He did.”

I closed the file and shut down the feed. When I popped the microscopic camera back into its frame and reattached it to my shawl, I looked at my friend. "Hey Sophie, you don't think he—"

"I don't think nothing," Sophie said. She stuffed another donut hole into her mouth and chewed noisily.

"You don't think he's only asking me out because of . . . of what he heard. Do you?"

She tried to jam a donut hole into my mouth but I swatted her hand away. She ate it herself and grinned.

"I'm serious, Sophie."

She nodded. "So am I. I think he likes you," she said. "*That's it.*"

I tucked a strand of hair behind my ear. "But the pictures and the rumors. What if--"

She wiped her hands on a napkin and got to her feet. "What if you don't go out with him and you never give yourself a chance to find out?"

61.

On my way home to get my sewing supplies so I could start work on the costumes, I was about to cut through the Ferguson's yard when Joe Sanderson caught up to me.

"We didn't finish what we started," he said, putting his arm around me and pulling me toward him. "I wasn't done talking to you before."

He didn't scare me anymore. Not now.

Not when I had all the power.

My voice was firm. "Joe, I don't want to talk to you. Please take your hands off me."

He dropped his hand but curved it into my waist. "I think we should kiss, right here, right now, and get it over with so we both know what we've been missing."

Without even trying to mask him attempt, he snaked his free hand up my shirt and grabbed at my breast.

"You have no right!" I spun out of his grasp, stumbling forward on the grass. I was losing control. Fast. And I had to get it back. "Do not touch me again. I'm warning you."

He laughed.

"I'm going to go to the principal with this. You'll get suspended," I told him. "Expelled, maybe. You can't keep doing this to me, Joe Sanderson."

He caught up to me and plastered a slobbery kiss on my neck.

"STOP!" I yelled, swinging at him. "I don't want you to touch me!"

"Your word against mine, babe," he said, laughing, hands aloft. "And who're they gonna believe? Star athlete . . . or *slut*? Or maybe that was *whore*. I can't remember. Which name do you go by today?"

I straightened my shawl and brooch. It was now or never.

Showdown time.

"This abuse ends here, right now." My voice was restrained. "I am not a slut. I am not a whore. You and Tyler started those rumors and you know it."

He laughed as he took a step back. "Hey, we just didn't deny it when kids started talking."

"You took those pictures of me when I was walking home in the rain." I put my hands on my hips. "And I know those phone calls and horrible emails came from the three of you."

He shrugged. "You just try to prove it, Carracino."

Oh, but I could. His cockiness was exactly what I wanted. So I played it.

"Hey, Joe? Man up for once in your life," I challenged. "Admit it. You've done nothing but harass me every day for months. At home and at school. Does it make you feel big and strong to make a girl feel this way? To make her feel low and worthless while you walk all over her?"

"I'm walking now," he said, taking a few steps away.

I sucked in a deep breath and held it.

But then he turned back around, and stared straight at my breasts.

He licked his lips. "With juicy tits like yours, it's a whole lotta fun."

On that parting note, Joe was gone.

And I felt one hundred percent victorious.

62.

At Kerry's Cottage, I finally had a real budget to shop, and I'd brought my sketchpad full of ideas.

When I rang the bell to walk inside, she looked up at me then did a hard double take. "*Lili?*"

I smiled. "Guess what? I'm here to spend real money. And it isn't even mine!"

"Great shawl," Kerry said, nodding. "Let me take a look at that."

I walked over to her and unfastened the camera brooch, slipping it into my bag with the receiver. I'd yet to watch the footage of Joe, but I knew it was really strong.

"You are looking good, missy," she said. "Absolutely love that color on you."

The emerald green in my sweater played well against my darker skin. Of all the colors I'd tried on at Bebi's, it had been my favorite. "I love it, too."

I handed her my shawl and she smiled. "You leave me for a week, and look what happens. You grow up overnight."

"Had to happen sooner or later," I said, feeling really proud of myself as I gave her a twirl. I wandered over to the wall of chiffon and began touching the fabric to get a sense of its movement and drape.

Kerry joined me by the bolts of angelic fabric. "So, is this the new you? The hair up and the makeup and the perfectly tailored clothes?"

The new me? Was it, really?

I already knew the answer, and there was no going back to the way I was. Ever.

For the life of me, I could not imagine ever wearing again the dead rapper's pants or a sweatshirt meant for a 450-pound man.

I gave Kerry a huge smile. "Yeah, I think it is the new me."

"Well, good. It's about time you came to your senses." She draped the shawl over my shoulders and smiled. "But you've been holding out on me and I'm officially mad."

My brows pulled tight. "Why? What do you mean?"

She picked up an end of the shawl and let her fingers drift over the multi-layered embroidery I'd done. "You've got the gift, Lili. This handwork is good. Really, really intricate."

I glanced at her quilt in the window then waved her off. "Nah. You're the one with the real talent. I'm just learning."

She crossed her arms. "Then why are you here to spend somebody else's budget?"

I shrugged. "My Aunt Margaux wants me to design the costumes for *Cinderella*. She hired me, kind of like a real job."

Kerry stared me down. "She believes in you."

"And my friend, Sophie, wants me to make her dress for the after party."

"Two clients already?" Kerry said with a laugh. "That should tell you what they think of you."

"Yeah," I said. "I guess it does."

I nodded slowly, glancing at the pencil drawing on the first page of my sketchbook. The costume might not be spectacular . . . yet. But my rags-to-riches princess was beautiful. Especially on the inside.

A big smile brightened Kerry's face. "Don't guess about what you have to offer, Lili. *Know*. So show me your ideas and let's get started. You don't have much time before the big night, hmm?"

As I picked up the pale silver chiffon, I did know.

I would shine.

63.

We dropped Tony off at football practice and made our way to Asia House, where Sophie's family had invited Grand-mère and me to dinner.

"Have you ever had something like this happen to you?" I asked. We took the exit from the highway.

In the half-darkness of the October night, she nodded. "When you have fame, *les insignifiants* will always look for something to tarnish your good name. When they cannot find a scrap, they invent one." She shook her head as she turned a corner and bumped the front tire against a curb.

"Did you know that a magazine once said I must be a man because I was so tall?" she laughed. "And the newspapers reported that I had forty lovers at a single time. Forty! Can you not imagine how tired I would be with that many men?"

I laughed, but gossip like that wasn't a joke. It hurt. It always hurt.

And I knew just how much.

She ran a yellow light to turn a corner. I braced for impact, but we slid through the intersection miraculously unscathed.

"I have found it is best to ignore the affront," she told me. "A lady always knows who she is, Liliana. That is enough to carry on."

Grand-mère pulled the Mercedes into a parking space, avoided a squirrel but hit a bush, then put it into reverse to drift back into position. My mother's car had seriously suffered while she was on Italian soil and would probably need a whole lot of body work and a new set of tires by the time she got back in two weeks.

But my grandmother was nothing if not earnest. At least she made an effort to do what I needed. And tonight, I needed a little levity. The Fishkins were the ticket.

"Be prepared," I told my grandmother. "You probably won't get to finish a sentence the whole meal. The Fishkins aren't exactly like our family."

"It will be another adventure for us both," Grand-mère said. She shut off the ignition and dropped the keys into her jet-beaded clutch. "Let us be wildly entertaining, yet polite."

"There they are," I said, pointing to the animated group walking toward the door. "As you always say, hold your head high and hang on for dear life. It's going to be a bumpy ride."

My grandmother laughed. "I may say many things, but I do not say that."

"Well, I added the last part, but it's good advice tonight. The Fishkins can be a handful if you're not used to it. But they're really great people."

She smiled and smoothed her hair as she checked her reflection in the rearview mirror. "But I shall be on my very best behavior and make you proud."

I found it funny that she was concerned by how I'd feel, *about her*. "You always make me proud, Grand-mère." I paused, thinking. "You always have."

She touched my cheek and smiled. "And you are a very sweet girl, *ma chérie. Merci.*"

We got out of the car, smoothed our clothes and waved to them.

Sophie ran to our side and greeted my grandmother with a warm hug.

"Great dress," she said to me.

I smiled in the half-light of the parking lot and showed off the chocolate square-neck sheath that hugged my body. "It's my go-anywhere dress, as Bebiane said. Dress it up, or dress it down. All depends on the accessories."

"I approve of the chunky necklace." She spoke in a whisper to us bothand pushed back her glasses. "But watch yourselves. The 'rents are in rare form. Murray just won a major sale so he's ready to celebrate, but don't ask about my Ma's heart, godforbid. It was just *agita*, and if you mention it we're all doomed to an entire meal discussing her most heinous bodily functions."

Grand-mère smiled but looked confused.

I touched her arm. "Sophie's dad sells big computer systems, but her Ma is a bit of a hypochondriac with a high need for attention."

"That's an understatement," Sophie said with a laugh.

Grand-mère nodded and we moved forward as a threesome through the shining red double doors of the restaurant and into the dim light.

We stood stock still, watching the exchange.

"Put us at the table over by the window," Sylvia Fishkin was instructing the *maître d'* with a gesture, "right over there between that lovely family and those boys with those funny eyeglasses."

"I'll get a chill," Bubbe Ruth interrupted and shook her head at her daughter. "I'm just saying."

"But you brought a little sweater," Sylvia retorted to her stone-faced mother. "Oh, never mind. Just put us at that other round table, over there by the woman with that horrible yellow jacket. God, what a color!"

Bubbe clutched her chest. "The table by the kitchen with the swinging doors? You won't be thanking me when they spill wonton soup on your dress."

"You're right," Sylvia said, nodding at her mother. "This is silk, and you know they have a heck of a time dry cleaning grease stains. Last time they left a ring, and I had to demand a refund, if you can believe it! They were planning to charge me anyway, but I said—"

"*Oy,* Lois, can we just take a seat already? My feet are killing me," Murray Fishkin said, running his hand over his bald head a few times. He pushed back his wire-rimmed glasses. When he turned to see us coming, he grabbed at the chance to escape. "It's the same thing every time with these two. *Meshugass*, I tell you. Always talking *bubkis*. You see what I married into?"

He got his first good look at Grand-mère in her fitted black dress, sheer black stockings and ultra-high heels, looking strikingly beautiful and serene. With her blonde hair piled high on her head in a perfectly sleek twist, she gave off an air of elegance that seemed painfully out of place in the restaurant with the cardboard take-out boxes lining the counter behind the cashier.

The expression on Murray's face was priceless.

"Well, hello," he said, nodding up at her and standing a little straighter. "You are a tall one, aren't you?"

Gracious as ever, Grand-mère held out her hand to him. "I am Camille Le Jeune. It is my pleasure."

"Murray Fishkin." He kissed her hand chivalrously, like they do in the movies, but his glasses nearly slipped off his nose.

Sophie and I giggled.

The normally talkative Murray studied her speechlessly while over his shoulder his wife and mother-in-law were directing the waiters to rearrange the tables to accommodate us at the restaurant's center.

"It is so very kind of you to invite us to join you this evening, Mr. Fishkin," my grandmother said.

"Call me Murray, please. French, are you? I've been to Paris," he said. "Didn't think much of those snooty Frenchmen and their attitudes, but you ladies are a sight for sore eyes."

My grandmother dazzled him with her smile.

I leaned over to Sophie and whispered. "Is Murray actually blushing?"

She snickered and took off her glasses to polish them on her napkin."Oh, yeah. He's crushing."

I smiled. "Ah, the amazing power of beauty."

64.

Ten minutes later, I'd made the proper introductions all around. We were finally seated with ten-page menus in hand, having moved tables twice because of the air conditioner draft and the parking lot noise, finally ending up right where we started.

Now settled, Sophie's Ma finally paid attention to her guests.

Her eyebrow arched with interest when she noticed how her husband was openly admiring my grandmother.

"Lili," she said, staring pointedly at me to divert his gaze. "You don't look half bad. I wish my Sophie would wear her hair up like that."

Behind her frames, Sophie rolled her eyes. "Ma, please. You know my ears stick out if I wear my hair up. And with glasses, it looks even worse."

"Oh, pish," her mother grumbled.

"The girl looks just fine like she always does," Murray said, finally turning to look away from my grandmother. "Will you leave her alone, already? Always nagging, this one here."

When they delivered bowls of crispy fried noodles, he immediately reached for a handful, only to get scolded by his ever-watchful wife.

"Murray, you need to watch your cholesterol."

His mother-in-law chimed in. "Do you want to be up all night with gas pains from those?"

He reached for the noodles anyway and deposited them on his bread plate. "I'm starving to death here!"

"Never listens, that boy," Bubbe Ruth said with a shake of her head.

“I don’t want to say I told you so,” Sylvia said, “but you know I will. Right when I’m handing you the bottle of Pepto at two a.m.”

Murray ignored them and turned to me. “So, Lili, tell me. Have you thought any more about Harvard?"

I shook my head. “I’m only a freshman, Mister Fishkin. I’ve still got plenty of time before I apply.”

I didn’t want to tell him that I had a lot of make-up work to do to finish out the school year with a decent record. I was making progress, but not fast enough for my taste. Harvard might be a long shot.

He shook his head. “Never too early to start planning ahead, right Camille?”

My grandmother put down her tea cup. “*Absolutement.*”

He swallowed hard. “You just call me when you’re ready, Lili, and I’ll put in a good word.” He nodded. “I know some people.”

“And what if she wants to go to Yale?” Sophie needled to get a rise out of him.

He slapped his hands on his head. “You’re killing me with talk like that!”

Sophie let out a laugh. “You’re so predictable, Dad.”

Murray Fishkin was a Harvard Business School legacy, and he’d pushed me toward his alma mater from the first day he met me. My own father hadn’t given much thought to where I’d go to college, I was sure. He just assumed I would, and that he would pay for it like everything else in my life, and that I’d make the right decision. He was far too hands-off for discussions like that.

But what if I wanted them to help me choose? To get involved with such a major decision? Could they?

“Perhaps Liliana might consider schooling at La Sorbonne University,” Grand-mère suggested. “In Paris.”

I stared at her. “Me? Go to college in Paris?”

Murray looked aghast. “Overseas? Do they even have a good program?”

“*Mais oui,*” she said with a smile and a nod. “To study *design à la mode* and become a proper *couturier*.”

"Fashion design?" I asked. I'd never thought of it as a career. But the possibility intrigued me, I had to admit.

She smiled and spoke quietly. "I know many people who could help you, *ma chérie,* to open the right doors and opportunities."

She did.

Fashion was *her* world, and she was offering to share it with me.

The waiter arrived to take our order, and the haggling began while I tried to imagine myself with my own fashion label and a shop near the famous Faubourg Saint-Honoré by the houses of Dior and Chanel and Hermès.

"Let me have the egg drop soup, but can you make it with extra green onion?" Sylvia asked, "but I want them on the side, and chopped up really fine."

"It's fabulous that way, it is," Bubbe Ruth said to no one in particular. "I'll have the same. And a plate of the egg foo yung, but go light on the egg. If it's scrambled, it's no good. I hate that."

"Is it hot?" Sylvia asked the waiter with a pinched expression.

"The egg drop?" he asked, confused.

"Spicy hot, or hot hot?" Bubbe asked her daughter.

"Spicy hot, of course!" Sylvia said to her mom. She clutched her ribs. "Ever since my gall bladder attack last winter in Aruba, I can't do the spicy, unless it's really good Mexican, and then only if they don't use too many of those tiny green peppers. *Oy*, those will be the death of me yet!"

Murray rolled his eyes and the poor waiter looked hopelessly confused as his pen hovered mid-air above the order pad. "Huh?"

"Just bring them the soup and the egg foo yung. We'll have the cashew chicken," Sophie ordered. "And a couple plates of eggrolls. And a big platter of pork fried rice with extra peas for the table."

"Sounds good to me," Murray said, folding his menu closed.

Sophie looked at my grandmother. "What do you want, Grand-mère?"

Grand-mère was a very good sport. She turned to Murray and smiled. "Perhaps you will order for me?"

Murray was dumbfounded. "*Anything*?"

She nodded at him, and I think Murray fell a little more in love.

"Please. If you would be so kind."

Bubbe Ruth and Sylvia were finally paying attention to their intercontinental dinner companion.

"You really shouldn't have the General Tso's chicken, unless you like the Szechuan peppers they sneak into every bite here," Sylvia told her in a conspiratorial whisper behind her diamonded hand.

"She might want to burn her mouth on the food," Bubbe said with a shrug. "We don't know how French people eat."

"But the General Tso's is much better at Hunan Palace," she said, putting her hand on her mother's arm. "I should know. I've been eating it there for years. It's absolutely to die for."

"Maybe we should go there," Bubbe Ruth suggested. "We haven't gotten our food yet, and these water glasses don't look none too clean. I think I saw lipstick. Isn't that a smudge?"

She held the glass up to the light for her daughter to inspect.

Sylvia gasped. "You're right, Ma. Don't touch it. Murray, let's—"

"Enough!" he barked. "We're staying!"

Turning to the waiter, he ordered my grandmother a dish of beef lo mein and shrugged in apology.

The waiter hustled back to the kitchen with a mixed-up order pad and a huge sigh.

In the hush that followed, my thoughts crystallized and I knew I had to seize the opportunity to talk to Sophie's father. He was a sharp-as-nails negotiator who always managed to get what he wanted and more. And right now I wanted to pick his brain and see if what I was planning made any sense.

"Mister Fishkin, I have a question for you," I said. "Hypothetical, of course."

"Sure, sure," he said, nodding. "Ask away."

"Say a person's been having some real trouble. At school, maybe. With some kids," I posed. "Boys."

Sophie put down her glass of water and paid attention. My grandmother shifted in her seat to hear me better.

"Tell me more," he said, sneaking a few crispy noodles into his mouth when Sylvia was turned toward the fish tank and talking about the bubble-eyed goldfish having ick and swim bladder disease, while her mother inspected the napkin for somebody else's leftover crumbs.

But I focused my thoughts on Murray. "Well, say these kids are doing things that are really bad to her."

Murray leaned forward, concern etched into the hard lines on his face. "How bad? Did these boys hurt her?"

He seemed to know I was talking about myself. I could tell just by the look in his eyes behind those wire-rimmed glasses of his. And that made it somehow easier to continue.

I shrugged. "Not really in a physical way, but yeah, let's say they did hurt her. Emotionally." I paused, catching my breath. "A lot. And they've left some deep scars that are pretty hard to heal."

He nodded and pushed his glasses back on his nose. "I'm listening."

"So, let's say this girl wanted to stop them so they couldn't do it anymore. To anyone else."

He smiled, sat back and started talking in a gravelly voice as he adjusted an imaginary tie. "You want I should break their knees for you?"

Sophie snorted. "Is that supposed to be Brando, Dad?" She poked me in the arm. "He does the worst Godfather impression I've ever seen, don't you think?" To him, she said, "It's really bad, Dad. You should quit it before you embarrass yourself."

I twisted my crystal earring while Grand-mère, sitting next to me, put a hand on my back.

"Go on, Lili," she said softly. "You can ask him. He will know what to do."

I looked up at her. As much as she loved her son-in-law, she knew my father's limitations, and she was all for tapping into resources to get the job done. She'd proven that to me this week.

Grand-mère gave me a small smile. "It is all right."

I turned back to Murray. "Well, what if she wants to make these kids learn a big lesson? So that they can't hurt someone else the way they hurt her?"

Sylvia and Bubbe Ruth were suddenly unnaturally quiet as they gave me their full attention.

I reached for my water glass and took a gulp as I listened to the distant clink of silverware and the faded whispers of other people's conversations.

Murray folded his arms across his starched shirt and watched me with fatherly concern. "Maybe this girl could go to the principal?"

I licked my lips. "Let's say she did and they told her to solve it herself or turn them all in?"

"Dad, turning them in isn't an option," Sophie said. "It wouldn't change much in the long run." She glanced nervously at me. "Let's just say."

He smiled and leaned forward. "And I'm guessing that this girl would rather take matters into her own hands?"

My breath came out in a rush of air. "No doubt about it. She's got some proof, but it's not enough. Making them learn not to do it again would be infinitely more satisfying."

Grand-mère stroked my back with a reassuring hand.

Murray laughed. "Well, if she were my daughter, I think maybe I'd tell her to find a way for the whole school to know about what these kids did. Show them for the kind of boys they really are."

I thought of my brooch cam and the locker surveillance tape.

And regardless of the outcome, I was absolutely certain about what I needed to do.

65.

The next day after school while Grand-mère was folding towels in the laundry room, I nearly got on my knees to beg for forgiveness.

"Tony, I need your help." I pleaded with him as I entered his sanctuary, the self-proclaimed "man cave" at the top of the stairs. The room was filled to the walls with old toys he couldn't bear to part with, mountains of Legos and Bionicles, sports apparatus of all sorts, and shelves of gleaming trophies engraved with his name and stats. My mother told our housekeepers to keep out on cleaning day, or enter strictly at their own risk. Right now, the room smelled vaguely of Cheetos and sweat socks – not a particularly good combination.

He looked pouty. "Why should I help you?"

My brother glared at me as he flopped back on his leather sofa littered with comic books. He started tossing an old tennis ball at the ceiling and apparently didn't notice the brown, smudgy rings he was leaving in the paint. Or he didn't, in fact, care.

I sat next to him, put my bag on the floor and gave him a hug against his will. "I know you love me. And because when I explain what I've been going through these past few months, you might even feel a teensy bit sorry for me."

He caught the ball and held it. With a few shifty glances at my face, he spoke softly. "Are you talking about . . . the pictures?"

I sat back, stunned and feeling sick. "What did you see?"

He shrugged.

"Tell me, Tony," I said. "It's okay."

He got up and started throwing the ball against the wall, oblivious to the extent of my embarrassment.

I spoke in a firm voice. “Stop that, please. This is important.”

Letting the ball go still, he turned to face me. “Somebody in my class sent me an email they got about you off their brother’s computer. It wasn’t very . . . nice.”

I sighed. “I’m really sorry you had to see that, Tony.”

He shrugged. “Who took that picture?”

“A few boys have been harassing me, pretty much all the time. They did it without me knowing it that night I got caught in the rain and broke Mom’s vase. And you saw how they used it.”

My brother got red in the face. “They the same guys who were all over you that day I wanted to kick their butts?”

I nodded. “Yeah. Those were the ones. And I hate that we’re even having this conversation.”

“Well, those guys suck,” he said, crossing his arms. “They’re nothing but stupid buttheads.”

I nodded. “That’s why I need your help.”

He came to sit beside me. “I don’t know what I can do. They’re a lot bigger than me. If I punched them they’d flatten me.”

I gave him a huge smile and put my hand on his shoulder. “I don’t need you to fight them with your fists, but I do need you to help me fight. And I’ll make you a deal, too.”

He looked up at me. “You’ll do all my chores for a year?”

I laughed. “Nice try. I already do most of them.”

He grinned impishly and I ruffled his hair.

Then I leaned closer to him. “I promise to get you the biggest, bestest cheering section for your football playoffs than any other kid on the Tigers. You deserve it, Tony. And I won’t let you down.”

His face brightened. “You mean it? You’d do that? For me?”

I nodded and held up three fingers. “Scout’s honor. But you have to agree to take what I give you.”

“Give me?” he asked, confused. “I thought you wanted something *from* me.”

Instead of telling him, I reached into the bag I’d brought and began to lay out the devices in a row between us.

"Hidden cameras, microscopic recorders, spy stuff and all that. It's all yours."

His face lit with excitement. "This is so cool! Where'd you get this stuff?"

"From a friend's shop downtown," I said. "And imagine the football videos you can make with these. You'll be the only kid in the league with helmet cams, sound effects and all sorts of neat stuff. You'll be a real director making your own Play of the Week reels."

He was on his feet and smacking his hands together. "All right. That's the best, Lili! Thanks! What do you want me to do?"

I sat back and crossed my legs. "We need to make a video and post it online, and it's got to be really, really awesome."

He grinned and gave me a high five. "Let's do it!"

And for once it felt like my brother and I were on the same team.

66.

"Stop wriggling, will you? I don't have time for this," I said through a mouth full of pins as I fitted the muslin dress pattern to Sophie's thin frame in the studio my Aunt Margaux had created for me near the practice room. Already, it was crowded with the tools of my trade. Bolts of fabric, scissors and pins, sketches of costume variations taped to the wall.

But I would not show Sophie the design for her dress. I was kneeling and trying to work out just the right hemline, experimenting with different effects.

She kicked her leg out with a flourish and I almost stabbed her.

"You'll be a pin cushion if you're not careful!"

"I'm too excited!" Sophie cried, dancing in place. "It'll be so good. Adam is coming to opening night. And he said he wants to pick me up before the performance so my parents can take pictures of us, which you know they'll take a million until we're blinded by the flashes, and then he's going to take me home after the party, just like a real date."

"It *is* a real date, you loon, if you don't count the fact that you'll be lighting up the stage with your magnificence for half the night," I assured her. "He'll be beyond impressed."

"From your lips to God's ears, I should be so lucky," she said, hands over her heart.

I laughed. "You don't watch it you'll turn into your mother, Sophie Fishkin," I said as I re-pinned the hemline for the third time. "You're starting to sound exactly like her."

She nudged me with her knee until I looked up. "I could say the same about you, you know, Lil. You're turning into a regular workhorse. A real woman on a fashion mission."

Me? Like my mother?

Maybe I was, just a little. Maybe we had more in common than I thought.

"I'm having a great time," I said. "Seriously. This is more fun that I've ever had, and you get to wear one of my creations! And my grades are getting much better, too!"

But a big part of me still felt empty. Even though I couldn't gauge what her reaction might be, I wanted my mother to see what I'd been doing in this small studio, to be proud of the work I'd been doing without her guidance.

I wanted to share my life with her again.

"Between my rehearsal schedule and your work hours I hardly see you anymore," Sophie complained. "How much more make-up work do you have to do?"

"Finishing up my last social studies paper tonight on the formation of bonds within human communities. It's really deep. Want to read it?"

"*No*. But are you almost done with that stupid project you've been filling your nights with? And when are you even going to tell me what it is? I'm going into Lil withdrawal over here! *Oy*, the palpitations!"

I thought about my project, which had turned into a family endeavor. When I told Grand-mère and Tony what I planned to do, they were shocked, but eventually they came around to my way of thinking. The promised to help me, and they had, every night after dinner.

We'd filmed interviews. We'd made slides. We'd compiled audio clips.

We were almost ready, and what I had to say would change lives at Middleton. Or at least that was my hope. All I knew for sure was that I was *finally* feeling better.

But right now, I had to focus.

"I've still got to sew your dress and get the costumes done." I sat back on my heels while she gave my pattern a spin. "And there's so much more I want to do with the designs. They just haven't captured the look I'm going after yet."

I glanced over to wall of raw classical costumes, each perfectly shaped and stitched, but lacking a certain spark.

Right now they looked ordinary, and I hated what they represented.

I didn't want my costumes to be like everyone else's.

I wanted them to bear my creative signature.

My personal style.

I needed them to tell people something about me. . . as a designer. As Liliana Carracino.

"They look great," she said. "Why are you being so critical?"

"They'll be even better." I nodded up at Sophie. "I don't know what it is yet, but the final idea will come to me. I just need to break through."

67.

Mrs. Alban, the lunchroom supervisor, was busy stapling collated papers on her desk when I knocked on her office door.

The first thing I noticed was the neat row of family pictures on the wall behind her. She and her kids, with a husband beside her and a golden retriever at their feet, smiling for the camera like any other all-American family.

We'd assumed certain things because of her super short hair, stocky build and strict demeanor, but we'd never taken time to get to know her, or even ask.

We just made up our own truth . . . and we were so wrong.

And after intercepting yet another note being passed around my social studies class about me, I knew firsthand how much those kinds of rumors could hurt.

"Can I help you, young lady?" she asked as she shuffled a stack of stapled papers into a neat pile.

I cleared my throat, feeling sick to my stomach that I'd misjudged this woman so badly. I knew then that I was guilty of exactly the same behavior that people had inflicted on me. And the realization was horrifying.

"Are those your kids?" I asked, pointing at the pictures.

She glanced at the boy and the girl in matching rugby shirts. "Yes, they are. Madison and Everett."

I nodded, feeling so incredibly ashamed of myself, but she was staring at me. I had to say something, and I couldn't change the past.

But I could change the future.

"Miz Alban, you're the faculty advisor for assemblies, right?"

She piled the papers into her out tray. "That's right. What do you need?" She laughed. "Extra tickets for family and friends?"

I felt wobbly, but I knew I needed to finish what I'd started, to remember why I came. I just couldn't do it standing up or I might collapse. "Can I sit for a minute?"

"You okay?" She nodded to an empty seat and leaned back in her own chair.

"Umm," I started, shaking my head and letting the sound trail off. "I'd like to be involved with the next one. The assembly, I mean. There's a special project I've been kind of working on that I'd, umm, like to share with the school."

"We don't usually ask for student participation." Mrs. Alban pushed up the sleeves of her sweatshirt and gave me an appraising glance while shaking her head. "And I'm afraid our speaker roster is full, Miss . . . ?"

"Carracino," I volunteered. "Liliana Carracino. I'm a freshman. I was hoping you could make an exception."

"I'm afraid not." She shook her head. "So, is there something else I can help you with?"

Closing my eyes for a second, I swallowed my fears and plunged in head first. "This next time the topic is bullying, isn't it?"

When she nodded, I drew a deep breath.

"Then you'll want to talk to me." I sighed as I met her concerned gaze. "You're talking about every single day of my life."

Mrs. Alban sat back and studied me carefully.

"So, Lili, tell me your story."

68.

My mother called after dinner the next day, and as soon as I heard her voice, I felt my body go tense.

"Have you been very good, *ma chérie*?"

I leaned against the kitchen wall and slid to the floor. "Define 'good.'"

She laughed. "I do not know. Normal, I suppose."

"Normal?" I repeated.

Had my days been normal? Did she even know what normal was for me? The headaches, the anxiety and the stress that school caused me on a daily basis?

Then again, had I ever given her the chance to know?

I'd shut my mother out of my real life, keeping everything important from her, kept our relationship superficial. I'd made it too easy for her to devote her energies to work, but now I wanted more, I *needed* more, and I didn't want a long-distance relationship with the woman who brought me into the world.

"Lili?" she asked tenderly. "Are you all right? What is wrong, my darling?"

I blinked back the tears of regret for the relationship that had been so strained between us. "I think I just miss you. That's all."

"*Ma chérie*, we miss you desperately, but our trip is almost over."

"That's not what I mean, Mom."

My mother and I could be so much more. So much better together.

I just had to start by letting her in.

I swiped at my eyes. "So tell me how's it going for you and Dad?"

"*Très bien,*" she said. "We are wrapping up the negotiations and should finish our work here very soon. And

I promise you, I will be home to watch you perform in *Cinderella*. I cannot wait to see you dance again!"

Grand-mère came into the kitchen and folded her arms to watch me.

I blew out a steadying breath and knew that I couldn't lie to my mother any longer. I couldn't keep hedging by changing the subject or letting the conversation drop. "About dance. . . ."

My mother's voice was excited. "How are the rehearsals going? You never did tell me which role you were assigned, and Margaux will not say a word, that minx!"

"Mom." I closed my eyes and prayed for strength as I killed her excitement.

"Yes, *ma chérie*?"

I bit my lip, weighed my options, and plunged into the truth about my choices. "I don't dance anymore. I'm not in the production."

I heard her sharp intake of breath. "*Pourquoi?* Did something happen?"

If she was disappointed in me, I couldn't tell. Her voice was too soft.

With a deep sigh, I looked up at my grandmother and smiled as I told my mother the very first truth I'd learned about myself.

"I'm not a dancer, Mom," I said. "A lot of stuff has been going on here since you've been gone. Things you should know about."

And while my grandmother looked on and smiled, my mother and I finally really talked.

And it was very, very good.

69.

The daily abuse from the Middleton masses continued at an unrelenting pace as the hallway shouts got louder and the emails got more intense, but the more involved I became with projects outside of school, the more my shell had hardened to my situation. The harassment was just one more pressure I had to deal with.

Tyler could walk past me and try to grab whichever of my breasts was closest to him.

Joe could corner me in the hallways and whisper lewd suggestions while he tried to rub up against me.

They could both follow me until my neighbors got suspicious and came out of their houses, and they could make the obscene calls that I'd begun to record to eventually play for the police, and they could gang up on me and crowd me and belittle me and chip away at my self-esteem in front of others. Through all their degradation, they could try to make my life a living hell.

But I would get through this phase and move beyond their abusive behavior. I'd begun to separate myself from the harassment, to transport myself into a different zone.

And I always remembered what my grandmother told me.

A lady knows who she is.

I was *not* going to remain their victim.

And at the end of all this, I would be someone new.

Just like Cinderella after the ball, I would fully transform into the woman I was supposed to be. At least that was the grand plan.

But standing at my locker listening to a steady stream of whispers, I tried to convince myself that total transformation takes time, and convincing people you were someone different than they thought could require a whole lot of sparkles from the fairy godmother wand.

Twelve hate notes had been stuffed into my locker today, each of them obnoxiously rude and mean, and each of them attacking me or my body on an even more personal level than the last.

Steeling my nerves, I took a steadying breath and gathered the notes into the folder in my leather backpack.

Then, I smiled as I removed and wrapped up the last surveillance camera for the data to be processed and our video to be wrapped.

My perpetrators would have their day of notoriety, too. I'd put them into the spotlight and see how they liked it.

Somebody tapped me on the shoulder, and I turned to find Billy Martin standing there.

"Hi, Billy," I said, smiling up at him as he adjusted his baseball cap.

"Hey, Lili." He blushed. "I was wondering if you wanted to . . . umm . . . walk with me for awhile?"

I slipped on a jacket and wrapped my scarf around my neck. As I adjusted the folds to showcase the embroidery, I smiled. "I'm going downtown to work."

He nodded as he watched me pull on my red leather gloves. "That's cool. Fall ball is almost over, and coach cancelled practice today."

Sophie and Adam came into view behind him, and Sophie was giving me a huge thumbs up while Adam nodded. I tried to ignore them both, soI smiled at this nervous boy who'd been quietly shadowing me for weeks.

"Then walk me to work?"

"Sure." Billy Martin grinned. When we headed for the door, he placed his hand protectively on the small of my back.

"Are you going to the football playoffs?" I asked as he led me outside.

"I'll be there," he said. "My little brother's pumped for a win."

I felt Billy's touch, gentle, reassuring . . . protective.

And I smiled and leaned back against Billy's hand.

70.

The last six texts I'd sent to my father about coming home for Tony's playoff game went unanswered, but another check had arrived in the mail for Tony and me to "buy something nice."

My father's hands-off definition of fatherhood was wearing on me, and right now my brother needed more from his dad.

We both needed *him*, to be here for us, emotionally.

My brother and I deserved our father's attention, and not just his money.

I took the phone out into the backyard where my brother wouldn't hear, and called my father after school. Dried leaves blew in crispy eddies across the lawn, swirling up the last bits of a season that had not been kind to me. As winter approached, I knew that life would be different, so very different, from this moment forward.

A lady knows what she wants and is not afraid to ask for it.

My father's secretary answered and tried to put me off with the standard "he's very busy today" line.

"I'm sorry, Miss . . . Nolomoglia, is it?" I asked as sweetly as I could.

"That is right," the woman said distractedly over the backdrop of corporate noise.

I could hear her typing. "Can you stop what you're doing and type a really important note to my father, please? And can you make one hundred percent sure you deliver it to him personally? *Today?*"

I waited, and the secretary finally responded.

She sighed. "What would you like me to tell him?"

I drew a breath. "Tell him it's Lili calling. His daughter."

She typed. "Yes?"
I exhaled, feeling relieved.
"And tell him that if he cares about being a father, he'll be home on Saturday afternoon by noon. His son and daughter need him in their life."

71.

Digital photographs of the collection I'd created for Aunt Margaux's dance troupe were hanging on my bedroom wall. The costumes for Cinderella were practically done. Technically, they were fine. I'd added bits of lace and hand-stitched sequins to catch the stage lights as the dancers did their pirouettes, but I still wasn't pleased.

These outfits didn't say anything about Cinderella and what she endures to find herself at the end.

Now the afternoon light was fading as I manically paced back and forth in my room, desperately trying to figure out how to improve what I'd sewn. I nearly tripped over one of the black bags of old clothes I'd emptied from my closet.

Looking into the castoffs, I shook my head. The clothes I'd chosen to wear for so long were such threadbare rags. With a deep sigh, I sat on the floor and spread the neck of the bag, reaching inside to pull out a handful of cloth.

The garments in my hands were faded, worn out, blend-into-the-wall dull like the girl I had tried so hard to be.

I smiled. I could never go back to being that girl.

The sunlight shifted and caught a glimmer in the corner to draw my eye toward the pair of shoes my mother had made for me.

Simple, beautiful and elegant in ivory and mother of pearl.

They were my very own glass slippers. Step into those shoes and become someone different.

I glanced at the dull fabrics in my hand again and noticed the sharp contrast between the two phases of my life.

An idea clicked and I shot to my feet, dumping the clothes back into the garbage bag and grabbing as many bags as I could carry.

Excitement ripped through me as my heart began to race.

Running to the hall, I threw open the door and shouted. “Grand-mère, get the car! We need to leave right away! And call Aunt Margaux to let us into the studio!”

72.

Mrs. Russell was organizing patterns in the sewing room supply closet when I found her.

"Oh hi, Lili. Aren't you supposed to be at the assembly?" she asked as she flipped through the bulging paper packets and rearranged them by size. "I thought I saw the crowds headed that way."

"It starts in a few minutes." I nodded. "But I was hoping you would come with me."

She put down the patterns and paid attention. "Is something special going on?"

I smiled at her. "Yeah. It kind of involves you."

She looked surprised. "*Me*? I don't have anything to do with assemblies."

"This time, it's because of something you said." I put my hand on her arm and pulled her toward the door. "And I don't want you to miss it."

73.

“Ladies and gentlemen take your seats,” Mrs. Alban said, tapping the microphone to get the crowd’s attention. “We’ve got a busy morning ahead of us.”

I stood at the back of the auditorium with Mrs. Russell at my side, too nervous to sit. My teacher studied me, and I gave her a smile.

“Thanks for coming, Mrs. Russell,” I said quietly. “You’ve always been there for me. And I just want to tell you that I appreciate it.”

She gave me a hug. “You’re a very special girl, Lili. It’s been a pleasure to watch you blossom through the years. And I’m so glad you’re getting back on track.”

“That I am,” I said quietly. “That I am.”

I nodded and caught Sophie’s eye behind her glasses. She and Adam were sitting a few rows ahead of me, holding hands. Turns out, he needed glasses, too. Even Sophie had grown this past month. She set aside vanity for practicality. Now she didn’t think twice about wearing glasses to school.

I was really proud of my best friend.

She gave me a questioning expression, and I nodded toward the stage until she turned around again.

Mrs. Alban’s booming voice sounded on the loudspeakers. “As you all know, we have been delving into the many facets of a person’s character. Those elements unique *to you*."

A few kids in the crowd groaned and conversations began.

She held up her hand. “Instead of the usual presentation on honesty or integrity and another lecture by one of our staff, I’ve decided to share with you a video I discovered last night on a popular video website. Even though the individuals you’ll see are not named, and some of their faces are concealed, I think this piece will give you some incredible insight into the true meaning of a person's character." She paused. "And while you watch this, I want you to ask yourselves two important questions."

Murmurs rippled through the crowd.

"Are you the victim?"

The word hung in the air as the murmurs got louder.

"Or are you the guilty one?"

I held my breath until the music started to play and the video projected. My grandmother's beautiful face filled the screen. She was dressed in a silk blouse and jewels, sitting at a table by the window in our kitchen where Tony and I had filmed her. Behind her, framed copies of her more famous advertisements and photographs lined the sill, including the nude one for Balcroix diamonds.

Guys whistled and hooted obnoxiously.

"What a MILF," someone yelled.

Another called out, "I'd do her!"

I slowly exhaled and clenched my fists, praying that this would work. It had to.

My grandmother's voice was lyrical, soft and French as she spoke.

In the world of fashion and beauty, people feel they know you.

To live life in the public eye as I have is to know that they believe they have the right to judge you, as a person.

A bunch of people shushed others to calm the chatter.

But I am here to tell you that what people believe to be true is often nothing more than illusion and suggestion.

Slander.

Rumors and lies.

She shifted to face the camera that zoomed in on her flawless face.

What many people wish to believe is nothing more than . . . gossip.

The film screen faded to black as the word "gossip" appeared in white letters, floating from one side to another. The sounds of a noisy school hallway filled the room, one sound clip merging into another.

A girl's voice, whispering to a friend. *"I heard she had sex in the boys' bathroom, right after lunch! Then she went to class like it was no big deal!"*

A boy's deep tone, bragging to a buddy. *"She'll do it, no problem. She did it with half the hockey team, didn't she? Why not you?"*

The video played sound of footsteps and idle chatter. Then, louder, the voice of another girl.

"He's got HIV, I swear. Look how skinny he is! And he's always got a cold!"

People in the audience started looking at each other, whispering.

But I could tell. They were paying attention.

The screen faded again, and a girl appeared. We'd shot her from behind, her face shielded and her hair concealed under a big hat.

It didn't stop at just the gossip or the picture.

They tormented me.

Teased me every day and ruined my reputation.

Her voice broke and she wiped away the tears.

Someone a few rows ahead of me whispered. "Is that Zoe Graham?"

The vulnerable girl on screen cleared her throat and steadied her voice.

I had tantrums. I screamed.

I tried to ignore them, but they wouldn't stop.

And when the pain got so bad, I . . . I . . . couldn't take it anymore.

The camera caught her struggle with an uncomfortable silence. Her voice was barely audible.

I just wanted to die.

So . . . I . . .slit my wrists.

A collective gasp swept through the crowd and Mrs. Russell put her arm around me for support.

The screen faded to black until a single word appeared.

Harassment.

Voices sounded while the word loomed on the screen.

First, a girl's, covered by a cough.

Slut!

Then a boy's, barely disguised at all.

Nice tits, baby!

Mr. Kellerman, the physics teacher who'd discovered the destruction to my locker, came to stand beside Mrs. Russell and me.

"Did you have something to do with this, Carracino?" he asked me, his face stern.

I shrugged and turned back toward the screen.

Harassment faded out to the sound of a boy's imitation sex-moan.

My own face filled the screen and the kids instantly started talking.

Someone laughed and called out a name.

Do you know how it feels to be bullied every day of your life?

As the word lingered, images began to fill the screen.

Still shots of stacks of printed emails containing the photograph of me in the rain.

Video clips of faceless, laughing people stuffing notes into my locker.

A rolling shot of those hastily-scribbled messages they'd left behind.

Mrs. Russell gave my shoulder a squeeze.

Mr. Kellerman shook his head. "You're a brave girl, Carracino. I gotta give you that."

The film sequence closed with a single close-up image of my locker, the black thong, and the horrible word that had been painted there for everyone to read.

An uneasy silence drifted through the auditorium as Sophie scrambled from her seat to stand behind me.

She hugged me, crying. "I'm so proud of you, Lil."

"It's not over yet," I said, nodding.

On the big screen, another word appeared.

Bullying.

Nobody in the room said a word.

The video rolled to show Tyler, his face fuzzed through the miracle of technology. People saw him laughing as he spray-painted my locker for the second time. The image on screen shifted to reveal Tyler walking away, paint can still in his hand.

And when the camera revealed this written assault against my character, people started looking for him in the audience.

Still, the video pushed the audience's comfort zone as I took the screen again.

Do you know what it feels like to be touched against your will?

To have your personal boundaries violated?

The video played back my encounter with Joe in live-action but with his face blurred.

My voice, panicky but firm.

Please take your hands off me.

His response, cocky.

I think we should kiss right here, right now.

The camera picked up a scuffle of hands and a pulling of my clothes.

My words, strong and sure.

You have no right!

Footage of my legs stumbling backwards, away from him.

Him laughing. The shot of him coming toward me, mouth puckered and ready to attack.

The sound of my flailing arms and more scrambling steps.

Panic in my voice.

STOP! I don't want you to touch me!

Righteousness in his.

Your word against mine, babe. And who're they gonna believe. Star athlete . . . or slut? Maybe that was whore. I can't remember. Which name is it today?

Stillness crept over the school auditorium.

A quick cut to the end of our conversation and my challenge.

Man up for once in your life. Admit it. You've done nothing but harass me every day for months. At home . . . and at school. Does it make you feel big and strong to make a girl feel this way?

The camera showed the blurry-faced boy licking his lips.

With juicy tits like those, it's a whole lotta fun.

And then he laughed and the scene faded out.

Music began to play as I walked toward the camera and folded my arms.

So ask yourself before you go to sleep tonight.

Are you a victim?

On screen, I opened my hands to the audience.

Or are you . . . the problem?

I turned to Mr. Kellerman and spoke. "Tyler Jackson. Joe Sanderson. Jimmy Barnett. I'll tell you everything. Just don't let them do this to anyone else."

After letting the word linger a few seconds longer, I delivered my final words and pointed at the lens.

Know. Who. You. Are.

My name is Liliana Carracino. I am a freshman at Middleton High.

And I will not be a victim anymore.

74.

Game day in Middleton High Stadium was cold and crisp when the Tigers prepared to take the gridiron against the Saints. The boys from our town and those from New Canaan were tucked in their respective borrowed locker rooms listening to pep talks from their coaches, and using the older boys' lockers to feel like they'd made it to the big time.

Outside, my adrenaline was riding high, and though we hadn't yet heard from my parents, nothing could dampen my mood.

Everything was going perfectly.

I'd promised my little brother something special, and with the help of Grand-mère, Sophie's parents, and my neighbor Mrs. Ferguson and her eight kids, I'd reserved an entire section of the grandstand for our cheering section. I'd even saved room enough to house a contingent of the Middleton High School band, whom had volunteered to play during the game when they heard what I was doing. I'd quickly learned, after showing the video at assembly, that more than a few members of the band felt indebted to me for putting a face and name to the bullying that had been happening to them for so long. Now, the thankful brass section was warming up to play as soon as our boys burst through the banner in the end zone.

I stared into the stands at the group I'd assembled, each holding a water bottle noisemaker and colorful pompoms, and wearing Tiger orange and brown to support my brother's team. Kerry and Brian sat side by side to anchor the middle of the stands, ready to do their part. Mr. Nabors and Mr. Wilbanks sat next to Mrs. Alban and her family who had rounded up another row of fans on my behalf. In the front row Mrs. Russell and the girls from my sewing class made up their own cheering squad, with Susi Nichols perched on the bleacher front and center. Mr. Kellerman had even made it to the game with his wife and four kids in tow, introducing me to them as the bravest girl he'd ever met. And Sophie's brother Leo and his girlfriend had put in an appearance, albeit reluctant, but of course they were already lip-locked and oblivious in the back row.

But what touched me more than anything was the fact that Zoe Graham and her parents had come, thankful that someone had cared enough to share her side of the story. And Zoe herself had reached out, taking the first huge steps toward healing and re-integrating back into high school life.

"I have made certain that every person has a letter or color card and knows exactly when to show them," Grand-mère said as she handed me the last few cards. "And Missus Ferguson has sent her husband across to the other side to take video pictures for Tony."

As soon as the team took the field and Billy's brother signaled Tony to watch the stands, we would roll the letter and color cards until the entire section became a "Tony the Tiger: You're GRRREAT!" living and moving banner of cheering fans.

"It's absolutely perfect," I said, wishing Sophie was here to see what was happening. But her parents had come in her place instead, a little dubious but cooperative as their dedicated daughter did a final dress rehearsal before her big opening night. Mrs. Fishkin was already directing the crowds and sharing her endless wisdom whether they wanted it or not, while Mr. Fishkin was surreptitiously watching my grandmother and smiling.

"Everyone knows exactly what to do," Billy Martin said, coming up to stand beside me. "This is a really cool thing you're doing, Lili."

I looked up at him, glad that he was here with me. Grand-mère smiled sweetly at us both, drifting back to her seat next to Murray Fishkin and his beside-herself wife.

"Most people wouldn't do all this for their little brother," Billy said. "But I'll bet you're a good sister, aren't you?"

From the step below us, a man's voice answered. "Yes, she is the very best."

I turned to see my father standing there, smiling in his Italian suit, looking hopelessly out of place amid the sweater-clad crowd in the stadium.

"Daddy! You came back to us!"

I threw my arms around him and he wrapped me in a hug. He smelled of expensive aftershave and wool, and the aroma instantly comforted me.

"*Bella,* oh how I have missed you."

I glanced behind him. "Is Mother with you, too?"

My father shook his head. "I am afraid we were only able to get one seat on the flight. She had to stay behind in Rome."

I tried to hide my disappointment with a smile."Oh."

When my father noticed Billy standing attentively next to me, waiting, he smiled at him. "*Buongiorno.* Are you . . .a friend of Liliana?"

Billy nodded and extended his hand to my father. "Yes, sir. Billy Martin, sir. We go to school together."

They shook hands firmly, and my father glanced back and forth between us, his smile growing and his thick black eyebrows rising just a bit. Amid the growing noise of the stands, the silent bubble settling over the three of us was more than a little awkward.

I clapped my hands together to break the unexpected tension and let out a cheer. "Go Tigers! Umm. . . the game's about to start. It's almost time!"

"Right," Billy said, nodding. He stuffed his hands into his pockets and cleared his throat. "So maybe we'll . . . umm . . . see each other around. At school, or something?"

I smiled at him, painfully aware that my father was watching us far too closely. But I couldn't let Billy to leave so soon. I didn't want him to.

Billy started to walk away, but I caught him by the sleeve and he spun to face me.

"Hey, Billy?" I asked as I let my hand drop. "About that movie you suggested?"

He smiled and gave me a nod as a faint blush crept onto his cheeks. "I remember."

I swallowed my nerves and took a deep breath."How would you feel, like, coming to tonight's party after *Cinderella* instead? In the club ballroom?"

My father looked hopelessly confused as he stared at his dress shoes, but Billy nodded. "That'd be great, Lili. It's a date. See you after the show?"

"Until ten o'clock." I smiled happily, a warm feeling in my bones. "See you later, Billy."

As I watched Billy take his seat and start rallying the crowd, my father put his arm around me and lowered his voice.

"It seems you have done much changing while I have been away, my beautiful daughter. In just two short months, you have grown up on me, have you not?"

I looked down the row at my grandmother and smiled, knowing I had her to thank for waking me up to my true potential. She caught my eye and gave me a wave, then turned her attention back to Murray and his steady stream of flirtation.

"I think I have grown up, Daddy." I looked into my father's dark eyes. "I'm a different person now. A lot more confident than I was." I paused, letting my words sink in."But I want you to know me. I *need* you to know exactly who I am. Because I do now. *I know who I am*."

He led me to a pair of empty seats. "Then we must make the time to get to know each other."

I leaned my head against him and let him pull me close as we sat and the cool autumn wind blew across us.

"Can you forgive me for staying away so long?" he asked quietly, his voice suddenly thick with emotion. "I am sorry I have not been a better father, Liliana. I have been so busy. But I will try to do better."

I shook my head. "Daddy, you—"

He stopped me. "Liliana, I have made many mistakes and have much to make up for . . . if you will let me."

I nodded and blinked back my tears as my brother's team took the field and the band began to play. "I'd like that, Daddy. I really would."

75.

The house lights were nearly dim as my grandmother and I made our way past the Fishkins to our seats in the front row next to Tony and my father.

My brother was playing back the recording of today's playoff game for my dad, more excited and proud of the outpouring of attention he received than I'd seen him in years. And my dad was completely absorbed, shoulder to shoulder with his son and not a cell phone in sight. There would be plenty of time for my father and me to get to know each other later. But right now, it made me really happy that my brother was so content after winning his big game.

With Grand-mère beside me in a crisp Christophe St. Pierre suit and pearls, I settled in my seat and arranged the soft folds of my dress. For tonight, for my debut as a brand new and very scared novice designer who had way too much to learn, I'd made a simple ivory sheath to showcase my hand-beaded organza wrap. I crossed my legs and caught a glimpse of the beautiful shoes my mother had made just for me, and my heart pulled tight.

So many emotions crossed my mind when I thought of her, so many moments I wished I could take back, harsh words I'd said, apologies I hadn't, fears I should have revealed but wasn't brave enough to speak aloud.

But I also knew that if one element had changed about the way I'd been treated or the way I chose to act, if one event in my life had turned out differently, I might not be sitting where I was right at this moment, waiting for the show to begin.

But even that realization didn't stop me from desperately wishing my mother were here with me now to share in this very special moment of my life.

Murray Fishkin nudged me. “You don’t clean up half bad, kid. Looking spiffy in that dress.”

I smiled as I adjusted my wrap over my shoulders. “Thanks, Mister Fishkin.”

He nodded and pushed his glasses back on his nose. “So, tell me. Hypothetically speaking, did that girl we were talking about go public against the boys who . . . *hypothetically* hurt her?”

I thought about the aftermath of showing the video and revealing the extent of my pain, the outpouring of support, the apologies and the regrets and the promises of so much friendship. Then I recalled what had happened right after the assembly, the crowds of people pointing fingers at Tyler and Joe and Jimmy, how the boys were rushed by Mr. Kellerman and the security officers to the principal’s office with half of the guidance staff.

I thought about the ultimate message Mrs. Alban and Mrs. Russell had helped me deliver to my peers when I learned the boys had been suspended and directed to serve their community for a full year by teaching younger kids how to defend their rights against bullies.

I thought about how justice was served.

And I thought about exactly how strong the entire experience made me feel.

I turned toward my friend’s father. “That girl did expose the abuse the boys had been getting away with and the rumors they perpetuated . . . and the whole school paid attention.”

Mr. Fishkin put his palms up. “And?”

I gave him a smile and nodded. “And I don’t think anyone will be hurting her anymore. Hypothetically speaking, of course.”

He shrugged. “Of course." With a pat to my hand, he whispered to me. “A girl’s got to stand up for herself to feel good about looking in the mirror every morning.”

I smiled as I thought about how much my own reflection had changed. “So true, Mister Fishkin. So true.”

He nodded.“You did real good, kid.”

Just then, the house lights dimmed and the room fell into a hush as the curtain rose and the dancers took the stage in costumes I had designed and made for them with just a little extra sewing help from Kerry.

My grandmother took my hand and smiled at me in the dark. We watched together as with each *rond de jambe relevé* and *saut de basque* Sophie transformed into the princess before our very eyes.

I studied her costume. I'd interpreted Sophie's Cinderella in a completely new way. Strong. Independent. A little bit fierce for defending herself in the face of the wicked. I clutched my grandmother's fingers and Sophie glided across the stage in the costume made of rags . . . *my very own rags.*

My eyes filled with tears as the music swelled, the colorful pieces of my old clothes and my old mixed-up life moving and swaying before my eyes, strips and tatters of mistakes and memories and events ready to be peeled away and shed. And when Cinderella's fairy godmother finally sprinkled her world with shimmering light and grace, Sophie began to pirouette beneath the lights, arms outstretched and face toward the sky. Then like a wave of magic, the costume's rag layers began to ripple, and lift, and pull away in a continuous stream as Sophie spun, turn after turn after beautiful turn, until the lights grew soft and warm and shone down on her and she struck a beautiful pose, a transformed Cinderella in a glittering gown woven from strands of her own wishes and dreams.

Her transformation . . . and mine . . . was complete.

Applause thundered in our ears and beside me my father clapped and cheered "*Molto bravo!*"the loudest–for Sophie, for me, for what we'd been able to achieve together.

The emotion of the moment overwhelmed me and tears began to trickle from my eyes.

Grand-mère leaned close and kissed my forehead. "You are a shining star, *ma chérie.*"

I shook my head. "It was all Sophie, Grand-mère. She was wonderful, wasn't she?"

My grandmother stroked my cheek as I looked into her eyes. "No, my darling. This is *your* moment, completely."

"Liliana," she said with a smile. "Embrace all that you have become."

76.

In her makeshift dressing room at the club, Sophie stood before the mirror in the gown I'd created for her, a frothy confection of the palest pink, just warmer than the tone of her shoulders but not quite as rich as the blush in her cheeks.

She looked ethereal as she met my eyes in the mirror.

"You're amazing, you know," she said to me. Then she smiled wickedly. "For a shiksa, you're not half bad."

I laughed at my very best friend in the world, knowing I'd be lost without her. "And for a princess, you're okay yourself."

She shrugged and lifted her foot to show off the sandals my mother had made. "Hey, if the fancy shoe fits . . . ."

I smoothed the length of her skirt, where it fell in delicate ripples behind her knees.

"Ooh!" she said suddenly. "Look what Ma got me just for tonight."

She reached into her beaded evening bag and slipped out a pair of slim glasses with a rhinestone at the corners. When she put them on, her eyes sparkled even more than her smile. "Too much?"

I shook my head. "No way. They're perfect. But Adam is waiting for you out there."

She nodded. "And Billy's waiting for you."

I smiled. My very first date, on the most special night of my life, and I was sharing it with everyone in the world who mattered to me.

Except my mother.

A fleeting sadness took hold, but I tried to brush it off. I didn't want to be sad now, not on a night like this. She would come home when she could.

Sophie turned to look at me and shook her head. "I'm not going out there first."

I pushed back my emotions and blinked the tears from my eyes. "Why not?"

"Because that whole crowd needs to see you. You're the reason I can ever look good on that stage. You make me a better person."

My tough-as-nails friend got tears in her eyes. "I'd be nothing without you, Lil."

I nodded as I pulled her into a hug. "You're my absolute rock, Soph, and I love you like a sister. Don't go changing on me, you hear?"

A knock sounded at the door and my Aunt Margaux ducked her head inside. When she saw us standing together, she rushed forward and took us into her arms.

"My darlings, what a grand success we have had!" she exclaimed. "You were both magnificent! And look how lovely you are! Let us go celebrate with everyone!"

Sophie pulled herself together and headed for the door, but I held my aunt back. "You go on ahead, Soph. I just want a minute with Aunt Margaux."

My friend looked at me and nodded, then slipped quietly outside.

Through the door, my aunt and I listened to the muffled round of applause that greeted Sophie as she made her grand entrance into the ballroom.

I looked at the floor. "Aunt Margaux, I just want . . . I need to say . . . thank you."

She brushed a lock of my hair into place and smiled. "No. Thank *you, ma chérie*. We could not have done the performance without your vision. I would have been lost."

"That's not exactly what I meant," I said, shaking my head. "I wanted to thank *you*. For believing in me. For seeing something I was too stupid to see in myself."

Aunt Margaux smiled and put her arm around me, leading me toward the door. "This beauty you share has always been within you, Liliana. You just had to open your eyes enough to see."

We reached the door and she led us into the hall. With a sweep of her hand toward the ballroom, she tilted her chin, smiled broadly, and said, “Now let us greet our guests and be our most entertaining.”

I smiled up at her. “You are your mother’s daughter, aren’t you?”

She glanced down the hall and nodded. “And so, my darling, are you. In more ways than you know.”

Then she let me go and drifted away.

77.

I turned and came face to face with my mother, standing under a light and carrying a shoulder bag.

All of the pent-up emotions of the past two months crashed through my system and I rushed to her.

She folded me into her arms and whispered. "Ah, Liliana, you are so *beautiful*. I have missed you so very much, my darling."

I nodded, overwhelmed by her words, by her appearance here tonight, and by the tenderness I'd never expected from her.

"But Daddy said you couldn't come."

She shook her head. "Just not on the same flight. I would not have missed this night. I just arrived from Paris and came straight to the theater."

I laughed. "You saw?"

She nodded. "Aunt Nina and I were in the back, and we did not miss a single step of the ballet. Tonight you showed everyone what I have always known. You are a creative genius, my daughter. I am very, very proud of you."

My mother was proud . . . *of me*.

The satisfaction filled me to the core, and I couldn't hold in my apology.

"I'm sorry, Mother, for being so . . . so horrible."

"Ah, I went through the very same phase with my mother at your age. I understand how difficult it can be to sort your emotions."

She took me by the hand and led me to a pair of chairs in the hall. "Let us sit for a moment, hmm?"

I nodded and took a seat as she set down her bag.

My mother reached inside the bag and handed me a thick book.

"What is this?" I asked, running my fingers over the embossed design on the cover. "It looks like the books I made on Grand-mère and the rest of you."

"It is." She cleared her throat and wrung her hands. "Liliana, I must make a confession. I have often not been a good mother to you. This I know."

I shook my head.

"*No*. This is not for you to argue. I am driven. Successful. Ambitious."

"Glamorous. Scary beautiful. Fierce," I added.

She smiled. "I may be a strong woman, but I can admit where I am weak." She took my hand in hers. "But that does not mean I have ever stopped loving you, or knowing who you are, or seeing the woman you could become someday."

Tears pricked my eyes with heat. "But—"

She leaned closer to me and opened the book. On the very first page was a picture of me, dressed up in my mother's clothes and shoes when I was about three-years-old.

I had wanted to be just like her then. I had looked up to my mother.

As I stared at the picture through a blur of tears, I wondered.

When had my attitude changed?

When had I become so indifferent?

She turned the page, and I saw us sitting together on a picnic blanket, pictured in red sundresses and matching sunglasses, our laughter brightening the page.

"When you were very little, you would not leave my side," she told me. "You followed me wherever I went, and I loved the attention."

I knew she spoke the truth.

My mother dabbed at her eyes as she flipped to another page. I was older now, maybe seven, a little more physically distant and dressing my own way. We looked straight ahead to the camera, but not at each other.

"As my business grew, you and I grew less close. You pulled away," she admitted, "and I failed to see you and all that you needed."

She paused, considering her words. "It is the price I have paid."

I turned the pages of the album, one by one, and studied the visible growing rift between us, the chasm filled by her success. As my mother grew more stylish and confident, I withdrew, a fraction at a time, pulling deeper into myself until I was barely there, disappearing into bad clothes and hiding behind my hair.

"I have let you down as a mother, Liliana," she said humbly, tears sliding along her cheeks. "And I have done it again, just now when you needed me most, by leaving you at such a tender time when so very many things went wrong."

When I turned another page, a new picture began to emerge. One of me, coming into my own, on my own. She told this story not through images of me, but of my embroidery, my needlework and my love of working with fabric, my escape from everything I hated about myself and my life.

"What is all this?" I asked.

"As you became a young woman, you would never let your father or me take your picture any longer," my mother said quietly, wiping away her tears. "And you would not talk to me about what you were feeling. You shut yourself off. So I began to photograph your work while you were at school so I could study it. To get close to you, in some small way."

I ran my fingers over one of the pictures and looked up at her. "I didn't think you ever noticed me." I swallowed back my own tears. "I didn't think you even cared."

My mother closed the book and took my hands.

"Oh, *ma chérie*, you have no idea. I have always loved you from the fullness of my heart, and I always will. We just need to learn how to talk to each other again."

I hugged my mother then, long and hard, building a bridge for communication with the first tiny brick.

It wouldn't be easy, to forgive our mistakes and share and let each other in, but together we would try.

"There is one more thing I must show you before we join the others," she said, clearing the emotion from her throat.

She reached into her bag and withdrew a large black and white photograph.

I dabbed at my own eyes and took it from her.

The girl in the picture looked like *me.*

"Is this . . . *you*?" I asked, studying the image. It wasn't posed, but the camera had captured a moment, a slice of time in which my mother had relaxed and revealed herself. Her eyes were honest, her expression open. "It's really beautiful."

"I was fourteen, as you are now." She leaned close to me. "Let me tell you about this picture. I hated having my picture taken, just like you. Nina had the confidence, and Margaux had the talent, and posing for photographs was natural to them. I was . . . more shy."

"You were shy?" I asked, surprised.

She laughed. "Goodness, yes. I was not always the boss, you know. I did not even date until Nina made me. This photo was taken when I did not know."

"Natural."

"*Absolutement.*"She opened the scrapbook again and began flipping pages."But that is not the point. I want to show you something."

When she reached the middle of the book, she turned to the portrait Richard Ranesford had done of me. I let out a tiny gasp.

"You . . . you saw this? When?"

"*Mais, oui.* Grand-mère sent it to me right away," she said. "You are always with me now in my office in Italy, and your father and I carry it with us everywhere," she said. "This is *you*, Liliana. The real you. *Naturel. . .* beautiful inside and out."

She took the old photograph from my hand and laid it side by side with mine. "*Regardez, ma chérie.*"

We stared at the images together. Though our coloring was different, our faces bore a striking resemblance to one another's.

"Wow," I said. "I never realized how much we look alike."

My mother hugged me. "We will always be part of each other, *chérie*. But right now, we are missing your big party. And you deserve to celebrate!"

Over her shoulder, I glanced toward the ballroom and felt the tug of what was to come.

"I have a date tonight," I told her through my tears. "My first."

She pulled back, surprise on her face. "What? And you have kept this boy waiting? To talk to me?"

I smiled at her as she wiped my cheeks.

"You're much more important to me, Mother." I paused. "I love you."

"And I you." She gave me a broad smile and dabbed my eyelashes and my nose with a tissue. "Now, show me the boy who has captured my daughter's eye."

Feeling suddenly whole, feeling good about my life, I got to my feet and we made our way to the ballroom where music played and people danced and life had carried on while we took the first steps to get to know each other all over again.

We saw Billy then, waiting nervously by the punch bowl, sipping a delicate cup of something pink. He was talking to Sophie and Adam, and they were all smiling. I pointed him out to her and she drew me close.

My mother whispered in my ear. "You must tell me all about him later. Now go enjoy your first dance."

I nodded, assuring her that I would. But when I started to walk toward Billy, I tilted my head and recognized my grandmother, standing tall and serene with her blonde hair shining beneath the glow of an overhead light.

"Billy can wait," I said. "There's someone I need to talk to first."

My mother let me go and I crossed the dance floor with steady steps toward the woman who had changed my life.

When my grandmother spotted me approaching, her smile for me could have lit the room.

"What a picture of happiness you are, *ma chérie*," she said, taking my hands. "Just a vision of beauty."

I smiled. "I think I am. *Happy.*" I drew a breath and gave her hand a squeeze. "I'm really happy, Grand-mère, and it's all because of you."

We stared into each other's eyes then, knowing that our special time together was coming to an end. We had discovered so many of each other's secrets, and in the process found something vital . . . and very real.

"I don't want you to leave me," I told her quietly. "Ever."

She shook her head. "But I must go home, Liliana. Life must keep moving on if we are to grow."

I nodded, saddened that she would be returning to France far too soon. "When will I see you again, Grand-mère? It won't be another few years, will it?"

"No, *ma chérie.*" She pulled me into a hug. "Ah, perhaps you might consider spending the summer with me . . .*avec les couturiers*?"

I pulled back to stare up at her. "You mean come to *Paris?* Really?"

"Ask Sophie to come along, and we will shop and go to the ballet together."

I smiled. "I'll have to ask Mother and Daddy if it's okay."

My grandmother nodded. "I think your parents would agree that you are quite a young lady now."

I leaned against her with my arm around her waist as we stared out over the crowd.

The girl I used to be was fading deep into the shadows of my memories.

But the girl I was inside now was strong.

Confident.

Proud.

I nodded as I cast my gaze on Billy, on my friends and my family, all around me and so very much a part of my life.

"You know, Grand-mère," I said. "I know exactly who I am."

The End

Grand-mère's Rules

1. A lady holds herself with dignity and pride.
2. A lady appreciates.
3. A lady is always tidy.
4. A lady works with her assets.
5. If a lady cannot fix something, she conceals it.
6. A lady is never vulgar.
7. A lady does not eat while walking and never chews gum.
8. A lady holds back strong words and smiles.
9. A lady uses her intellect to make a point.
10. A lady has strong lips or strong eyes – never both.
11. A lady's lips would not shine.
12. A soft chignon will complement every lady's face.
13. A lady's hair is always natural and glorious.
14. A lady's clothing endures the test of time.
15. A lady's skin is always nourished.
16. A lady starts the day well with juice, a baguette and fruit.
17. A lady always respects her curves.
18. A lady eats when she is hungry, but she should strive never to overindulge.
19. A lady knows to be clean imparts elegance.
20. A lady keeps her knees together, ankles crossed.
21. A lady helps and doesn't hurt.
22. A lady shares her creativity.
23. A lady's confidence imparts strength.
24. A lady holds her head high.
25. A lady knows who she is.

Lili

Reader's Discussion Guide

1. Talking to a parent can be hard, and everyone goes through phases when it seems impossible. But communication is one of the most important things a teen can learn to perfect. Does Lili do the right thing by not confiding in her mother? Why or why not?

2. Having someone objective to talk to away from home can get teens through very tough times. Why do you think it takes so long for Lili to share with her teacher? Does she make a mistake in waiting? Why?

3. Lili has a best friend in Sophie. But when her life becomes almost too difficult to bear, she doesn't tell Sophie what she's feeling. Why do you think Lili holds back from the one person who really understands her?

4. Younger brothers and sisters can be a lot of work, but at the same time, the relationship you have with them can be fantastic. Lili and her brother bicker, but at their core they love each other. What is your relationship like with your siblings? Do you think you might behave any differently after reading Lili's story?

5. When Lili's body begins to develop before those of her friends, she is subject to ridicule, harassment, and bullying by boys who make assumptions about what type of girl she is. Have you

ever made assumptions about people before you got to know them? Has anyone made assumptions about you?

6. Rumors hurt, and reputations are quickly damaged by gossip. Think about a time when someone said something about you that wasn't true. How did it make you feel? How did you react?

7. The internet quickly spreads the lies being told about Lili as her classmates share unflattering images and untrue stories. Has this happened at your school? Have you ever participated by distributing something electronically that might not have been true? Afterwards, how did that make you feel? If you were regretful, did you apologize?

8. When harassment turns to bullying that becomes physical, Lili reaches her emotional limit. Have you ever felt this desperate? Have you ever considered hurting yourself ? Why?

9. Lili's grandmother comes back into her life at a vulnerable time. Instead of lecturing Lili about how she should behave, Grand-mere leaves her simple notes. Do you think this is more or less effective than talking about Lili's problems? How do you think it affects their relationship?

10. Lili struggles to learn to love her body, one small acceptance at a time. We know that over half of all American girls are unhappy with their body image, yet less than one third are actually overweight by insurance industry standards. Can you be truly objective about your own body, or are you influenced by the images you see in the media? What do you love about yourself?

11. Personal style is all about expression, but the meaning of fashion is different for everyone. Some

girls go all natural and lead an athletic lifestyle, some dress clean and plain with very few frills, others live to wear the newest, hottest, trendiest clothes, jewelry, and shoes, while still others, like Lili, set their own style that doesn't fit any one category. What is your personal style?

12. When it comes time to take a stand, Lili gets creative to draw attention to what has been happening to her. Do you think her video was the best way to express herself and see justice served? How else could she have handled her situation?

13. If you witnessed a classmate being bullied or sexually harassed, what would you do?

14. At the end of the book, Lili can hold her head high and feel good about herself. Do you think this type of transformation is possible? Do you think rumors can be forgotten and people can overcome the side effects of gossip? What do you believe is in store for Lili?

Andie and Mitch

A new Michelle Lane novel
coming
in November 2012

ACCELERATION

If everything seems under control,

you're just not going fast enough.

Mario Andretti

1.

Some days I felt way older than my 16 years, and not in a good way.

I was seriously stuck . . . and it was nobody's fault but my own.

Like right now, at 6 a.m. on a bright Saturday morning in March, when other kids my age would be deep in a dream with no intention of waking up until a respectable hour sometime after lunch, I was tackling the dirty kitchen.

Skip out of the job and sleep? *No.* I was the only one my family could count on.

All. The. Time.

My older sister and I had so little in common in the reliability department it made me want to scream. But I held in my tension as I flipped on the coffee and stared at the mess.

My family owned a restaurant not 200 feet from our house. So why was there a constant mountain of dishes in our kitchen here? And how exactly did I get elected the Queen Bee of Cleaning?

Oh, yeah. I volunteered.

My life was so predictable it was positively scary. I followed rules. Stuck to schedules. Kept everybody organized. Churned out lists by the dozens. Created systems for order in our busy lives.

I couldn't help it . . . and I didn't know how to change.

I hated my life so much sometimes it made me just want to cry.

"Andie, start the coffee, will ya?" my sister shouted from upstairs. "I need a major dose of caffeine."

"Already brewing," I responded automatically, cursing myself for being so dependable.

But I rolled up my tee shirt sleeves anyway and wrapped my ponytail into a loose knot of curls. I grabbed a garbage bag from the pantry and tackled the take-out containers on the table first. My sister must have downed this meal last night before going to bed. Staring at the leftover grease, I knew exactly why I'd heard her getting sick this morning. The sight was making even me queasy.

I carried the smelly garbage bag to the trash can on the back porch. While I tightly secured the lid, I gulped in a breath of fresh Spring air. The crocus had sprouted early this year and the hyacinths were on their way to pushing up, dotting the edge of the path with bright spots of purple and yellow and the palest of lavender petals. This was the best time of year, when everything was fresh and crisp and every green shoot had the potential to turn into something beautiful.

But when I turned back toward the sink, my sigh was involuntary. Some days it might be better to stay in bed and call it a day. I could do it, if I tried. But then I'd just lie there against the pillows making lists of all the things that would never get done around here unless I did them myself. And *that* would be a fate far worse than another case of dishpan hands.

A vigorous hour of scrubbing, drying, and mopping later, the coffee was brewed, the dishes clean and put away, and the countertops sparkling as much as they could considering their advanced age.

As I finally sat to review the grocery list, my sister bustled into the kitchen on a cloud of hairspray and Maybelline.

"You are a miracle worker," Persie said as she sat at the polished table. Toying with the sugar bowl, she sighed. "I just didn't have the energy last night."

Ever the light sleeper, I knew her schedule intimately. "Four twenty-seven. You came in right before Mom got up to shop. That's kinda late, even for you."

She shook her head and her dark curls swayed. "Don't give me shit, Andie. You know I've been working hard. We both have. I was just blowing off steam."

"You can't do it every night." I poured two mugs and slid one toward her as I sat down. A few drops sloshed over the rim. Without thinking twice, I wiped the spill away with a paper napkin. My sister's face was pale beneath the makeup. "Seriously. You're looking tired, Persie. Like no-amount-of-concealer-will-help tired."

"Tell me something I don't know. I feel lousy."

"Well don't breathe on me," I said quietly, warming my hands with my mug. "You've got to work front of house, and I can't get sick with Theo and Risto in Greece and me cooking at the restaurant. You know we can't afford to hire a replacement chef. Papa's always complaining how broke we are as it is."

Persephone Aphrodite Karras, my never-say-no older sister with the notoriously bad reputation and no college plans, needed a whole lot of mothering sometimes.

Like right now.

"I'm worried about you. This is the second time this week you've been sick. We should tell Mom," I suggested. "She's at the market picking up tonight's vegetables. Want me to call her cell?"

"Good God, don't you dare," Persie said, violently shaking her head. "All I need is another lecture about looking harder to find my true nature from our precious saint of a mother."

I laughed at her description. "Saint? Hardly. A little flaky, yeah. Mom's got a penchant for the dramatic exit maybe, but she's definitely not pure."

Persie snorted. "*And* she never seems to be around lately. She spends more time at her stupid women's center than here."

Mom and my sister were the original oil and water combination. So any mothering Persie got these days tended to come from me, her younger sister, Pandora Cosima Karras.

Unfortunate, but true.

Our names were real.

Our poet mother was dead serious when she named us in some grand tribute to mythology. She insisted on honoring our father by giving her daughters good Greek names, but she never bothered to investigate their symbolism or tell him what she'd decided when she filled out our birth certificates. She liked their poetic flow. So, from our very first come-into-the-world birthday forward, we were forever branded as those weird home-schooled kids with the dark curly hair and screwed up names.

My sister, named for the goddesses of the underworld and love, lived up to her given name with a slew of self-proclaimed vices, including an almost unhealthy addiction to bad boys.

And my curiosity succeeded only in me having an appetite for new and improved office supplies and my father's cooking.

Naturally, my brain circled back to food.

"When's the last time you ate a decent meal? You need some--"

"Uh-uh. Do not mention eggs." She nodded as she doctored the coffee with cream and sugar then cradled the mug. "I don't feel right."

"I'll pick up some multi-vitamins, and you need to take them every day without arguing. And oranges for Vitamin C. I'll remind you," I said. I added a few entries to my neat shopping list under the nutrition category. "What about girl stuff? Need anything besides tampons?"

Persie averted her eyes.

I put down my pencil and studied her. "What?"

She drank from her coffee.

"Persie?"

I stared at my sister with her overly made up face, shirt buttoned just to her cleavage, jeans hugging her thighs too much. She looked like she always did, but something about her appearance seemed . . . *off*.

And then it hit me.

She looked *guilty*.

I leaned forward and glared at her. "What did you do, Persephone?"

She hedged. "I . . uh. . ."

"Spit it out," I said, stealing her coffee from her. "You'd better tell me. *Now*. Or you're not getting your caffeine back!"

My sister wrung her hands together. "Well . . . *um* . . ."

"Persephone Aphrodite Karras!" I slapped my hand on the table so hard the sugar spoon jumped from the bowl and spilled some onto my jeans. "Talk to me!"

She wailed her confession. "*I might be pregnant, okay*!"

I gasped and covered my mouth. "Oh my God. Oh, Persie." I whispered, even though I knew we were alone in the house. "This is so . . . *bad*."

She nodded. "I kind of lost count, but I think I'm late."

I tried to calculate myself, but suddenly I couldn't remember either. My voice was barely a murmur as I glanced quickly toward the back door, praying no one would walk in. "You *think* you're late? How can you not know absolutely for sure?"

I knew my own cycle forwards and backwards. 25 days like clockwork. Never missed a beat. I pulled my calendar from my purse and saw the days marked with a tidy row of red Xs every month. A girl has to know these kinds of details.

She shrugged and got to her feet. Walking to the window, she pulled back the lace curtain to stare at the restaurant. "You know I don't remember to write stuff down. I'm too busy."

As I replaced my calendar in its slot in my purse, I cleared away the spilled sugar and sensed this was not the time to lecture her about developing better life skills.

Instead, I did what I always do. I took charge. "Okay. We need to formulate a plan."

My heart was thumping in my chest. There was so much to do, and fast. I stared at my shopping list, crossed off tampons and replaced them with pregnancy test. "First step is to find out."

I shook my head. "But wait a minute. I need to know. Why weren't you using protection? I bought you condoms and put them in your purse so you'd always have them with you. You still had plenty the last time I restocked you."

"I know. I'm so stupid. Got carried away." She fisted her hands, trying not to cry. "What am I going to do, Andie? I didn't think this could ever happen to me."

Her naiveté stunned me. I muttered. "You and ever other single mom. If you're going to have sex, at least make him wear a raincoat."

My sister made an unhappy whine. "I know, I know. I'm the poster child for slutty teenagers everywhere. *I know!*"

She wiped away a tear and sucked in a jagged breath. Getting frantic wouldn't help the situation. I forced myself to calm down by straightening the pictures on the wall beside the table and polishing a spot from one of them with the hem of my sleeve. When I only ended up smearing it, I rubbed the glass with a clean paper napkin. Once I folded the napkin into neat little triangles, I could deal with my sister again.

Shaking my head, I added more birth control to the shopping list. Too little too late, maybe, but I had to keep trying for her sake. I sighed. "We'll deal. I just need to work through some strategies to figure out what's best. Give me a little time."

"We're a good team, aren't we?" she asked quietly. "You and me?"

"Yeah," I said, letting the word linger. "We are. Did you tell Mark yet?"

Slowly, Persie turned to face me. "He broke up with me last week."

My breath escaped in a rush. "I'm really sorry, Persie. He was a good guy. You should have told me."

She tried to act tough with her chin tilted up, though I knew she was hurting inside. "Our relationship was fizzling anyway." She shook her head. "But promise not to be mad?"

I shrugged and she avoided my eyes.

I held my breath for what was coming next.

Her voice was soft. "Well . . . I'm not entirely sure it's his."

Her admission caught me totally off guard. *"What?"*

"It could be Brian's," she admitted. Then in a shame-filled whisper added, "Or Steve's."

I flew to my feet. "Steve from the gas station, Steve? Are you kidding me? He's like twenty-five and you're only eighteen!"

"And?"

I couldn't hold back. "God, do you have to sleep with *everybody*?"

"That's not fair, Andie. He gave me a ride and we had a few beers . . . and, well, I was . . . I was feeling lonely after Mark dumped me."

I didn't even want to ask when she'd found time to have sex with Brian. Sometimes there weren't enough good answers.

Instead, I reached out to her and wrapped her in a huge hug. I got a lung full of her perfume as she leaned her head on my shoulder.

"I love you, Andie," she said, sounding more young than she had in years.

"I know. Me, too," I said. Then I let out a sigh and brushed back one of her curls. "How could two girls who look so much alike be so completely different?"

She sighed. "Night and day, right? I'm the darkness and you'll always be my sunshine."

Then I made the mistake of glancing at the wall clock.

"Oh, Persie. My sister the loveable slut," I said. "We've got to go to work. Mom and Papa are going to kill us."

2.

Dev Patel was a dick, no two ways about it. And I, Mitchell King II, was stuck sharing a 12x12 room with him whether I liked it or not.

It's character building, my father said.

The work world has all kinds of people, he explained.

If you want to succeed, you have to learn to accommodate, he added.

Accommodate my ass. Living with such a prick was severely trying my patience, and I was one microsecond from decking him right in front of his pathetic fan club.

The concept isn't hard to understand, really. Room. Desk. Homework. Come back from class to room, sit at desk, attempt homework. End of story.

I went through my same routine every day, and he went through his.

Brag. Belittle. Bribe. He blustered on and on about his alleged sexual conquests, never did his homework, insulted his lackeys, then bought them off so they kept coming back for more.

So today, when I was trying to get through my physics chapter on Newton's laws of motion so I could finally retreat to the kitchen, Dev just wouldn't shut up.

I mentally tested Newton's Third Law: *For every action there is an equal and opposite reaction*. Pop Dev in his blabbering mouth. Stunned silence follows.

So the law works. Damn, that Newton was a smart dude.

"I could have done her right there on the pool table," Dev said, scrolling through his iPod and adjusting his earbuds. "She was begging for it."

Sandhurst Fennimore sputtered. "Then why didn't you?"

"The Prime Minister came into the room and interrupted," Dev said with a tilt of his chin. "Thought it might be inappropriate to be banging her while he wanted to play pool with my dad."

"You are so full of it," Harrison said. "No way did you get that close."

Dev looked at the retail magnate's son and cocked a smile. "Like you know, limp dick? Better stock up on hand lotion at your daddy's store. It's going to be a long winter."

Harrison threw a shoe at him, missed and hit Cooper in the head.

"What the hell was that for?" Cooper snapped, dropping his PS3. "I was on the last level, too!"

They all laughed while I breathed and counted to ten at my desk.

Hayward Academy was overrun with jerks like these. Privileged. Snotty. Useless.

I did not belong here.

A pillow hit the back of my head.

"You gonna ignore us all day, Mitch?" Dev asked. "I'm starting to think you might be a serial killer with all that brooding you do."

I turned to face the little prince. "I don't brood. I do homework. There's a difference."

"Humorless SOB, aren't you?"

Only with you, my man. Only with you.

Dev cocked one of his black eyebrows at me and gave me a shit-eating grin. "You gotta figure out the system, dude. Find someone to do the work for you. It's the way of the modern world."

They all laughed, and I gave him a tight smile to get him off my back. "Whatever."

Dev shot to his feet and rubbed his hands together. "Time for lunch. I'm in the mood for Greek today."

"Speaking of Greek, did you do her yet? You never told us," Cooper asked, standing and shoving the handheld in the cargo pocket of his khakis. He scratched his crotch and readjusted.

"Who?" Dev answered. "The slutty waitress?"

"*Yeah.*" He nodded. "The one with the nice tits."

Dev laughed. "Last month. In the parking lot on her smoke break."

"Nice," Harrison said, impressed. "Man you get 'em all, don't you?"

Sandhurst, the pasty-white kiss-ass with the liver lips, swallowed hard in awe of his Indian idol.

I wanted to laugh out loud, but I held it in. This entitled son of a cabinet minister was so full of shit it wasn't funny, and they were too stupid to figure it out. In my opinion, they all deserved each other.

Dev smacked me on the back. "You coming, Mitch? I'm buying."

Staring at the impossible challenge of two pages of physics problems, I knew my mind was hopelessly off task now. I'd heard the taverna in town was good, so let the jerk pay for my lunch. I was hungry.

Tossing my pencil to the desk, I stood. "I could eat."

To be continued . . .

Please keep reading
www.michellewrites.com for
news about
the Fall 2012 release of
Andie and Mitch
And in Winter 2013,
you will meet *Grace*.

Meet Michelle Lane

I know what it's like to grow up on the edges of beautiful towns filled with beautiful homes and beautiful people, but that hasn't stopped me from writing about what it's like to be the one on the outside looking into those circles. Life can be bumpy for a kid who's struggling to fit in and find the way, but staying true to yourself and what you believe in is the best reward. Meeting your soul mate, best friend, and future husband in seventh grade is pretty great, too. After a happy high school courtship, I married my senior prom date, Ed. We live with our sons, Mike and Nick, and a pack of rowdy shih tzus in Atlanta.

The writing bug bit me early. To survive the daily traumas of middle and high school, I started writing novellas for friends and submitting spooky stories and romantic tales to magazines at the ripe old age of 13. Literary magazines, yearbooks, college newspapers, freelance writing assignments, a hearty imagination, and fierce determination led me to write countless magazine articles and books about lifestyle passions - home, entertaining, cooking, interior design and family life.

If I'm not tapping away at my keyboard reliving the angst and joy of my teen years, you might catch me behind the camera or at the stove. An avid photographer, I'm also an award-winning chef who racked up medals and the grand prize in an international competition. But if you ask my husband, the most memorable meal I've ever made was the fettuccine Alfredo and Tater Tots he convinced me to make on one of our first dates. And as we dug our spoons into the carton of mint chocolate chip that night, we promptly fell in love forever.

Why did I write *Lili*?

Why did I write **Lili**? Because I know what Lili feels like. It's hard enough to be a teenager, but growing up can be even more traumatic for a girl who gets her curves too early. Kids can be beyond mean, and the emotional damage they cause can last a lifetime. **Lili** shares what it feels like to be victimized by rumor - and find the strength to come out on top.

Call me the champion for the regular kids of the world who don't thrive on human blood or wear shoes that cost as much as their parents' mortgage payment. Regular kids have a lot of talking to do, and I'm here to give them a voice in books like **Lili**.

What's my writing process?

I like to plot on long car trips. I'm an unintentional eavesdropper in grocery stores, on trains and anywhere people are interesting – and different than me. Some of my most amazing scenes have been inspired by overhearing a single comment. If I'm on deadline, you'll probably catch me baking something delicious while I mull over details. I read my character's dialogue out loud. If it doesn't sound real, it's not good enough. I carry a camera with me wherever I go so I won't forget cool details to enhance a scene. I always listen to audio books to appreciate the rhythm and flow of words. I never go anywhere without a pen and paper. Inspiration often strikes in strange places and my bag is always stocked with blank index cards, just in case the next great idea comes when I'm least expecting it.

And, one thing is for certain.

Until I take my last breath, I will always be a writer with a great story to tell.

14648324R00155

Made in the USA
Charleston, SC
23 September 2012